ALSO BY TINA FOLSOM

SAMSON'S LOVELY MORTAL (SCANGUARDS VAMPIRES, BOOK 1)
AMAURY'S HELLION (SCANGUARDS VAMPIRES, BOOK 2)
GABRIEL'S MATE (SCANGUARDS VAMPIRES, BOOK 3)
YVETTE'S HAVEN (SCANGUARDS VAMPIRES, BOOK 4)
ZANE'S REDEMPTION (SCANGUARDS VAMPIRES, BOOK 5)
QUINN'S UNDYING ROSE (SCANGUARDS VAMPIRES, BOOK 6)
OLIVER'S HUNGER (SCANGUARDS VAMPIRES, BOOK 7)
THOMAS'S CHOICE (SCANGUARDS VAMPIRES, BOOK 8)
SILENT BITE (SCANGUARDS VAMPIRES, BOOK 8 1/2)
CAIN'S IDENTITY (SCANGUARDS VAMPIRES, BOOK 9)
LUTHER'S RETURN (SCANGUARDS VAMPIRES – BOOK 10)
BLAKE'S PURSUIT (SCANGUARDS VAMPIRES – BOOK 11)

LOVER UNCLOAKED (STEALTH GUARDIANS, BOOK 1)

A TOUCH OF GREEK (OUT OF OLYMPUS, BOOK 1)
A SCENT OF GREEK (OUT OF OLYMPUS, BOOK 2)
A TASTE OF GREEK (OUT OF OLYMPUS, BOOK 3)

LAWFUL ESCORT
LAWFUL LOVER
LAWFUL WIFE
ONE FOOLISH NIGHT
ONE LONG EMBRACE
ONE SIZZLING TOUCH

VENICE VAMPYR – THE BEGINNING

QUINN'S UNDYING ROSE

SCANGUARDS VAMPIRES – BOOK 6

TINA FOLSOM

Tina Folsom

Quinn's Undying Rose is a work of fiction. Names, characters, places, and incidents are the products of the author's imagination and are used fictitiously. Any resemblance to actual events, locales, or persons, living or dead, is entirely coincidental.

FOR MARK

1

With a look at the calendar, Rose Haverford sighed heavily. Even without reading the date, she would have known what day it was. Every year, she felt it as though it had been carved into her bones, her skull, and her flesh. Already days before, heaviness had started spreading in her heart, and melancholy had soured her disposition. But tonight, she felt the old bitterness well up in her again and move in like an unwelcome relative who would stay too long and stir up too many unpleasant memories.

Over the last two centuries, she'd learned to deal with it. Indeed, she'd found an outlet that helped her evict the painful recollections of the events that had shaped her life and made her into what she was today, what she would always be: a creature of the night, hungering for the blood of humans. A vampire.

Every year on the anniversary of her turning, Rose put pen to paper to write a letter she would never mail. The recipient was long dead, yet the loss was still as fresh and painful as ever.

Dearest Charlotte, she began the letter to her daughter.

Another year has passed and I miss you still. I've kept my promise to you even though I could never be the mother that you deserved. You would be very proud of your great-great-great-grandson Blake. He's a smart young man, ambitious and well-educated, and he'll one day make something of himself.

Rose groaned. Maybe she should cross out that last sentence. After all, she would only be lying to herself.

He's a smart young man, well-educated, and . . . he's arrogant and self-absorbed. When I established the trust fund for Blake to make his life easier, I never imagined he would use it to live a life of excess rather than draw on it to further his career and establish himself. But then, what do I know about men?

Nevertheless, he is my flesh and blood, and I've sworn to protect each and every one of my descendents. However, considering his lifestyle, our line might end with him. I don't see him settling down and starting a family.

From my words you might think I don't love him, my dearest daughter, but I do. It's only . . .

She lifted her pen from the paper and heaved a sigh.

. . . he reminds me too much of your father, even though he looks nothing like him. Blake's hair and complexion are dark, whereas Quinn had the fairest looks in all of England, so handsome, so charming.

And in the end, so deadly.

I wish you could have met your father, but I could never risk him knowing. You do understand, don't you? He would have made you into one of us, and I couldn't allow him to deprive you of a normal life, of the chance to have children and a family.

Rose pushed back an involuntary tear. She'd promised herself not to cry, not to wallow in self-pity, but whenever she thought of Quinn Ralston, the second son of the Marquess of Thornton, the man she'd loved with such passion, she couldn't maintain the icy composure everybody knew her for. She'd been called the coldest vampire this side of the Mississippi. Yet hot blood ran in her veins, and her heart beat for the ones she loved, the family she'd lost, and her only living descendent, her great-great-great-great-grandson Blake.

Despite her misgivings about Blake's lifestyle, she cared about him. Blood was thicker than water, and to her he was like a son, one who needed guidance.

I plan on following him to the West Coast shortly. My bags are packed. There's nothing left here for me in Chicago since Blake decided to move to San—

With a loud bang, the French doors leading to her little garden behind her two-story house were thrown open with such force that the panes shattered, scattering shards of colored glass over the priceless rugs and furniture. But there was no time to concern herself with such trivial details. Without losing a second, Rose shoved the unfinished letter into a fashion magazine on the desk and glared at the intruder.

In burst the man she'd hoped never to see again. For once, she would have liked the rumor to be true that vampires couldn't enter a home uninvited, but alas, this was only a fairy tale.

With eyes flashing red and fangs extended to show his intent, Keegan charged into her living room, his three thugs right behind him. Great, the asshole obviously counted on a fight and was stacking the deck. No surprise there. Why she had ever fooled herself that this man was anything but evil, she couldn't recall now. But then, she'd slept with plenty of jerks in her long life, and Keegan was no exception. At least she'd finally seen his true character and made a quick exit, but apparently he wasn't going to let her slip away so easily. She should have followed her instincts and left the night before.

Too late now.

His nostrils quivered as he stalked toward her. Pure fury shot from his eyes, eyes that were trained at her. She'd seen him look at others like this before, unfortunates who were now dead. Instinct urged her to retreat, but her pride dictated that she stand her ground. She had long ago stopped cowering to men; she wasn't going to start again.

As fast as a bullet, his hand encircled her throat, and as tight as a hangman's noose, he squeezed it, lifting her up.

"Where the fuck is it?" he pressed out from between clenched teeth, his vile breath ghosting over her face.

"I don't know what you're talking about," she managed to say with the limited supply of air he granted her.

He squeezed harder. "You lying whore!"

His other hand came up and slapped her hard across the cheek. The force of the impact whipped her head to the side. At once, she smelled her own blood as it ran down her nose, trickling over her mouth and chin. The sensation tickled just the way she imagined Chinese water torture felt like: annoying as hell. Yet she felt no pain. Too much adrenaline coursed through her veins, equally preventing her from feeling the fear that should drench her body from head to toe at the knowledge of what cruelties Keegan was capable of when he knew he'd been betrayed.

And he had been betrayed. By her.

His eyes drove into her as if he thought he could find the answer to his question there. She would have to disappoint his arrogant ass.

"Call me what you will," she spat with barely any air left to breathe. It didn't matter: vampires couldn't suffocate. They might lose consciousness for a while, but death would have to be delivered by different means.

"I asked: where the FUCK is it?"

When she attempted to shake her head but couldn't, his grip preventing her, he tossed a glance at his men. "Search the place!"

The three vampires, with more brawn than brain, firmly licked their chops at being ordered to tear her home apart. She didn't care. She had planned on leaving it all behind anyway. Her real estate agent was going to put the place up for sale tomorrow. Looking at how the three thugs went about their search, it appeared that some major restoration would be necessary before her house would be suitable for viewing by any potential buyers.

"I don't have it," she lied.

Another blow broke her nose—she would have to set it before her restorative sleep to make sure it didn't grow back crooked.

"I saw it on the security camera, you fucking bitch!" Keegan thundered.

Shit! She'd known that his office was wired, but what kind of freak had a camera hidden in his bedroom?

"You recorded us in bed? Fucking perv!"

The thought that tapes of their sexual encounters existed, sickened her. If she had any opportunity, she would go back there now and erase whatever he had recorded. But unfortunately, that plan was dead in the water.

"Oh, I'll keep watching those tapes whenever I want to. And there's nothing you can do about it."

Rage boiled up in her. Without thinking, she jerked up her knee and kicked it into his nuts. Satisfaction flooded her as his hand around her neck loosened and he doubled over, his face contorted in pain. But her glee was short lived.

Witnessing their master's predicament, two of his vampire minions instantly charged her. Despite her own speed and agility, they made mincemeat of her efforts to do a runner. Not that she had earnestly thought she stood a chance, but she had never been one to throw in the towel without trying.

By the time the goons had restrained her, bending her arms backwards and holding them in a decidedly uncomfortable position, Keegan had recovered from his temporary pain. She attempted a shrug. Seeing Keegan in pain had been worth it, even though she wished it had lasted longer.

Rose couldn't bring herself to regret the action even though her erstwhile lover now looked even more pissed off than when he'd stormed into her home.

"Try that again, and you'll end up at the end of my stake."

She raised a mocking eyebrow. "Go ahead. Kill me."

Clearly furious at her taunt, he pulled his stake and launched himself at her.

"But you'll never find it. Because it isn't here," she added calmly, stopping him in his tracks.

"Where did you hide it?"

She let out a bitter laugh. "Do you really think I'm stupid enough to tell you? . . . Men."

"I'll make you," Keegan threatened.

"I'm not afraid of dying. I've had a long enough life. I'm tired of it."

In part, it was the truth. She'd had a long life, and she wasn't afraid of dying. She'd died before. In fact, tonight was the anniversary of her death as a human and her rebirth as a vampire. But what wasn't the truth—and what she could never let him guess—was that as much as she hated being a vampire, she wasn't tired of this life, because she had a purpose.

"Everybody can be forced to talk." He tossed a wild look around the room, scanning it, searching for something.

"Not I. You have nothing on me, Keegan. You should know that."

"Even you have a weak spot. Even you, Rose." The vein in his temple throbbed, attesting to his quick temper.

"If I did, you'd never know. I'm the coldest vampire this side of the Mississippi, don't you know that? I don't form emotional attachments. Go ahead, destroy my house. See if I care."

She didn't. As a human she'd grown up in wealth; as a young vampire she'd lived on nothing until she'd carved out an existence for herself and finally amassed more wealth than her parents had ever dreamt of. Yet material things meant nothing to her.

Keegan's eyes narrowed as he swept the room once more with his searching gaze. When his eyes fell on the antique desk where she'd penned her letter only minutes earlier, he paused.

The desk was clean of clutter, except for two items: a fashion magazine and a pen.

He crossed the distance to it with the preternatural poise their species was graced with and picked up the ink pen. Its cap lay on the pristine surface of the desk.

"Been writing your memoires, have you?"

She tried for a nonchalant shrug. "Would you like a copy when I'm done?"

"And read what? The drivels of a whore who's as cold in bed as a block of ice? A frozen turkey would have provided a more welcome hole for my dick."

"Don't flatter yourself," she countered. "Your dick won't even fill the cavity of a rabbit."

A partial chuckle escaped one of the thugs, before he could stop himself. Big mistake, as it turned out: in vampire speed, Keegan leapt at the guy and plunged a stake into his chest, turning him to dust.

His eyes were glaring red when he turned back. "Anybody else have an opinion on that?"

Rose felt the two vampires who were still restraining her freeze at their boss's question.

"Didn't think so." Keegan returned to the desk. "So where were we?"

He tapped his finger against his temple in mock thought. "Ah, I remember, we were discussing what you were using this pen for." He motioned his hand to the otherwise empty desk. "Considering that I don't see any unpaid bills here, I have to assume you weren't writing checks."

She lifted her chin and kept her face expressionless. Inside, she was shaking. But decades of having to lie and cheat, to bluff and pretend, had taught her how to keep her poker face. And how to change the subject.

"Maybe I was extolling the virtues of your minuscule dick by writing a poem about it."

This time, her insult didn't have the same effect. Keegan merely chuckled. "Nice try, Rose. But even you don't beat a dead horse, and—" He turned and motioned to the spot where he'd only moments earlier killed his associate. "—we've already laid that subject to rest. But thanks for telling me that I'm on the right track."

With horror, she watched as he rummaged through the desk, pulling out drawers and emptying them, tossing their contents to the ground. Bills, pens, and office supplies fell on the carpet. When the last tiny drawer and its contents tumbled to the floor, Keegan let out a frustrated huff.

"Fuck!" he cursed.

An involuntary sigh of relief escaped her tense lungs, so tiny she thought nobody had noticed, but Keegan's head snapped to her. He tried to penetrate her with his look.

"It's there, isn't it? Your Achilles Heel."

His head turned back to the desk and the only item that remained on it. "Of course."

He picked up the magazine and shook it. From its pages, a single sheet of paper fluttered to the floor. He caught it before it reached the ground. "Gotcha."

Rose's heart sank.

With a triumphant grin, his eyes flew over the words she'd written, before he looked back at her, chuckling. "Well, well, Rose. Who would have thought that you had a heart? Had me fooled long enough."

Then he pointed to the letter, snapping his fingers against it. She knew what was coming. He now had a means to force her. To use her love for her own flesh and blood against her.

"The way I see it, you have two choices: give me back what you've stolen from me and I let your little grandson live . . . " He made a dramatic pause. "Don't, and I'll kill him."

A helpless gurgle escaped her throat. Because of her, Blake would suffer. But she couldn't sacrifice so many lives in exchange for just one, could she? If she gave Keegan what she'd taken from him, he would have the means to control so many lives and destroy those who opposed him. He would grow too powerful to defeat. She couldn't allow that, not to save just one single life.

"I can't be blackmailed. If you have to kill him, do it." Her heart bled for Blake. Despite all his faults, he didn't deserve this. He deserved a full life, a long and happy one.

Keegan's eyes narrowed into small slits as he approached. He studied her, but she knew all he would see was her determination to fight him. Then he looked back at the letter, reading it again. When he looked up, he had a self-congratulatory smirk on his face.

"My apologies, Rose. I believe I didn't use the right means to entice you. Let's try this again, shall we?" His casual voice turned to ice with his next words. "If you don't give it back to me, I'll turn him."

Her throat seized, robbing her of the ability to breathe. "No," she managed to choke out.

He moved closer to her, dropping his voice to the same volume as hers. "Yes."

"Don't do this."

Keegan smiled, and had she not known him so well, she would have thought it was out of kindness. "You hate your own species so much you want to save your great-great-whatever-grandson from becoming one of us. Then save him."

She swallowed. There had to be another way. "It's not here. I hid it."

"We'll go together."

Quickly, she shook her head. "I've left strict instructions: if I don't go to pick it up on my own, it will be destroyed."

Keegan's eyes flashed in obvious distrust. The cords in his neck strained as he fought for control. She held her ground and didn't flinch.

"I give you two hours to retrieve it."

Desperate to buy herself more time, she added another lie to her earlier one. "There are other . . . safety precautions I put in place. There are only certain times during which I have access."

When Keegan narrowed his eyes, she added quickly, "Similar to a time-delay lock at a bank. I need at least twenty-four hours."

Keegan let out an angry huff. "If you cheat me, I'll find this Blake. And I'll make his turning the most horrific event of his life. Do you understand me?"

Rose simply nodded.

"I'll be watching you. You have twenty-four hours or I'm hunting down your boy."

He ushered his two henchmen outside and disappeared into the night.

Trembling, her stance faltered. With her last ounce of strength, she reached the sofa and let herself fall onto it.

Tears freed themselves from her eyes and rolled down her cheeks like an avalanche. She couldn't allow Blake to meet the same fate as her. She'd promised Charlotte and herself that her children and children's children would lead normal lives. Nobody would be cursed to be a vampire. Never again.

"Where are you when I need you?" she cried out. "Quinn, you have to help me now. You owe me. He's your flesh and blood too."

2

Quinn slunk into the passenger seat as Oliver took the driver's seat of the SUV and started the engine.

"Wish you could stay longer," Oliver said as he pulled onto the unlit country lane, leaving the house behind where the inner core of Scanguards had been celebrating yet another blood-bond.

Only vampires and their mates had been invited—well, and Oliver. Not to forget a few dogs: Zane had brought Z, and Samson and Delilah had brought their baby daughter Isabelle's little puppy too. If they weren't careful, Scanguards would turn into a circus.

"Gotta get back to New York. Besides, what would I do here? Watch how Zane makes puppy eyes at Portia the same way his dog does?" Quinn chuckled. "Better get out of here. Whatever's going on here might be contagious."

The human kid next to him gave him a sideways grin—yeah, he was a kid, barely in his mid-twenties, and while Quinn too looked rather young, he carried the experience and memories of two centuries on his shoulders. Two very long and lonely centuries, despite the fact that he'd never been alone and had always surrounded himself with the hottest pieces of ass available. But being surrounded by others hadn't chased away the emptiness in his heart. He'd felt it physically tonight. Seeing so many of his friends happily tied to their blood-bonded mates had driven reality home once more.

"Like you would ever settle down," Oliver claimed. "Hey man, the life you're living—that's what I want. Women left, right, and center. You're doing it right."

Quinn caught his admiring look and forced his usual charming smile onto his lips. He'd perfected it over the last two hundred years, and by now, even he couldn't tell how fake it was. If that wasn't an accomplishment in itself!

"Hey, kiddo, I just make it look easy. Being a playboy takes a lot of work—and energy." He winked, forcing his thoughts about his past to retreat into the dark recesses of his mind.

Oliver burst out in laughter. "Right! I don't mind *that* kind of work." He wiggled his eyebrows in Groucho Marx fashion. "And energy I've got plenty of."

"The young!" Quinn rolled his eyes. "No appreciation for the art of seduction. It takes skill and cunning to coax a woman into your bed."

"It takes money, good looks, and a big dick!"

Quinn couldn't help but chuckle. "Well, that certainly helps. But then of course that leaves you short on two things."

Oliver turned his head away from the winding road ahead of him.

" 'Cause the looks you've got!" Quinn added.

His young colleague snorted, showing his outrage. "You haven't seen my dick!"

"Yeah, and by the grace of God, I hope I never will." Quinn laughed, unable to contain himself.

Oliver glared at him. "I have what it takes!"

"Whatever you say, kiddo!" His eyes started tearing, and he could barely get the words out without bursting into laughter.

"You don't believe me? What? You think cause you're a vampire and I'm not, I don't have the equipment?"

Quinn shook his head. "I can't believe we're having this conversation."

"Well, is that it? You think you're better at it because you're a vampire?"

Quinn decided not to let Oliver goad him into a comparison of their two species. With a grin on his face he winked at him. "Once you've been at it for as long as I have, I bet you'd be even better than me. I think you'd be a natural."

A proud sheen of excitement radiated from Oliver's eyes. "You really think that?"

"Sure I do. I've seen how girls look at you." He ruffled his dark hair, which as usual stood in all directions as if he'd just gotten out of bed. "Of course at this point they all just want to tame your wild mane. But trust me, that's an advantage: you reel them in with your innocent, cute-boy looks, and badabing-badaboom, you've got them in the sack."

Oliver grinned from ear to ear. "Yeah!"

He looked so innocent and fresh-faced, Quinn felt his heart clench for a moment. He'd been like Oliver once: full of excitement for his life ahead. Full of hope. In love. And then he'd lost it all: his life, his hope, his love.

He cleared his throat, desperately trying to push down the rising memories and reached for the first words that came to him. "You should come visit me in New York. We can hang out and pick up some babes."

"Really?" Oliver's voice was full of awe as if he'd just been presented with the keys to a Lamborghini. "You mean that? Man! That's awesome!"

Quinn sighed. Now he'd unleashed something in the kid that would last at least until they reached the airport, where a private Scanguards jet was waiting to take him to New York. Better that than wallowing in his own thoughts. And maybe a visit from Oliver would be fun. Jake, who was currently holding down the fort in the New York office of Scanguards, could join them, and the three of them could go hunting.

He could teach the kid a thing or two, just for the hell of it. When he was older, he would understand that it wasn't about how many conquests he made, but who he conquered.

"Why don't you talk to Samson and ask him to give you a couple of weeks off? I'm sure he'll be okay with it. Now that Zane's all domesticated, I really have nobody else to go partying with."

Oliver's face lit up like a Christmas tree. "You mean I'm going to be like Zane? Like I'm taking his place?"

Quinn howled. "You've got to be kidding me, Oliver! Nobody can be like Zane!"

"But I'm taking his place, aren't I?" he hastened to repeat.

Quinn gave him a slap on the shoulder, secretly happy about the kid's enthusiasm. Nevertheless, he couldn't stop needling him. "Those are big shoes to fill. You're up for that?"

"You say when and where, and I'm your man!" Oliver proclaimed, beaming at him.

Quinn nodded, his head turning sideways, when he perceived something in the corner of his eye. His head whipped toward the dark road in front of them. Shit!

"Oliver! Watch out!" he yelled.

Oliver's head snapped to the obstacle in front of them: in their lane, cones cordoned off equipment for road work, resting there for the night, but the flashing lights that usually accompanied such blockages weren't flashing—they appeared dim and barely recognizable in the dark night. To the right of it there was no outlet: a wall of rock rose next to the shoulder.

"Fuck!" came from Oliver's mouth.

"Swerve!"

Just as Oliver yanked the steering wheel to the left to avoid the excavator, the light of another car speeding toward them, blinded them. In vampire speed, Quinn jerked the wheel back to the right, just as Oliver slammed on the brakes.

The tires screeched, and the back of the car fishtailed out. Loose gravel from the construction site suddenly made the tires spin without finding purchase. The car advanced, virtually unimpeded, heading straight for the excavator. Wildly turning the unresponsive steering wheel and pressing down the brakes, Oliver tried to avoid the inevitable. With a loud thud, the car crashed into the side of the small excavator, which toppled to its side. Only now, Quinn noticed the crane next to it.

The power of the impact deployed the airbags, but the windows blew out and with horror, Quinn saw how Oliver was thrown out of the car. He hadn't worn his seat belt.

Quinn was held back by his own seat belt, the air bag suddenly obstructing his view.

He fumbled for the release of the belt and realized that it was jammed. He forced his fingers to turn into claws, but just as he sliced through the material, he heard a snapping sound and looked around him when he perceived a movement outside the passenger window. As he whirled his head to look through it, he saw a large plate of steel, suspended from the beam of the crane, swinging toward him.

He froze in mid-movement. Shit! There was no way out of this. The steel plate would decapitate him. It was over.

His life didn't flash before him; maybe it wasn't that way for vampires. Only one thought filled him now. He was finally going home.

Rose.

With a last breath, he sighed.

Rose, we'll be together again. Finally.

Then he felt the impact as the car got hit. He was knocked sideways, hitting the steering wheel to his left. All went black.

3

London, 1813

"Rose," Quinn whispered from behind a hedge as he saw her emerge from the ballroom and step onto the quiet terrace, where at present nobody else sought refuge from the crowd.

She looked lovelier than ever. Her golden hair was piled high on her head, soft ringlets pulled from it to surround her perfectly oval face. Her skin was alabaster—not a single wrinkle anywhere, flawless. Her dress was cut fashionably low, her small bosom enhanced by the bodice that pushed up her flesh as if presenting it on a platter. With each step she took, it threatened to escape the silken fabric of her dress, bouncing merrily up and down, driving any breathing man insane in the process. More so Quinn, for he was in love with the delightful creature.

"Rose."

When she heard his voice, she hurried in his direction, cautiously throwing a glance over her shoulder toward the ballroom, making sure nobody had followed her.

In the seconds it took her to come to him, he admired her graceful walk, which seemed as light as that of a gazelle. The sound of her slippers was absorbed into nothingness as soon as she stepped off the terrace and onto the manicured lawn below.

Quinn reached for her and pulled her behind the hedge with him, hungry for a touch. A kiss even.

"Quinn." Her voice was breathless as if she'd danced one of the more energetic country dances the lower classes enjoyed and not the sedate dances their hosts, Lord and Lady Somersby, preferred.

When he dragged her against him, disregarding all manners and decorum, the rays of the moon lit her face, presenting her heated cheeks to his gaze. But his eyes dipped lower to those lips that waited, slightly parted, for his touch.

"Oh, Rose, my love. I couldn't wait another moment."

He sunk his lips onto hers, taking in her pure scent, her innocent response. With a sigh, he slid his hand to the back of her head and pulled her closer. When he nudged his tongue against her lips, a soft whimper issued from her mouth. He welcomed it and slipped his tongue between her lips, sliding it along her teeth, coaxing, tempting, urging. Her taste was intoxicating, her scent mouthwatering.

Finally, her timid tongue met his, and life stood still.

"My Rose," he mumbled and slanted his mouth, diving into her, his passion unleashed, his control shattered. This was the third time he kissed her, and just like the first two times, the moment she responded to him, he was lost.

His other hand went down to her buttocks, palming her curves through the thin layers of her ball gown. A shocked gasp escaped her, but a moment later, she molded her heated body to his, her soft breasts rubbing against his evening coat. And lower down, where his trousers were bulging with a shaft as hard as a blacksmith's iron rod, he nestled against her soft center. Was it the summer air or the fact she'd danced all night that he perceived her so hot there? Or did the heat have an altogether different reason?

The thought nearly drove him to madness. But he couldn't take her here, where any moment now, another amorous couple or some unsuspecting guest might stumble upon them. Reluctantly, he released her lips. Yet he couldn't let go of her body.

"We must be careful," she whispered, her voice hoarse, her lips looking thoroughly red and abused. He was responsible for that, but by God, he couldn't regret it.

"Papa will soon notice that I am gone."

"Nonsense, your father is occupied at the tables. And I've made sure your chaperone is otherwise engaged."

Her eyes widened. Was it surprise or delight he saw in them?

"Pray tell, what did you do?"

He winked at her mischievously. "I made sure she had an ardent admirer this evening who will claim all her dances and ply her with punch."

She flicked her fan lightly against his waistcoat. "You are cruel. What if she believes in his insincere attention?"

Quinn took her hand and led her fingers to his lips, kissing them one-by-one as he replied, "Who says his attention is insincere? Mayhap he simply needed a little encouragement to overcome his shyness."

"You, my lord," she said in mock-reprimand, "have not a single young man in your acquaintance to whom the label of 'shy' might

apply. The company you keep is considered most . . . " She hesitated,
looking for the correct word. " . . . debauched."

"Does it matter what company I keep? All I truly desire is yours.
And once you grant it, I shall be with only you."

"You mean to say, once my father grants it."

Quinn sighed, his chest heavy with what he had come to tell her
tonight. He'd thought long and hard about it, had even discussed it with
his older brother, who had thought the idea a viable one.

"What is wrong?" Her voice carried the sound of concern.

"Ah, perceptive as always. Is there anything I can hide from you?"

Rose gave him a coquettish smile, one that made his heart melt. "Do
you *want* to hide anything from me, my lord?"

He pulled her closer. "If you call me 'my lord' one more time, I
certainly shall. But when my name crosses your lips, I will be utterly
incapable of doing so."

Her eyelids fluttered as her cheeks colored in a deeper red. "Quinn."
More breath than sound, the word tumbled from her lips.

Capturing her chin between thumb and forefinger, he brought her
mouth to his. "Ah, Rose, you tempt me so."

He sensed her lift herself onto her tip toes, and he had no restraint
left. All he could do was kiss her, take her soft lips, caress her wicked
tongue, all the while pressing her soft curves to his body, fueling the fire
inside him until he realized that he could not take leave of her tonight.

Nudging back from her lips, he put his forehead to hers. "My love, I
will be leaving tomorrow. For the continent."

A shocked gasp escaped her as she pulled her head back to stare at
him in surprise. "Leaving?"

With his knuckles, he brushed over her cheek. "I purchased a
commission and shall be joining Wellington's army."

Her lips quivered. "You are going to war?"

She pulled from him, but he dragged her back.

"It's the only way. Your father won't give his consent. I spoke to
him. He simply laughed in my face."

"You spoke to Papa? About me?"

He nodded. "I asked for your hand. He refused, saying I have
nothing to offer you, no title, no wealth of significance. My brother will
inherit the title; all I have is a small estate from my mother's side. Your

father doesn't deem it sufficient."

And why should he? Rose deserved so much more. She was the daughter of an Earl, a beauty at that, and suitors lined up wherever she appeared. Her father would be a fool to allow her to marry a second son, a man without a title.

"But he must understand." Her eyes reddened, a sign that tears were imminent.

Quinn laid his finger across her lips. "Shh, my love. Hear me out. I have a plan. It will work."

Rose raised her lids in hope. Ah, how he could see the love shining in her eyes, a love that burned for him. It was all worth it, just to see this.

"I have spoken to several officers in Wellington's army. I can rise in the ranks very quickly. I'll be fighting by Wellington's side soon and come back a decorated war hero. Many doors will open for me; I will be wealthy, and despite the lack of title, your father won't refuse me then."

He could see the little wheels in her pretty head turn, the way frown lines showed on her forehead told him as much.

"But you can get killed."

Of course, she would be worried about him. He hadn't expected anything less. "You know me. I can look after myself. I promise you, I'll come back in one piece."

She gave him a doubtful look. "They all say that. And then they come back, limbs missing, or worse, they don't come back at all. I have heard of the accounts, of the terrible things that happen on the battlefield." She turned away from him.

Quinn sighed and put his arms around her from behind, pulling her against him, her soft buttocks fitting perfectly against his groin. "My love, I will come back to you. I promise you that. I won't allow anybody to kill me. And you know why?"

"Why?" she asked, her voice quiet and resigned.

He dipped his head to her neck. "Because I love you, and I plan on spending my life making you happy."

"You promise?"

"Yes, if you promise me one thing too."

"Yes?" She turned her head to meet his gaze.

"You won't entertain any other offers of marriage. You are mine, no other man will ever touch you."

She closed her eyes. "Papa will force me."

Quinn shook his head. "No, he won't be able to." Tonight he would make sure that Rose could never accept another man.

He turned her to face him. "Because tonight, you'll become mine."

He witnessed the exact moment when Rose realized what he was saying. First, shock spread over her lovely features, then a furious blush, her bosom heaving in concert with her excited breaths.

"You are planning on ruining me?" she whispered.

"Not ruin. I'm going to make you mine; I'm going to make you my wife and love you like a husband."

"A husband," she murmured in disbelief. "Without the blessings of the church and society?"

He chuckled. His sweet Rose! How could she believe he would even contemplate such a thing? He patted his breast pocket. "Of course not, my sweet, I have procured a special license, and have a minister and a witness waiting for us this minute."

"But I don't understand. If we were to get married tonight, why do you need to go to war at all?"

With a heavy heart, Quinn looked at her. "Because I want your father's consent. For you. I don't want you to be shunned by your family and by society. This will remain our secret, and only should your father force you to marry somebody else during my absence, will you reveal to him that you're already married to me. Only then. And once I return a war hero, I will ask for your father's permission. And we shall marry a second time. And nobody except you and I will be the wiser."

She contemplated his words, her intelligent eyes studying him. "So you are proposing to me?"

He nodded. "And your answer?"

She flicked her fan at him. "Has nobody taught you how to propose?" She clicked her tongue, clearly amused. "Well, on your knees then."

Laughing, he dropped to one knee. "You're not making this easy, my love. But since you insist."

"I do indeed. Since this will be the only offer of marriage I shall entertain, I would at least like to enjoy the performance."

Her encouragement lifted his worries about a possible rejection.

"My darling Rose, will you marry me and let me love you for the rest of our lives?"

"Yes!" She threw herself at him, making him land on his back, with her on top of him.

"Ah, I like this position."

"Quinn Ralston, you are a scoundrel!"

"Yes, a scoundrel on his wedding night. Now my sweet bride, release me from this utterly compromising position, so we can meet the minister and *enjoy* the rest of tonight's *performance*."

As he repeated her words, she let out another delightful laugh.

The minister was waiting at a little chapel only a short stroll from the grounds of the Somersby's estate. Next to him, his friend James Worthington, stood patiently.

If anybody asked him to recount the ceremony later, Quinn would be unable to do so. He was too mesmerized by the sight of his alluring bride. All he could do was look at her, knowing that shortly she would be his wife in every sense of the word.

"I do take thee, Quinn Robert James Ralston . . . "

4

When the door to the chapel shut behind the minister and his friend, Quinn lifted Rose into his arms.

"My wife."

"My husband."

He started walking them toward the door.

"Where are we going?"

"To a small cottage." Quinn had arranged for a place nearby, where they could spend a few hours alone, knowing there would be no time to take her to his own townhouse, which was clear across town.

When they reached the house that was tucked away in a side street, he wasn't disappointed. The owner had made sure the inside of the small cottage was clean and comfortable. He headed for the door that led to the bedroom. Clean linen covered the bed in the corner, and a single candle burned on a chest of drawers nearby.

While he'd hoped for a more lavish environment to make Rose his, he knew there was no time to lose. He was leaving at first light, and consummating their marriage was paramount. It was the only way of making sure that her father couldn't marry her off to one of the titled suitors who, even now, were hovering in the ballroom for their chance at claiming her. She would have to wait for him and him alone.

He set Rose back on her feet and closed the door behind them. When she turned to him in the dim light, he recognized her heavy breathing and her flushed face.

"Don't be afraid, my love. I won't hurt you. I'll be the gentlest of lovers. Your pleasure is my pleasure." He meant it. Now that he knew she would surrender to him, he would take his time to create a memory she would look back at with joy until he returned.

"I'm not afraid," she whispered, her lips trembling nevertheless.

She was so brave, his beautiful Rose.

Slowly he lifted his hands and stroked along her neck down to her shoulders, where the puffed sleeves of her gown sat like little butterflies, delicate and nearly transparent. Gently, he took hold of the thin fabric and tugged on it, inching it down her arms.

Her breath hitched, her lips parting in the same instant as she lowered her lids to avoid his gaze.

"Rose, look at me."

She lifted her eyes.

"You should feel no shame. What is between us is pure and honest."

He moved his hands to her chest, slowly pushing her bodice lower. Without the restraints of a corset, the fabric moved out of the way, freeing her breasts, delivering them to his hungry eyes. Dark rose buds sat on pink mounds of flesh that despite the lack of any support were firm. Her breasts weren't large, but they were perfect in shape and form. He feasted his eyes on the sight, unable to get enough.

Rose's eyes squeezed shut. He bent to her, kissing her lids one after the other.

"Oh, Rose, you are beautiful. I am the luckiest man in all of England."

Then he allowed his hands to roam. As he palmed her breasts, feeling her warm flesh in his hands for the first time, his cock twitched in anticipation.

"Tell me, my love, what am I holding in my hands?"

Her eyes widened.

"Tell me," he coaxed.

"M . . . my br . . . breasts."

He gave her a soft smile. "Men call them tits."

At the crude word, he saw her pull in a breath.

"Yes, and you have gorgeous tits, my beautiful wife. The most beautiful tits I have ever seen."

Her cheeks flushed even more, but there was no anger in her eyes, instead he saw signs of desire there, of passion, of lust. Yes, Rose, his lovely, proper Rose, had a wild streak in her. He'd always known it; in fact, it was what had made him fall in love with her. And it was why he'd known she would surrender to him, because she wanted it too. She wanted to experience that wildness, that passion. With him.

Bending his head, he captured one beautiful taut nipple with his lips and sucked on it.

"Ohhh!" she exclaimed, almost immediately thrusting her chest out so he could take more of her.

"You like that?" he mumbled, continuing to lick and suck her responsive breast.

"Yes, oh yes, Quinn. It feels . . . it feels so . . . good."

He released her breast only to lavish the same attention on the other one. When he felt her hand on his neck to hold him to her, he couldn't suppress a grin. Oh yes, she would be a wonderful wife, and an even more amazing lover. And knowing that he would never get enough of her, they would have many children, a whole estate full of them.

Not taking his mouth off her breast, he lifted her into his arms and carried her to the bed, where he set her on her feet. Hastily, he took off his coat and opened the buttons of his waistcoat, feeling his body heat up as if a furnace were burning inside him.

Only when he'd freed himself of his waistcoat, did he allow himself to lay his hands on her again. Instantly, she melted into him. He tugged on the dress, loosening a few of the fastenings in the back, and pushed it to the ground. Her petticoat and chemise followed. When she stood before him only in her drawers, her arms went around her torso as if to protect herself.

He took them and gently moved them to her sides. "Never hide yourself from me. Beauty like yours should never be hidden."

Moments later, she lay on her back on the bed with Quinn slowly untying the strings of her drawers. Her hand clamped over his, making him look at her face.

"I'm scared."

He pressed a kiss on her hand. "I am too."

"You are?" Her eyes stared at him, wide and surprised.

"Yes, because if I can't pleasure you, if you don't enjoy what I'm going to do, I will lose you. And I can't lose you. I need you, Rose."

A relieved smile spread on her face and all the way to her eyes. "If you do anything close to what you do to me when you kiss me, I'm certain I will enjoy it."

Her words made his heart stutter. Was she telling him that she found his kisses arousing?

"Tell me what you feel when I kiss you."

Her eyes closed half way. "I get this warm feeling. All warm and . . . tingling."

"Where? Where does it tingle?" he urged her.

Rose pulled her lower lip between her teeth and that action alone brought him to the brink of release. How much longer he could hold back before he had to thrust his hard cock into her, he didn't know.

"There," she whispered almost inaudibly, hesitantly moving her hand lower, releasing his and bringing it to the apex of her thighs. "There."

A moan escaped him at the knowledge of what his kisses did to her. Because they did the same to him.

"I can do more than just make you tingle there," he promised and slowly moved her drawers over her hips, revealing her most secret place, then pulling them down her legs. He discarded them carelessly and quickly looked at what he'd unveiled.

The canopy that guarded her sweet cunny was a dusting of blond curls, barely hiding the rosy flesh beneath. The scent of her arousal wafted to him, enveloping him in a cocoon of desire and lust. He'd been with other women, sown his oats, but never before had the scent of a woman caused him to lose his senses as with Rose.

He tore his shirt from his torso, perspiring at the mere thought of what he was about to do.

"I will cherish this, cherish you," he whispered, spreading her thighs as if he'd done so a thousand times before.

Then he sank between her legs, lowering his head to her sex.

"What are you—?"

But he cut off her surprised question by placing his lips onto her soft curls and soaking in her intoxicating scent.

"But you can't . . . " she tried to protest, her voice dying with a moan before it came to life again. "Surely, this is not proper."

He lifted his head for a moment and unleashed a satisfied grin. "Oh, my love, but it is very proper. A man who doesn't want to eat his wife's sweet cunny, is a Philistine. He has no sense of taste or pleasure. And I pride myself on both."

With a moan, he brushed his lips against her sex and took his first lick. His tongue swiped over her nether lips, those plump folds that glistened with her desire, and carried her taste into his mouth. Her nectar was sweet and tangy at the same time, so many different flavors bursting in his mouth in a symphony of delight. Ah, yes, she would be a wonderful wife, one whose bedchamber he would visit nightly. In fact, he didn't see the need to have his own bedchamber. He would simply move into hers, sleep with her in his arms every night. A shocking proposition, yet one he hoped she would agree to.

When he felt her twist under his mouth and heard soft moans and sighs—hers not his—fill the small chamber, he knew that he could give his sweet Rose a night to remember. Taking his time, he spread her legs wider, opening her folds, testing and tasting, exploring her, never neglecting the bundle of flesh that sat just at the base of her curls. Her pearl was engorged, red and swollen, and with each lick he delivered, with each swipe of his tongue over the sensitive organ, she issued sounds of pleasure.

Her naked breasts heaved, her breaths coming in short pants, and her skin started to glisten, a thin sheen of perspiration spreading over her entire body, evidence of the heat that was building inside her. The same kind of heat that was inside him, ready to burst to the surface.

His cock pulsated angrily against the flap of his trousers. He tried to ignore it as best he could. First, he wanted to give her pleasure. And he could only do that as long as he kept his own lust leashed. Once his cock was thrusting into her, there was no way he could keep the passion inside him under control. He would pound into her like a wild animal, unable to see to her pleasure. He'd desired her for too long to destroy this perfect moment with haste, despite the fact he was starving for her.

"Oh, yes," she moaned, her hands digging into his hair, holding him to her, urging him for more.

His tongue lashed against her pearl, rapidly and with single-minded purpose: to show her ultimate ecstasy, to teach her the pleasures her body was capable of. Pleasures he could unleash in her, share with her.

With his finger, he stroked against her cleft, gently probing. God, she was tight. He would split her in half if he tried to plunge into her. How could she possibly get used to him? There was so little time; he had only tonight.

With trepidation, Quinn slowly pressed his finger between her plump nether lips, parting them. His tongue never ceasing to caress her swollen pearl, he drove his digit into her tight opening. An instinctive tensing of her muscles was her response, so he doubled his efforts on her precious button, licking it harder and faster.

Rose's body relaxed. It allowed him to drive his finger into her to the last knuckle. Warmth and wetness engulfed him, and the knowledge that his cock would feel those same muscles gripping him tightly in a few minutes made his heart race like a wild horse galloping to escape a captor.

When he started moving his finger in and out of her, her hips undulated, moving in rhythm with his gentle thrusts. Yes, she was a natural, her body telling her what she needed. Her panting became more pronounced, her breaths faster and shorter, sounds of pleasure spurting from her lips like water cascading over a waterfall.

"Ah, Rose, my Rose," he murmured against her flesh.

Her body tensed. "Quinn . . . I need . . . I . . . I want," she whispered.

He knew what she was unable to express. With his tongue he pressed hard against her pearl while his finger delivered a deep thrust.

A strangled cry filled the cottage. Not one of pain, but one of pure pleasure, for her muscles started convulsing around his finger, her hips moving wildly as her climax took her.

"Oh God!" she cried out.

Seconds stretched longer as he continued to gently move inside her, continued to lick her quivering pearl, wanting to extend, to prolong her ecstasy.

When he finally looked up as her body started to calm, he gazed into the face of a new Rose: one who looked at him with wonder and amazement in her eyes. He'd done that to her, and he swore that he would do everything in his power to make her feel this way for the rest of their lives.

"Quinn, my Quinn."

He lifted himself. With an efficiency that was new to him, he discarded his trousers. When he stood in front of her with not a stitch on him, Rose's eyes dropped to his groin.

His hand went to his fully erect cock. It was so rigid, so pumped full with blood that it curved against his stomach. And his balls were pulled just as tight.

"You're so . . . so . . . big."

A flash of fear crossed her features.

Slowly he lowered himself to her, sank down between her spread legs.

"You're wet for me now. I'll slip into you without resistance. I'll fill you more completely than my fingers ever could. And you'll hold me there until we both experience ecstasy together."

Slanting his lips over hers, he kissed her gently, let her taste herself on his tongue. She moaned into his mouth and he went deeper, driving his tongue into her sweet cavern just as his cock nudged against her nether lips. As if she knew what to do, she pulled up her knees, adjusting her angle.

Unable to restrain himself, he thrust inside her. Her muffled cry made him stop instantly. He'd burst through her maidenhead. She was his.

"Easy, my love," he cooed. "The pain will disappear in a second."

She nodded, her eyes squinting.

"My brave Rose. You're my wife now. Say it, call me your husband."

Her eyes opened wide. "My husband. You're my husband now."

"Yes," he whispered and pulled back, withdrawing almost completely from her warm sheath. "And now your husband will make love to you until you come apart once more."

As he plunged back into her welcoming depth and took her lips once more, her arms and legs wrapped around him as if she were trying to make sure he didn't leave her.

With every thrust, every stroke, and every moan, their bodies moved more in sync, adjusting to each other, learning each other. Every stroke brought him deeper into her warm cave, her muscles gripping him like a tight fist, imprisoning him in a cage he never wanted to escape.

It was like a dance. At first unsure and uneven, uncertain what the other would do, but with every minute that their bodies moved together, with every thrust he delivered, every kiss he captured, they fused, became one.

Quinn felt her hands on him, roaming his back, moving to his buttocks, her fingernails digging into his flesh, urging him on. But he tried to hold back, knowing her flesh was too fragile to go any harder than he was already taking her. If he did, there was no telling what would happen. He wanted their first time to be perfect, to make her want more, to wait for him.

But Rose continued to pull him harder to her as she slung her legs tightly around him, digging her heels into his backside.

"Oh, God, Rose! You have to stop doing that or I'll forget myself."

She gave him a startled look. "You don't like it? I'm not doing it right?"

When he noticed her retreat into herself, he stopped her. "No. No. You're doing this too well. It's better than I ever imagined. But if you continue like this, I won't be able to pull out when it's time."

He wasn't a cad. Taking her virginity was one thing, but risking leaving her with child while he wouldn't come back for at least a year was unacceptable.

"When it's time?" she whispered back, her forehead creasing.

"Before I spend."

"Oh."

Quinn pressed his forehead to hers. "I love you, my Rose, my wife, my everything."

Then he took her lips and allowed himself to forget everything except the woman in his arms. With more passion than before, with more determination and fervor, he kissed her, showing her that she belonged to him, that she would always be his. And her response was equally untamed.

Their bodies intertwined, they moved as one. The makeshift surroundings forgotten, the dire circumstances pushed to the background, Quinn allowed only one thought to remain: Rose was his. The woman he would love forever, the woman who would bear his children one day.

Her glistening skin sliding against him, her hands stroking his heated flesh, he felt as if he were in a dream, but this was real. Rose was in his arms, connected to him. She had accepted him, his love, his body. And she had given him her most prized possession: her virginity.

That thought made him plunge deeper and harder into her. The knowledge that she wanted him, despite the fact that he was a nobody, despite the fact that her future with him was uncertain, made his heart swell. She possessed his heart now, she owned him. Just as he was the keeper of her heart now.

"I love you, Quinn."

At her words, his balls tightened, the fire in them threatening to incinerate him from the inside.

"Always!"

With a hard thrust, he drove into her again, then slid his hand between their bodies, searching and finding her sensitive pearl. He stroked his finger against the moist flesh.

"Once more, Rose, once more. Fly with me."

When he felt her muscles spasm, squeezing his cock even tighter than she already was, he lost all coherent thought. Only pleasure mattered now. Release was all he could think of. Unable to hold onto his control, he let himself fall.

The burning in his balls signaled his imminent release. With a groan, he pulled from her sheath, too late to avoid spilling his seed over the insides of her thighs, rather than into the sheets. His heart was racing.

Rose was his wife now. His lover. His forever.

5

Quinn blinked. Before his eyes, everything was tinted red. Had he landed in hell? To tell the truth, he'd hoped for heaven, not that he'd gotten his hopes up too high. After all, he'd led a thoroughly debauched life, even though he'd never committed any violent crimes. Well, killing while defending one's own life wasn't considered a crime. If there was a god, then he hoped he—or she—would cut him some slack. After all, hadn't he always donated to charities and taken care of orphans and other less fortunate people? Didn't that count for anything?

"Thanks a lot!" he cursed and winced instantly.

His lip was split, and the taste of his own blood was in his mouth.

"What the . . . ?"

If he was dead, why was he injured and feeling pain? His head shot up, quickly assessing his surroundings.

"Shit, I'm alive!"

His gaze darted to his right. There, where the metal beam should have entered the car and decapitated him, another metal pole was wedged between it and the shattered car window. It had stopped the beam's path. Where it had come from, Quinn wasn't sure. Maybe it had been catapulted off the nearby stack of supplies when the crane had toppled.

Relieved, Quinn straightened, pushing away from the steering wheel and easing back into his seat. His hands made a quick assessment of his body: no major injuries. His heartbeat slowed somewhat. He'd escaped mostly intact. His vision was still blurry, though, and everything appeared with a red tint. Carefully, he wiped his eyes with the sleeve of his jacket, then blinked a few times. The tint disappeared, only leaving a faint red at the edges of his vision.

Sighing, he looked past the nearly deflated airbag and through the blown-out windshield. His heart stopped and his stomach lurched. If vampires had any content in their stomachs, he would have lost it now.

Oliver.

What he saw, chilled him to the bones: Oliver was impaled on the shovel of the dipper, one of its jagged teeth sticking out through his stomach. Blood gushed from him. His body hung there, suspended like a limp rag doll.

Quinn scrambled forward, lunging through the remnants of the windshield, ignoring the crumbled pieces of glass.

This was all his fault. He'd distracted Oliver while he was driving. He should be the one impaled on those spikes now, not Oliver, not the innocent boy who had an entire lifetime ahead of him.

Within seconds, he reached his friend.

"Oh, God, Oliver."

Why did he have to die so violently? Why so young? He hadn't even begun to live yet. Out of its own volition, Quinn's hand touched the boy's cheek, where dirt and blood had mixed. His skin was still warm.

"I'm so sorry. I would do anything to make this undone."

He would have gladly given his own life for Oliver's. He'd lived three normal lifetimes, and he was tired of it. Recalling Rose in the moments before the beam had hit the car, had brought it all home for him: he couldn't continue like this, whoring his way through life in the hope he would one day forget her. He knew he never would. He'd always known that his heart belonged to her, that she'd taken it to the grave with her. She would never release him, just as he could never release her.

He should have died tonight. Maybe then he would have finally found peace. He would see her again—if there was such a thing as heaven. Maybe he would get one more glimpse at her, see her, touch her, love her one last time.

"God, why? Why are you so cruel?" he screamed, lifting his head toward the night sky. Stars glittered in the dark, unaware of his turmoil. Mocking him in his despair. No help would come from that direction.

Resigned, he wrapped his arms around Oliver and held him, cheeks touching, wanting to give comfort even though the life had already left his body. All of a sudden, he felt a pounding, beats of two different rhythms dueling. Startled, he pulled away, his hand instantly sliding to Oliver's neck, pressing against it.

There! A movement against his fingers. Was he dreaming? Imagining it? A beat. Then another one. Faint and growing more irregular, it was barely recognizable, but it was still there: a heartbeat.

Oliver was still alive.

There was no time to lose.

As gently yet as quickly as he could, Quinn drew Oliver forward and pulled him off the spike, bringing him down on the ground where he kept him in his lap.

"If there was another way, I wouldn't do this," he said to his unconscious friend. "But there's no time left."

The kid had only seconds to live. His pain would soon be gone. He would surrender this life, but in its stead, he would be issued a new one—a less vulnerable one.

Quinn brought his own wrist to his mouth and extended his fangs, piercing his skin so the blood dripped from it. Touching Oliver's neck again, he listened for the heartbeat growing fainter, anxiously waiting for the short window during which a human's body would be susceptible to a change, when it could accept what Quinn offered. When the time between the beats stretched longer and longer, he brought his bleeding wrist to Oliver's lips.

The first drops of blood entered his mouth. Quinn pumped his fist, causing more blood to drip from his wound and into his dying friend's throat. When he saw the boy swallow for the first time, he expelled a sigh of relief.

"More," he commanded.

Relieved that the unconscious Oliver obeyed, Quinn brushed a wayward strand of dark hair away from his face. Glass splinters had left him with cuts to his young face, but they would heal quickly. Once the transformation was complete, Oliver would bear no sign of the accident—if he survived the turning. A fair percentage of humans didn't. He could only hope that Oliver's body didn't reject the change.

Still feeding him his blood, Quinn looked up at the night sky, searching it, yet finding nothing.

"Are you happy now? Are you?" he yelled out his frustration. But God didn't offer an answer.

Quinn had never turned a soul, never considered it. He didn't want this responsibility, didn't want to be the one who changed another's life for eternity. This had been thrust upon him. But now he was stuck with it, with his decision and the newfound responsibility it brought with it.

He would be a sire now. A maker. Something he never wanted to be. Would he fail in his duties the way his own sire had failed him? Would he desert his protégé just as his sire had deserted him soon after he'd been turned? Just when he had needed him most, when he had been in the depth of despair, his sire Wallace had disappeared, simply left him never to come back. Quinn had searched for him, but never found a trace. He'd felt alone and abandoned. And heartbroken.

Violently, Quinn shook his head and looked back down at Oliver.

"I won't do this to you. I won't abandon you like Wallace did. You understand that? You're my son now."

A son. God, how often had he dreamed of having a child, one that had the fair looks of its mother, of Rose. They could have been a happy family. But the war and what had happened on the battlefield had destroyed that dream.

In the distance the canons continued to thunder even though night had fallen already. Somewhere he heard drums, interrupted by screams of wounded men, dying men like himself. Quinn knew it was over. He'd fought, but this time, luck had deserted him. There would be no more decorations, no more medals, no more heroic deeds that would bring him closer to his goal of returning as a decorated war hero. All so Rose's father would accept his suit.

He had gambled and lost.

Now he lay in a pool of his own blood, life slowly slipping from his grasp. He was cold and wet, and from what he'd witnessed on the battlefield over the last few months, he knew it was a sign that he didn't have much time left.

"Rose," he whispered. "I'm sorry. I meant to keep my promise. I meant to come back to you."

"Is she waiting for you?" a voice suddenly answered.

With difficulty, Quinn turned his head and saw the man who stood over him. He squinted. The man wasn't a soldier but a civilian. The few times he'd seen him at the camp, he'd conducted business with some of the soldiers, and Quinn suspected that he was procuring whores for the privates. There was something commanding about him. An odd fellow, he'd always thought.

"Wallace, is it?" he asked.

The man nodded. "Does the lady love you?"

Quinn closed his eyes, pushing away the pain. "She professed it."

"You promised her to come back?"

"Yes," he choked out, at the same time wondering about the odd conversation he was having with a man he didn't even know.

"Then you shouldn't disappoint her."

Quinn tried a mocking laugh, but all that escaped his throat was a helpless gurgle.

"Don't talk. Just listen to me. I can save your life. But it will be different. You will only walk in the shadows, and the thirst for blood will be unbearable at first. But you'll be alive, strong, almost invincible. And immortal."

The words were outrageous, unbelievable. But Wallace looked serious.

"And if I say yes . . . if I agree, what do you want for this life?"

Nothing was free. He'd learned that long ago.

"A place to call home."

"I have a small estate . . . "

Wallace nodded his head. "That will do for now." He crouched down. "When your heartbeat becomes so faint that it is barely there, I will feed you my blood."

It was all Quinn remembered until he came to the next night. There was no pain, only the thirst for blood. The battlefield provided all the nourishment he needed.

He was different now, human no longer. But one thing that hadn't changed was his love for Rose. With Wallace's skill of mind control, a skill Quinn himself had yet to master, he secured an honorable discharge, which allowed him to return to England. Their travels were fraught with difficulties, since they could only travel at night and had to hide during the day. However, the need to see Rose, made everything bearable.

But Rose . . . she hadn't loved him enough to see past what he was, what he had become to survive. He'd done it all so he could come back to her. And it was all for naught. Had he known, he would have chosen death instead.

Quinn hugged Oliver tighter, pumped his fist harder to make the blood spurt from his open wrist with more pressure. A moment later, Oliver stopped swallowing, his head rolling to the side.

Quinn's heart stopped. Had Oliver had enough blood? Should he force him to take more?

He licked his own wrist to allow his saliva to close the puncture wounds then reached for the cell phone in his pocket. He speed dialed.

"Hey, can't get enough of us, can you?" came Zane's voice from the other end of the line.

"I need you now. I—"

"Whoa! I'm not sure Portia will like that kind of—"

"We had an accident," Quinn interrupted, breathing hard. "Oliver's dying. I'm turning him. I need help."

Instantly, Zane's voice was all business. "Where are you?"

"On Highway 1, about five minutes south of you. Use the GPS tracker."

"On my way."

The line went dead, and Quinn tossed the phone to the ground. The next few minutes felt like hours. Hours in which his entire life seemed to replay before his eyes. Was this what he wanted for Oliver? The same debauched life he'd led, all because the woman he'd loved with all his heart hadn't loved him back? What was in store for Oliver? Would he be rejected too?

Oliver was still in his arms. He neither stirred nor moaned. Quinn put his fingers to his neck. No pulse. It could mean one of two things: the turning had started, or he was already dead. There was no way of telling.

With his thumb, he pried an eyelid away from his eye to look at the boy's iris. It was still the way a human's eye looked. During the turning, it would turn entirely black, leaving not a single spec of white until the process was finished. But so far, the tell-tale black color was nowhere to be seen.

Quinn felt his hand shake. What if it didn't work? Or was it not meant to? What if Oliver wasn't meant to survive? Maybe it was better this way, better that he wouldn't be subjected to a life in the darkness. But who was he to judge? He wished he knew what Oliver wanted. But he'd never made the effort to really get to know him. After all, he'd only met him on a few occasions, and during most of those, Oliver had stuck to Samson and Zane, who he seemed to idolize.

Screeching tires and the beam of headlights alerted him that he wasn't alone anymore. Quinn turned his head and saw Zane's Hummer arrive behind the crashed SUV. From it jumped two people: Zane and

Amaury.

Quinn let out a deep breath. Good. Those two would know what to do. As they rushed toward him, another car door slammed, making him jerk once more. From the corner of his eye, he saw another figure emerge. He recognized him as Cain, the vampire who had joined Scanguards only a short time earlier after helping them eradicate a group, which had planned to create a master race of hybrids.

"Oh, fuck," Zane cursed as he reached him.

He instantly dropped down and examined Oliver's body. "You did the right thing." He pointed at the torn muscle and flesh in his stomach region from which even now blood was oozing. "He would have never survived it."

Quinn met his friend's gaze. He'd never been so glad to see the bald vampire than at this moment. "I was making jokes in the car. I distracted him."

He suddenly felt a big hand on his shoulder and looked up. Amaury towered over him. His linebacker-sized friend gave him an encouraging nod. "It's all good. He's young and strong. He'll make it."

Then Amaury turned to Cain. "We've gotta clean up before a passerby alerts the police or an ambulance."

Cain nodded, his dark hair looking almost black in the dim light. "No prob."

He and Amaury instantly went toward the toppled crane.

Zane reached for Oliver. "Let's get him in the car and take him back to Samson's."

Quinn pulled his protégé closer. "I can take care of him."

Zane raised his hands in capitulation. "Didn't mean to . . . " His voice died. "I know you can do it." Then he rose to his feet and motioned to Amaury and Cain.

"The tow truck should be here in a few minutes. If you need anything else . . . "

Amaury waved him off. "Go. We'll take care of this."

With Oliver in his arms, Quinn rose, accepting Zane's strong arm in the process. He briefly nodded his head at his two colleagues. "Thanks, Amaury, Cain."

"See you at the house when we're done here," Amaury replied as he braced his body against the crane, Cain at his side.

Slowly, Quinn turned, the weight of Oliver's body suddenly weighing him down. His knees buckled. If Zane hadn't grabbed his elbow and propped him up, he would have collapsed.

The realization of what kind of life he'd imposed on the young man in his arms suddenly crashed in over him.

"Oh, God, what have I done?" he murmured.

6

"You need to feed."

Quinn whipped his head toward Samson, who had quietly entered the guestroom. He stared at his boss, but barely saw his tall and dark features. Once more, he blinked, trying to wipe the remainder of blood from his eyes. He hadn't even cleaned up yet and still wore his torn clothes. The dirt of the accident site still clung to his skin and clothes.

He'd been sitting at Oliver's bedside for the last few hours, waiting for a sign that the kid would make it. His eyes had turned black, giving Quinn hope that things would turn out all right.

"Not now," he answered.

How could he think of himself now when Oliver needed him?

Samson stepped closer. "You shouldn't blame yourself."

Quinn expelled a bitter laugh. "And why not? Didn't Zane tell you what happened? Didn't he explain?"

His boss nodded. "It was Oliver's responsibility to drive. Just because the two of you talked and joked, doesn't mean it's your fault."

"I distracted him." How could Samson not see that?

"Why are you doing this to yourself?"

"Doing what?"

Samson drew closer, bringing his over-six-foot frame within inches of Quinn. "Don't play stupid with me! I know you're not. You're smarter than the rest of them, so what are you playing at?"

"I'm not." Rage boiled up in Quinn. He wanted to be left alone with his grief, his self-pity, his memories.

"You selfish bastard!" Samson accused him. "You're only thinking of yourself. Why am I even surprised?"

Quinn shot up from his seat. "What the fuck? How dare you? I'm only thinking of Oliver!"

His boss sneered. "No, you're thinking of yourself, of how this will change your life! Suck it up and don't wallow in self-pity!"

Even though he'd hit a nerve, Quinn wasn't ready to cave. Samson had no idea what was going on inside of him, and he wasn't one to share his innermost self. "Keep out of it! You might be my boss, but we both know I don't need this job!"

"Oh, ready to quit? Wanna throw it all in because it's getting too difficult? Are we interfering with your playboy life?" Samson hissed.

"How I conduct my life is none of your fucking business!"

Samson narrowed his eyes. "Is that what you're gonna tell Oliver when he wakes up?"

"What do you want from me?" Quinn ran a shaky hand through his hair, encountering a cluster of dried blood in the process. Shit, he was in a terrible state and in no mood to carry on this conversation.

"I want you to tell me what you're gonna do about Oliver."

When he locked eyes with Samson, he saw worry in them. But before he could say anything, his boss continued, "If you can't handle it, I'll act as his sire. After all, he's been with me for—"

"No!" Quinn interrupted. "He's my responsibility." Taking a deep breath, he tried to slow his heartbeat, tried to calm himself. "I'm sorry, Samson. I know what Oliver means to you. You lost your assistant, your right hand."

Samson let out a surprised gasp. "You think this is about me?" He shook his dark hair then rubbed his neck. "It was only a matter of time until this happened. I knew one day Oliver would ask for this. I've been grooming him for it. Of all the humans I know, he's the best prepared for a turning. But that doesn't mean he won't need your help to adjust."

Quinn let the words sink in. He squeezed his eyes shut for a moment, pushing back the memories of a happier time. A time long gone. "Seeing our life from the outside is one thing, living it is another."

Samson motioned his head toward the bed, where Oliver still lay motionless. "He knows that." Then he pinned Quinn with a stare. "But do you?"

Quinn didn't flinch. "I know what's expected of me." He wouldn't shirk his duty. "You can count on me."

"Good. Now go and take a shower. You look like hell. You smell even worse."

"But, Oliver . . . "

Samson waved him off. "I'll sit with him. Go."

Quinn turned and walked to the door.

"And Quinn . . . "

He paused without turning. "Yes?"

"I always thought you didn't care about anybody. Guess I was wrong."

Quinn swallowed, his throat dry as sandpaper. Had somebody finally figured him out?

Without another word, he left the room and closed the door behind him, wishing he could close the door to his past just as easily. Maybe then he would be able to start living again.

***

As soon as Quinn stepped out of the spare bathroom, freshly showered and wearing clothes Samson had lent him, he headed for the stairs to the upper floor, wanting to rejoin Oliver. But Zane blocked his path, holding out a cell phone to him.

"Gabriel wants to talk to you."

Quinn hadn't even noticed that Gabriel wasn't with the rest of the Scanguards gang, who lingered in the living room, anxiously waiting for any developments in Oliver's condition.

"Not now. I'm busy."

He tried to brush past him, but Zane didn't budge. "He said it's important."

Impatiently, he yanked the phone from Zane's hand and brought it to his ear. "What?"

"I need to see you. Now," Gabriel answered.

"I can't. Whatever it is, it'll have to wait."

Gabriel sighed. "I'm sorry to have to do this at a time like this, but . . . "

"I said I can't." He pressed the disconnect button and tossed the phone back at Zane.

By the time he'd made it up to the second floor, the cell phone rang again. Behind him, he heard Zane's footsteps following him, then his hand clamping over his shoulder.

"I suggest you take the call," Zane warned.

Pressing his lips into a tight line, he snatched the phone and answered the call. "What the fuck is so important?"

"I'm going to cut you some slack right now, because of what's happened, but another sign of insubordination, and I'm going to have your hide!" Gabriel said in a calm voice that betrayed the seriousness of his words.

Shit, did everybody have it in for him tonight?

"Do I have your attention now?"

Quinn cleared his throat. "Yes."

"Good. I have an assignment that just came in. You were requested especially."

"I don't have time for an assignment." Oliver needed him now.

"You'll be interested in this one. I get the feeling that there's something odd about it. It's worth checking it out. The woman says you're old friends and that you owe her a debt. Yet at the same time she's offering an outrageous amount of money to secure our—and in particular, your—services."

Quinn's ears perked up. "I don't owe anybody anything. Who is she?" He wasn't aware of any outstanding debt or favor. And certainly not one he owed a woman. He was always careful not to leave any loose ends.

"Her name is Rose Haverford. She . . . "

But Quinn didn't hear the rest of Gabriel's words, because blood suddenly thundered through is head, rushing past his ears like a freight train barreling through a quiet countryside. It drowned out all other noise.

Rose.

A voice from the grave. His Rose.

"Is she still there?"

"Yes, she's in my office, waiting."

"Keep her occupied. Make sure you're armed. I'll be there in a few minutes."

He disconnected the call before Gabriel had a chance to say anything else. As he pressed the phone back into Zane's hand, his friend stared at him.

"Something wrong?"

Quinn nodded. Everything was wrong.

"She's dead, long dead."

Zane gave him a confused look, but Quinn brushed past him and rushed down the stairs and out the door without another word.

This imposter would have to pay for the cruel joke she was playing on him.

7

Rose knew she had to be very careful. The wrong word and she would be toast. The less any of the Scanguards people knew, the better. Particularly Quinn. He could never find out what had really happened two hundred years ago, or he would never help her save Blake.

Nor was he allowed to find out what Keegan really wanted, not yet anyway. First she had to figure out which side he stood on: would he help her protect what she had stolen, or would he simply want it to attain power himself by using it? The Quinn she knew from when she was human would have never wanted that kind of power, but what about the vampire he was now?

Rose looked around the comfortable office, waiting for Gabriel to return. He hadn't wanted to make the phone call in front of her, which she couldn't really blame him for.

Despite the gruesome scar on his face, he had appeared very civilized, polite even. It could be a trick of course, just as Keegan's polished behavior had simply been a façade. Beneath it, he had hidden his brutality.

She was sick of violent men. They had crossed her long life too many times. This time she would be more careful. She couldn't afford to trust the wrong man again. There was too much at stake. Besides, she wasn't here to rekindle her relationship with Quinn. All she wanted from him was his help in protecting Blake. Once he was out of danger, she would disappear again.

Staying away from Quinn was the only way to protect her secret, because if he ever found out what she had done two centuries ago, he would kill her.

"Excuse the delay," Gabriel's voice came from behind her.

Pure instinct made her shoot up from her chair and reach into the inside pocket of her leather jacket. She stopped herself short of pulling out the silver blade she was hiding there.

Gabriel broke his stride and came to an abrupt halt, his eyes narrowing instantly. He had perceived her threat.

Not breaking eye contact, she slowly pulled her hand from her jacket, leaving the knife where it was. Even more slowly, she sat back down.

"I'm sorry," she purred, trying to play down her action. "I get startled easily."

He nodded before moving back to his own chair and sitting down behind the desk once more.

"Quinn will be here in a few minutes."

At the sound of his name, a tingling danced down her spine. Only a few more minutes and she would see him again. Would he have the same effect on her as he had then? Would her knees grow weak at the sight of him? Would her stomach turn into a nesting ground for butterflies?

"Why don't we talk about the assignment in the meantime? I'm afraid you've given me very little information so far."

"It's a very delicate matter," she insisted.

"You said that earlier. But we need a little more than that."

Rose pushed a strand of her long blond hair behind her shoulder. "Doesn't a million dollars suffice to douse your curiosity? I'm sure you don't get offered that kind of fee every day."

"On the contrary, somebody offering that kind of money always arouses my curiosity."

Gabriel leaned back, giving a relaxed impression, but she wasn't fooled. Underneath the calm exterior, he was watching her closely. Just as she was watching him.

"I prefer to defer disclosing the details until Quinn is here. I hate having to tell the same story twice." Besides, the more often she had to tell it, the more likely she would trip up and get caught in her own web of lies.

"As you wish." Gabriel straightened in his chair, a sign she interpreted as displeasure. "So, how long have you known Quinn?"

"That's irrelevant." Her relationship to Quinn wasn't up for discussion.

"If you do truly know him . . . " he insinuated. Gabriel leaned forward.

She wouldn't take the bait. If he wanted to know anything about her and Quinn, he could try his luck with Quinn. Maybe he would be more forthcoming. But she would remain tightlipped. Some things didn't need to be dredged up again. Her ill-fated relationship with the father of her daughter was one of those things.

It would be hard enough having to see him again.

A sound at the door made her whip her head around.

Oh, God, it would be harder than she thought.

Quinn was as handsome as he'd ever been. His blond hair seemed a shade darker, but maybe it was simply the way the light reflected on it. His hazel eyes appeared more alert and drained of the innocence that had inhabited them so many decades ago. While his body hadn't aged, she realized that his mind had. There was hardness in him now. The carefree young man she'd known, the one who'd gone off to war to make a name for himself, was gone.

Yet at the same time, he was still the same. Still the man she'd loved so fiercely, with all her heart and soul. The man she'd given her body to more freely than she'd done ever since. The man she'd called husband for one night.

Rose only noticed that she'd risen when she felt her knees wobble and had to reach for the backrest of her chair to steady herself. Had Quinn noticed? Had he seen her weakness?

She searched his eyes, looking for a sign of what was going on inside him. Did he feel what she felt?

She wanted to turn away, wanted to hide from him, from the feelings that welled up in his presence. But turning away would expose her even more. She couldn't allow him to detect her vulnerability.

She opened her lips, wanting to issue a greeting, something business like, but her dry throat was incapable of producing a single sound.

The silence was suffocating, and she yanked at the collar of her thin turtleneck top. The heat in the room was suddenly stifling, the air thick with unspoken words, the atmosphere laden with memories.

"Rose . . . "

Her gaze locked with his, and the room and their host melted into the background. Hesitant steps brought her closer to him, while he too moved toward her as if pulled by invisible strings.

For a moment she allowed herself to fall, to take in his scent, his presence. And for an instant of weakness, she wished it could be different, that she could be honest with him, tell him the truth. Confess everything.

When his hand came up to her face, she leaned in. She wanted his touch, craved it. When his fingertips connected with her cheek, she lowered her lids and took a breath. She didn't release it, because it would have come out as a sob.

Quinn's heart rejoiced at the sight of her. "You're alive!"

Happiness poured through every cell of his body, making him feel alive for the first time in two hundred years. At the same time, his eyes greedily roamed her body, not being able to get enough of this vision.

She was as young as when he'd seen her last. He'd come back from the war to claim her. She'd looked just like she looked now. Her hair was golden, her eyes sparkled in a bright blue, her red lips beckoned for a kiss. Not a single wrinkle marked her flawless face. And her body: slender, young, and utterly enticing. Back then, she'd been dressed in the fashion of the day, her legs always hidden beneath layers of fabric, and just as well. Had the men of that era seen her legs the way they were encased in tight fitting jeans right now, they would have made fools of themselves in public.

Yes, public ravaging would have ensued.

Just as he wanted to ravage her now. His feet carried him to her without him even realizing. When he stopped only inches from her, he lifted his hand, touching her golden hair. She wasn't an illusion his lovesick mind had conjured up—she was real. Flesh and blood.

His fingers connected with her skin, stroked over the silken softness of it.

His Rose was alive. As beautiful as back then, yet different: she was a vampire.

The realization took only seconds to sink in. What this meant took longer to digest: she'd been alive all these years, while he'd thought her dead, while he'd grieved for her.

At that moment something inside him snapped. The heart that had cherished her love for two centuries and kept it alive, suddenly cracked, a fault line the size of the St. Andreas fault carving itself through it.

His voice turned to ice when he addressed her again. "You made me believe you were dead."

All these years she'd been alive, and she'd never come to see him. Had she not loved him even a little? For two hundred years, he'd mourned her, pined for her, and she had been alive all this time.

"I did no such thing."

Hearing her voice for the first time in two centuries, nearly undid him. Despite the words, the sound was as sweet as a bird song. He knew he was a fool, but when it came to Rose, he would never truly be in possession of all his faculties.

"I went to your grave! I read the gravestone. You died shortly after I returned from the war."

She made a dismissive hand movement. "So I did." Then she straightened. "But I'm not here to talk about the past. I'm here to save our grandson."

Shock made him stumble back a couple of paces. "Our what?" he choked out.

"Well, Blake is our great-great-great-great-grandson, but that's just too long a word."

God, how easy it was for her to talk to him, as if it all meant nothing, as if she wasn't at all affected by this reunion. Her words sounded so matter-of-fact, whereas he could barely string a coherent sentence together. How cold had she become, the woman he'd once called wife?

"We had a child?" he managed to ask while he was barely able to keep upright.

"A daughter."

The clearing of a throat made him snap toward the sound.

"I think I'll leave you alone," Gabriel said as he walked to the door.

Quinn hadn't even noticed that he was still in the room, so taken in was he by Rose's presence.

"I'll be downstairs in Maya's office if you need me," Gabriel added before closing the door behind him.

Slowly, Quinn drew his gaze back to Rose, trying to digest her words. A daughter. He was a father.

"Where is she?"

A sad look crossed her face. "She's long dead. She lived a full life, a happy—"

Quinn pounced, slamming her against the wall behind her, before he even knew what he was doing.

"You deprived me of ever knowing my daughter? You kept her from me? How could you be so heartless? How could you lie to me like that?"

She didn't blink when she met his furious glare.

"This is exactly why." She motioned to his claws that pressed her against the wall. "You came back as a vampire. I was afraid for her. I was afraid you'd hurt her if you knew she existed."

"I would never hurt my own flesh and blood!" he shouted at the top of his lungs. "Never! Do you understand that?"

"Don't you remember what you were like then? How you reacted when I . . . when . . . ?"

"You mean when you rejected me because of what I had become?" he hissed, hatred filling his heart, where love and grief had lived for two centuries.

Oh, he remembered every painful moment of it. How could he ever forget?

"I snuck into your house that night because your father wouldn't receive me." He remembered it just as though it were tonight. She'd looked angelic. She'd glowed, smiled at him when he'd entered her chamber.

"You wanted to tell me something then, but I didn't let you talk. I wanted to tell you first what had happened to me. God . . . " He paused and shoved a hand through his hair. "I almost died on that battlefield. And had Wallace not been there that evening, if he hadn't turned me into a vampire that night, I would have been gone forever. But he offered me a way to come back to you. I did this for you. So we could be together again."

Quinn stared into her blue eyes, but he didn't really see her. He saw only what had happened that night. "You were afraid of me when I told you. You shrunk back from me, disgusted. As if you thought I would hurt you. I would have never hurt you. I promised you I wouldn't hurt you. You wouldn't listen. You didn't even see ME. You saw a monster, but I wasn't a monster. I was still the same man. I loved you!"

The last words made him choke. His heart broke a second time.

"And you trampled on my love. And as if that wasn't enough, you lied to me. You kept my own flesh and blood from me!"

Quinn's words sent a chill down her spine. Rose had never seen him so furious, so wild. And he had every reason to be. She would have reacted the same way.

The glare Quinn lashed at her cut deep into her heart.

Finally she pushed him away with both hands. Maybe she'd pushed him too far, but she couldn't stop now. She still needed his help.

"What was her name?" he asked, his voice suddenly calmer.

"Charlotte."

"That was my mother's name."

"I know." When she'd given birth, she'd still believed that everything would turn out fine. That Quinn would return. Out of love and respect for him she'd named their daughter after his mother, a woman he'd adored and loved.

"Where was she when I came back?"

She didn't really want to talk about those painful days, but she knew if she didn't answer his questions, he would never agree to help her. She had to pacify him.

Rose pinned her gaze at the window, looking out into the darkness. "When it was obvious to my parents that I was with child, I showed them our marriage certificate. My father was livid. They sent me to a country estate. They told everybody in London that I was sick. I gave birth there, but they took Charlotte away from me. They placed her with a farmer's family. It hurt to let her go, but I knew I would come back for her." She lifted her lids. "Once you came back, we would have collected her. But . . . " Her voice broke.

Undeterred by her anguish, he continued his questioning. "What happened to her?"

"She grew up as the farmer's daughter. She married and had children. Only one survived. Charlotte died at the age of sixty-eight."

Quinn turned away, but not before she'd seen a wet sheen suddenly covering his irises.

For the first time, she wondered whether it had been a mistake to hide his daughter from him. Maybe he would have loved her, cared for her. Doubts that had risen years ago resurfaced again. Had she been wrong? Should she have accepted him after he'd come back from the war, after he'd come back a changed man? No, not a man, a vampire. Could they have had a life together? No matter. It was too late now. She couldn't turn back time, even if she wanted to.

"Did she know you were her mother?"

Rose nodded even though Quinn remained with his back to her. "Not at first. But I told her later. I looked out for her. She was never in need of anything. I protected her. And she made me swear to protect all her offspring too once she was gone."

"She knew what you were?" he asked, disbelief in his voice.

"She was a brave girl. Never afraid of anything. When I told her, she accepted it. She made me show her my fangs. She showed no fear."

She'd been so proud of Charlotte then. To have a daughter who had accepted her, loved her. Her descendants hadn't been as welcoming. When she had told Charlotte's son who she was, he'd tried to stake her right there and then, his country bumpkin prejudices too deeply ingrained in him to listen to her explanation. She'd had to wipe his memory of her to make sure it wouldn't happen again. That was why she had not revealed herself to the others, but simply watched over them from afar, just as she watched over Blake from a distance. He had never met her, didn't know who she was. And she wanted to keep it that way.

"You were disgusted with what I had become," Quinn recalled in turning back to her, his face composed. "Yet you became a vampire shortly after that. Don't deny it: you look the same as you did when I came back. You must have gotten turned within a year of my return." His voice turned to stone again. "I want to know what happened. Everything."

The dangerous undertone in his voice was unmistakable. But she couldn't comply with his request. If he knew how she'd gotten turned, he would suspect what else she had done. And if he found out, she would be as good as dead.

"It's not important. What's important is that our grandson Blake is in mortal danger. I need your help to protect him. I can't do it on my own."

As hard as it was to admit that, she needed his expertise. After all, he was a bodyguard, and of all the things that she'd found out about Scanguards and the people he worked with, she knew they were the best. If anybody could prevent Keegan from digging his claws into Blake, it was Quinn.

"What makes you think I will help you after all you've done to me?"

She gasped. "After all *I* have done to you?" Had he already forgotten what he had done to her?

"Yes, you! Would you like me to make a list for you?" His glare intensified. He lifted his hand, counting with his fingers. "You tossed me out after I came back from the war. I professed my love. You stomped on it. You hid my daughter from me. And then you even made me believe you were dead when in reality you were living as a vampire. You became what you hated so much about me. Yet, you never came back to me, not even after you became what I was. Why is that, Rose? Why did you do all this to me? Did you hate me so much for taking your innocence, for leaving you with child?"

There was a haunted look in his eyes. Involuntarily, she reached out her hand, wanting to soothe his pain. He jerked back, as if he couldn't bear her touch.

"I can't talk to you right now."

He turned on his heels and stormed out faster than she could get another word past her lips.

"I'm sorry," she whispered, but he was already gone.

If only she could tell him the truth, but the truth would get her killed. And she wasn't ready to die.

8

Quinn inhaled the cool night air and fought to regain his composure. To no avail. His entire world had just been turned upside down. And by the looks of it, it wouldn't be fixed any time soon.

As he brought distance between himself and Rose, stalking through the night, more and more questions bombarded his mind. But no matter how long he pondered them, only one really mattered: why hadn't she come to him after she had become a vampire?

They could have lived a happy life together, a life full of love, companionship, and laughter. Instead, for almost two hundred years, he'd been lonely, his heart remaining cold despite the many women who had warmed his bed.

He felt betrayed by the only person who had ever mattered to him.

Rose had never looked lovelier or smelled more enticing. Even now, her scent still clung to his nostrils, eliciting a bodily reaction he had barely been able to suppress when he'd been in her presence. He hadn't allowed himself to give into it, not wanting to give her the satisfaction that he still desired her even knowing that she had been hiding from him all these years.

But now that nobody would be witness to his weakness, he let the feelings she'd conjured up wash over him. The result was instantaneous: blood shot into his loins, making him harder than the metal pole that had saved his life tonight.

"I wasn't finished."

The voice jolted him, made him whirl around in a split second. Rose marched toward him with a determined gait, her long hair blowing backwards in the light breeze.

"I was."

It was a lie, and he knew it. There were so many questions he wanted to ask her, but he knew himself well enough to realize that he was in shock. Therefore a continuation of their heated discussion should be postponed at all cost—until he had himself under control again, until he could treat her with coldness and indifference.

But clearly, Rose knew him too. And she was obviously bent on exploiting his weakness. Damn her for that!

"I still need your help. Blake is in danger. If you don't protect him, he'll perish. He's your flesh and blood, the only one who's left. Is that—?"

"What kind of danger?" Quinn interrupted, wanting to keep the focus on business rather than delve into the emotional baggage he and Rose shared.

A slight relaxation in her stance confirmed that she had been unsure whether he would respond. However, her face remained as impassive as before. Did she have any feelings left? Or had whatever had happened to her, purged them from her heart? Was *his* Rose still in there somewhere?

"There's a vampire. His name is Keegan. He's powerful, and wherever he is, his henchmen aren't far behind. He wants Blake harmed."

Quinn narrowed his eyes. "Why?"

She pulled in a breath. "Because he wants to hurt me."

"What did you do to him?"

"Nothing!"

He crossed the distance that separated them with two steps, bringing him flush to her. The heat from her body was pure torture as was the intensifying scent.

"Bullshit! He must have a reason, so spit it out, Rose. What did you do?" And he wouldn't take any crap for an answer.

Her eyes shifted to the side. "I left him."

Her answer came as a surprise. It instantly sent bolts of rage through him. How many men had there been? How many men had touched her after him? Had run their dirty hands over her perfect body? Had been inside her?

Disgust spread in his gut, mingled with the rage that boiled there, and mixed with the hatred that had started building. For seconds he couldn't speak, his fangs itching so badly, he couldn't prevent them from descending. He saw the red flicker of his eyes reflect in hers, and realized he was quickly losing control.

"He's evil. I didn't see it at first," she continued quickly as if wanting to drown out the unbearable silence. "He didn't want me to leave him. Nobody leaves Keegan. His ego is hurt. He wants to take it out on me by hurting Blake."

But the more she explained, the clearer one thing became.

He could see it now: the way her eyes drifted away, how her voice trembled almost unnoticeably, how the vein at her neck twitched. Even her scent changed, her glands emitting more of her clean sweat. She was nervous. Not because of Keegan, but because she was dishing him up a lie and was hoping not to be caught in it.

"You're lying to me."

"No!" she protested. "I left Keegan."

"So you did. But that's not why he wants to hurt Blake." Quinn paused briefly, pinning her with his eyes. "Not even you are that good in bed."

The barb hurt him more than it seemed to hurt her.

"Think what you want. The fact is that Keegan is bent on revenge. I need you to help me protect Blake."

He would get the truth out of her, one way or another. Maybe not tonight, but if anything, he was patient.

"Fine. Stick to your lie. What does he want to do to Blake? Kill him?"

Rose shook her locks, squeezing her eyes shut. "He wants to turn him." When she opened her eyes again, anguish had settled there. "I can't allow that."

Realization spread quickly, making him take a step back.

"You hate being a vampire."

She glared at him, not masking her feelings. "What's there not to hate?"

In disbelief, he shook his head. How could she have lived as one of their kind for such a long time and not seen the advantages, the benefits of such a life? How could she still hate it?

"It wasn't your choice, was it?" She'd been forced into this life.

"It doesn't matter now. What matters is Blake. Are you going to help me or not?"

The wounded look she tossed him was enough to slice his heart in half. Without thinking he nodded.

"Under one condition: you tell me how you got turned."

He could see the wheels spin in her head. Was she trying to construct another lie she could serve him up?

"Once Blake is out of danger."

"Why not now?" Quinn pressed. Why could she not tell him what had happened?

"Because you're not ready to hear it."

"Try me."

She shook her head, her lips turning into a hard line. "When Blake is safe, I'll tell you what happened."

He observed how her chest heaved with each breath she took. The knowledge that she was hiding something, something he felt instinctively, concerned him, gnawed at him. But he also knew that she wouldn't cave. Not yet anyway.

"Fine. Have it your way. But the moment he's safe, I'll demand to know."

She acknowledged his statement with a nod. "Good. Now let's talk about how we can protect him."

Quinn raised his hand. "Hold it. We're not done negotiating."

Her surprised look could have been droll, had he had any sense of humor. As it was, he was all out of humor, and no supply truck was on its way to deliver more. But what he had in abundance was anger. And he would unleash it on her.

If she thought she could just waltz back into his life without any explanation, without any remorse for the pain she'd caused him, he'd make her pay in his own way.

"Now to the payment for my services."

She raised an eyebrow. "I've already told your boss that I'll be paying Scanguards one million dollars for keeping Blake safe. Isn't that enough?"

Quinn suppressed his surprise at the large amount. Clearly, Blake meant a lot to her, otherwise why would she shell out that kind of money? However, he wasn't interested in cash. He had more than enough to see him through eternity.

"The million is for Scanguards, not for me. I prefer something more personal than cold hard cash."

He roamed his eyes over her lithe form. God, she was gorgeous. He remembered her glistening body as if it had been yesterday. He could still feel her muscles squeezing him, her heels digging into his backside, her hands caressing him. Despite the many women he'd had after her, he'd never forgotten his night with Rose.

But it would be different now. What he was planning wasn't meant to rekindle those sensations. It was meant to destroy them, so he would finally be free of her.

"What do you want?"

Quinn raised his eyes to meet hers. He noticed the apprehension that had taken over her face.

"You pay with your body. I'll fuck you whenever it pleases me until the assignment is over."

She gasped.

Only if he removed the mystique surrounding their one and only night together would he be able to stop thinking about her. When he'd taken her virginity so many years ago, he'd been a relatively inexperienced young man, and making love to Rose had been magical. Today he was well versed in all matters of the carnal arts. He'd slept with the most experienced of women. Sleeping with Rose now wouldn't elicit the same responses in him as it did two hundred years ago. It would finally rid him of the feeling that he'd lost something very precious.

Yes, he argued with himself, if he fucked her now, it would be no different than being with any woman. She would be nothing special. He had to prove it to himself, make it clear to his body and his heart, that he didn't need her, that whatever he needed, he could get from any woman.

Rose would finally lose the power she had over him. And he would be free to love somebody else. Free at last.

"You can't be serious!" she finally shot back.

"Take it or leave it!"

This point was non-negotiable. If she wanted his help, she would pay for it.

"But he's your flesh and blood. How can you be so callous?"

Quinn expelled a bitter laugh. "Callous? Don't go there, Rose. This Blake means nothing to me. He may be my flesh and blood, but what does that really mean?" He slammed his fist onto his heart. "I feel nothing here. Do you understand? Nothing!"

And she was the reason for it, but he didn't bother saying it, because the glint in her eyes told him she already suspected it. She was smart, his Rose. She'd always been bright. Brighter than the other young women that he'd met during the season in London. Her beauty had drawn him to her, her mind had made him stay. While the other women had been airheads, Rose had always stated her opinion, asked intelligent questions, and supported her arguments with logic. He'd loved sparring with her.

"I'm sure you're not short of women willing to share your bed."

Was she fishing whether he was seeing anybody? "I can name you a dozen who will jump right now if I make the call," he said icily. It was the truth, but he wasn't in the mood for any other woman. He was in the mood for Rose.

Her jaw tightened visibly. "Then what do you want from me?"

He took a deliberate step toward her, bringing his body within an inch of hers. "I wasn't aware that you were hard of hearing. But let me spell it out for you again: I want to fuck you. That's my condition for protecting Blake. You have until tomorrow at sunset to give me your decision. Then my offer expires."

Swiftly, he pulled a card from his pocket and stuck it into the pocket of her jeans.

"Text me."

He turned away.

"Fuck you!" she hissed.

Quinn grinned. "That's the spirit, Rose. Now let's put those words into action."

9

When Quinn's cell phone pinged hours after he'd left Rose behind, indicating a text message, his heart pounded excitedly, and he had to take an extra breath of air to steady it. He'd been wandering aimlessly through the city, trying to clear his head.

Pulling the phone from his pocket, he closed his eyes for an instant. He couldn't let her know how relieved he was that she accepted his ridiculous condition.

His eyes swept over the message.

Oliver is awake, it said.

For a split second, he didn't understand the significance of those three words, but then it hit him. He had responsibilities.

His interactions with Rose had made him forget what else had happened tonight. He was a sire now, Oliver's sire. And it meant that he had to help him through the transition, guide him, provide counsel. Never mind that he needed counsel himself; he had to pretend now that he knew it all, that he had the solution to every problem his new protégé would face.

Quinn shoved a hand through his hair. How he wished he could talk to somebody, to ask for advice. But he had nobody he felt comfortable confessing to. In those two hundred years since his transformation he hadn't made one true friend. Even Zane, his fellow bodyguard at Scanguards, wasn't close enough to him. Yes, they'd been out, whoring together, but all that was long gone. Zane was bonded to a hybrid now, Portia, a young woman, half vampire, half human. Besides, Quinn couldn't tell anybody what was going on inside him. All he could do was fake it, not let anybody know what a mess his life had turned into.

Determined to at least get one thing in his life right, he headed for Samson's house. Oliver needed him now, and he wasn't going to shirk his responsibilities.

Thomas greeted him at the door. The gay biker with the sandy blond hair and easy smile waved him in. Quinn glimpsed Samson and Amaury in the living room, both pacing with their cell phones pressed to their ears, talking quickly. He gave Thomas a questioning look. Why had they left Oliver alone?

"Zane is upstairs with Oliver." His friend motioned to the regal mahogany stairs that led up to the second floor.

As he marched up the stairs, he was surprised that Zane was still at the house. He would have expected him to return to his mate Portia. The two were practically inseparable since they had bonded only a short time earlier.

Zane's laughter greeted him as he opened the door to the guest room. Quinn furrowed his forehead. The last thing he had expected at a time like this was laughter. What was going on?

When he stepped into the room, he found Zane sitting in a chair next to the bed. Oliver was stretched out on the bed, holding his stomach with both hands.

"Stop!" he begged, his face contorted into a grimace. "That hurts!"

Zane waved him off. "Yeah, that's what he said too when I poured hot wax over it."

"What are you doing to him?" Quinn yelled, launching himself at Zane.

His colleague immediately jumped up.

"Who pissed on your grave?" Zane shot back, tossing him a surprised look.

"He's just . . . " Oliver's voice died amid fits of . . . laughter.

Quinn whipped his head to stare at Oliver. Now that he looked more closely, he noticed how his protégé's eyes were tearing as he held in another laugh.

"I was just telling him a joke," Zane explained.

Dumbfounded, Quinn just stood there. He had expected Oliver to be in shock. Most newly turned vampires were, especially those who'd been turned unexpectedly. However, Oliver seemed to be anything but. In fact, he looked positively . . . happy!

Suddenly, Oliver's face contorted in pain. "Shit. Still hurts." He motioned to his stomach.

Panicked, Quinn rushed to his side, but Zane's hand on his shoulder held him back.

"He's all right. His stomach wound will take a few more hours of healing though. Don't worry, we brought a live donor in to speed up the process."

"Who?"

"Wesley. He was closest."

Quinn blinked in surprise. "Haven's brother? He volunteered?" Wesley had hated vampires for a long time. But since his own brother had turned into one, it appeared his hatred had somewhat eased.

Zane shrugged. "Kind of."

"What's that supposed to mean?"

Oliver cleared his throat, making Quinn look back at him.

"Samson offered him a job at Scanguards."

Shit! "Wesley is a loose cannon!"

Zane chuckled. "I remember being called that myself not too long ago. And look at me now!" His bald vampire friend stretched his arms out to his sides as if presenting himself to an audience.

"You still are," Quinn answered in dry tones. "Fuck, I should have been here. Samson shouldn't have to clean up after me." Instead of making sure his protégé had everything he needed, he'd deserted him the first chance he got. What did that say about him? That he wasn't any better than his own sire?

He ran his hand through his hair, then let his eyes travel over Oliver's body.

"Are you okay? How are you feeling?"

"I'd be lying if I said I've never been better," Oliver started.

Quinn dropped his lids. "I'm sorry. I wish I could have given you a choice." Instead he had let himself be ruled by his own guilt. After all, the accident was his fault, not Oliver's.

"Don't be. As soon as this damn stomach wound has healed, I'll be better than new," Oliver claimed.

Quinn raised his head, meeting Oliver's gaze.

"But your entire life has changed."

"Yeah, for the better. Frankly, if this hadn't happened, I would have asked Samson to turn me." Oliver smiled. "It's not like I'm getting any younger and—"

"You're twenty-five!" Quinn interrupted.

"Almost twenty-six," his protégé corrected. "It was about time. I don't want to look older than the rest of you."

Quinn shook his head. "I don't believe I'm hearing this." He'd known that Oliver had always looked up to them, even toyed with the idea of becoming a vampire. But he'd never expected him to take to it as easily as a duck to water, to accept his fate with such grace. Even those who'd asked to be turned had found the adjustment hard and questioned their decision later. Oliver wouldn't be any different.

"You don't know yet what to expect from your new life. It won't be easy. Just ask Eddie."

Amaury's brother-in-law was a relatively young vampire, turned less than a year earlier.

"Eddie's doing just fine. He's got Thomas."

Zane chuckled at that. "Or maybe Thomas has him."

"Would you shut up, Zane?" Quinn snapped. "Thomas is downstairs. He can probably hear you."

Then he turned back to Oliver.

"There's lots to think about. For starters, you can't live on your own right now."

The opening of the door interrupted him. He watched Samson and Amaury enter.

"Hey Samson, Amaury. I was just telling Oliver that he'll have to make some changes. He needs to live with me for a while."

Samson nodded. "Already arranged."

Quinn raised an eyebrow. "Excuse me?"

Amaury interrupted. "An acquaintance of mine just renovated a mansion in Pacific Heights, made it vampire proof and all that shit. He wants to open it as a B&B."

Quinn took a breath. "Out of the question. I'm not living in a B&B with Oliver. We're returning to New York. We don't need a bunch of strangers around us."

"There won't be anybody else. He can't open the place yet—some issues with the building department. So he's offered us the place for exclusive use until the permits are final. Knowing this city, it'll take months," Amaury claimed.

"And it's better if you stay here for now, so Oliver can stay in an environment he's used to," Samson added, then turned to his erstwhile assistant. "Don't you think so, Oliver? Isn't that what you want?"

The kid nodded eagerly. "That'd be good." Then he looked back at Quinn, his facial expression one of dread. "I mean for now, right? Afterwards, it would be cool to go to New York with you."

Reluctantly, Quinn nodded. If it was what Oliver wanted, then he could at least do that.

"Then it's settled," Samson answered. "When do you want to move in? Tomorrow night?"

Before Quinn could answer, his cell phone pinged. Again his heart raced, because this time he was sure who was texting him. What he wasn't sure about was what her answer would be.

His pulse galloping, he looked at the screen.

I agree, was all it said.

He swallowed, not knowing whether to be happy or sad about Rose's answer, maybe both.

Slowly he tore his gaze from the phone and glanced back at Oliver.

"Hope you don't mind that we won't live there alone." He pushed down the lump in his throat that threatened to rob him of the ability to speak. "My wife will be joining us."

Oliver stared at him wide-eyed, shock plastered all over his face. "Dude, you're married?"

10

"That's him." Rose pointed toward the bar.

Despite the late hour, the popular nightclub wasn't completely packed yet. Soon, however, the clubbers would be lining up like sardines just to get a drink. And the dance floor would be looking like a can of worms, wiggling one way or another.

Quinn followed the direction of Rose's finger, letting his gaze fall on a tall guy who looked like he'd stepped out of a photo shoot for GQ Magazine. His dark brown hair was cropped short. Under his immaculate clothes, his muscles bulged. A tan, whether artificial or real, complemented his model looks.

Without looking back at her, he asked, "The clothes horse?"

From the corner of his eye, he noticed Rose's shrug. "I have no influence over how he spends the money in his trust."

Quinn rolled his eyes. "Great. A trust fund baby. What else should I know about him?"

Blake looked nothing like he would have imagined his grandson to be. Not that he had ever lost a thought on that particular subject until twenty-four hours earlier.

"He finished college, then did a masters."

"What subject?"

"Communications. Not something he could actually find a job in," Rose replied.

"So he's unemployed." Just perfect. His great-great-whatever was a loser.

"That's why he came out to the West Coast. He thinks he can get some job out here."

Quinn snorted. "Maybe he should have moved to LA."

"You don't like him," Rose said.

He turned to her to contradict her, but the moment he laid eyes on her, he was instantly distracted. Rose wore a low cut top that accentuated her small breasts and made them look larger than he remembered them. Her cleavage was more pronounced than he'd ever seen it when she'd worn those fashionable ball gowns so many years ago. Allowing his eyes to trail down, he wondered how long it would take to peel her out of the tight black jeans she wore. One second or two?

His mouth went dry at the thought. He smelled the blood of the humans all around him, yet at this moment no scent was as tantalizing as the scent of Rose's skin. He'd always preferred human women as his lovers, because the scent of their blood heightened his arousal, but now that he stood so close to Rose, her body getting hotter in the inadequately air-conditioned room, he realized that her blood smelled no less enticing. On the contrary: despite the delicious smells all around him, his body wanted to partake of only one.

"What?" she asked, staring at him.

Quinn tried for an indifferent look, hoping he wasn't drooling. God, he was pathetic. How would he be able to do this night after night? "Let's go to the bar. Might as well have a drink."

Rose gave him a confused look. "You drink ... uh ... " She lowered her voice. " . . . human drinks?"

"Just to blend in. Standing around without drinks will make us look suspicious. This is a nightclub after all. People come here to drink." Besides, his throat was so dry, he didn't care what kind of liquid moistened it.

Quinn headed for one end of the bar from which he had a good view of Blake and motioned to the bartender, then patted his hand on the empty stool, glancing back at Rose.

She followed him and took the seat.

"Two Boodles martinis, dry, no olives," he ordered, seeing what used to be his favorite brand of London dry gin behind the bar. "Stirred, not shaken."

The bartender nodded and went to work.

"I thought James Bond always insists that his martinis be shaken, not stirred."

Quinn thought she seemed to find her remark far more amusing than it was. "Bond knows women, not martinis."

He took a sideways glance at Rose. Now that she sat, his head was at the perfect height to allow him to look right down her cleavage. When he lifted his eyes, he collided with her gaze. It appeared that she had noticed the same thing. He felt heat shoot through his veins.

Annoyed at his own reaction, he focused his attention on the middle of the bar, where Blake was talking to a young woman. He tuned into their conversation, shutting out everything else around him out.

"I just moved here. Cool place," Blake said.

"Good for you," the girl replied, taking her nearly empty glass and pulling on the straw. Her gaze strayed away as if she were looking for somebody. She was pretty, and by the looks of it, she was well aware of that fact.

"What are you drinking? I'll get you another one," Blake said.

"Thanks, but I'll get my own drinks," she replied and waved toward the bartender, who just placed the two Martini glasses in front of Quinn.

"That's twenty-four bucks."

Quinn pulled out a couple of banknotes and tossed them on the bar. "Thanks."

As the bartender took the money, Quinn looked back at Blake and the girl.

"She doesn't like him," Rose said next to him.

"Maybe she's just playing hard to get," Quinn mused, wondering why Rose even bothered talking to him.

For the first time, he heard her chuckle. The sound trickled down his body like a soft caress. God, how he'd missed her laughter. How he'd missed that warm sound that could lift anyone's spirit.

"Guess it runs in the family."

"The playing hard to get?"

"The not being able to know what a woman wants." She paused. "Or doesn't want."

Quinn reached for his glass. "Ah, that's harsh, Rose, even for you." Then he took a generous sip and allowed the disgusting liquid to coat his throat. At least it would help make his voice sound normal again, or so he hoped.

"And there I thought I gave you everything you could dream of that night."

She narrowed her eyes. "And more."

Her words cast an icy chill against his nape. "Are you referring to the baby?"

"Among other things."

He set the glass onto the bar with too much force, making some of the liquid spill over the rim. "I pulled out!"

But even he knew that wasn't a foolproof method of preventing conception. However, two hundred years ago, short of using French letters, it had been the only one.

She withstood his glare without flinching. But she didn't grace him with a response. Instead she merely took her own glass and emptied it without grimacing.

"Is that why you're so pissed at me? Because I left you with child? I would have taken care of you and our daughter if you'd given me a chance."

Daughter—the word still sounded so foreign to him. Yet, he meant what he'd said. Had he known, things would have turned out differently.

"Having Charlotte was the only thing that ever went right in my life," Rose admitted.

Her admission surprised him. "Then what was it that I did wrong?" The words were out before he could take them back. He knew he was showing his vulnerability by asking a question like this.

A man's booming voice saved him from whatever comeback Rose might have had ready.

"Didn't you hear what she said?"

Quinn's gaze snapped toward Blake and the girl he was hitting on. Rose was right: the girl wasn't interested in him. Behind her, a tall guy was glowering at Blake.

"She doesn't want your attention. So beat it!" the stranger growled.

Blake glared back at him. "Don't get in my way. This is between me and her." He turned away from the guy and focused his attention back on the girl.

The timbre of his voice changed as he smiled back at the girl again. "So, you wanna dance? I'm told I'm a pretty good dancer."

The object of his attention rolled her eyes. "I'm not interested. Thanks." She turned away and accepted the drink the bartender put in front of her.

"That's ten."

Before she could pull out her wallet, Blake put some money on the bar. "Let me get that."

"No thanks," she insisted.

"Oh, come on . . . it's just a drink." Blake unleashed a charming smile, and Quinn could see how with most women he would do well.

Not, apparently, with this one.

Nor with the guy behind her, who had obviously decided to act as her protector.

"That's it!" the protector snapped and snatched Blake by his shirt, yanking him away from the bar.

Blake's elbow hit her cocktail glass, tipping it over. The red liquid spilled over the girl's dress, making her scream out in frustration.

"See what you've done now, you jerk!" Blake shouted at his attacker.

The next second, he launched a balled fist into the guy's face, whipping his head to the side.

"Well, great, look what your grandson is starting now," Quinn pressed out between clenched teeth. That's just what they needed: unwanted attention.

"Mine? He's just as much yours. And trust me, that temper doesn't come from my side of the family," Rose retorted.

It took only five seconds until the two men were in the middle of a full fist fight. Left hooks alternated with uppercuts to the chin, blows to the stomach and kicks to the legs. Both sides fought neither elegantly nor fairly. And neither held back. Almost as if they both had been waiting for an outlet to get rid of long-stored-up tension and frustration.

Quinn knew enough about that, about how a fist fight could ease pain by causing pain in other parts of your body.

Leaning against the bar, he almost enjoyed watching the two men go at each other, beating the shit out of each other. The other clubbers seemed to equally enjoy the exchange, forming a circle around the fighters, even cheering them on as if they were prize fighters.

Rose stared at the fight with an open mouth, then glared back at him.

"Aren't you gonna do something?"

"Do what?"

"Stop them, damn it. He could get hurt."

Quinn made a face. "He can take care of himself from what I can see."

In fact, it appeared that Blake's fighting skills, while unsophisticated, weren't bad. He was strong, and his instincts were good. Light on his feet, he had the agility of a dancer and was able to evade many of the blows his opponent dealt.

Maybe he had underestimated the boy earlier. Clearly, he had more brawn than brains, as well as the subtlety of a sledgehammer, but he seemed to be made to fight. As if he were born for it. With a little bit of the right training, he could be good, excellent even.

Rose jumped off her stool, looking impatient, and readied herself to interfere.

"If you're not going to stop them, I will," she threatened.

Quinn expelled an annoyed breath. "Don't get your knickers in a twist."

He grabbed her arm and brushed past her. "Stay here." Then he made a path through the crowd, effortlessly pushing people out of his way until he reached the two fighters.

With a lightning fast move he grabbed both men by their upper arms and pulled them apart, holding them to either side of himself. They struggled to get out of his hold, but their human strength was no match for his vampire power.

Stop fighting, you idiots. He planted the simple thought into their minds, making them stop almost immediately.

"Enough!" he called out. "Nothing more to see here." Slowly, the crowd turned away and went back to what they'd been doing before, dancing, talking, and drinking.

Quinn released the two.

"Get lost," he ordered the girl's protector while his mind sent the same command into the guy's head. Mind control was a handy vampire tool. He didn't like to overuse it, but he wanted to talk to Blake alone and wasn't in the mood to do more in terms of damage control than he'd already done.

"Who are you?" Blake spat.

Quinn looked him up and down. Besides the fact that his clothes were a little disheveled, there wasn't a scratch on him. "I might be just what you need."

Outrage glittered in Blake's eyes. "Hey, I don't swing that way."

"Neither do I, so don't get your feathers ruffled. I have a proposition for you."

Blake raised a questioning eyebrow. "What kind of proposition?"

Quinn motioned his head in the direction of the guy whom he'd fought with only moments earlier. "Looks like you're a good fighter. I wonder whether you'd like to apply your skills professionally."

"You mean like a boxer? Not interested. I don't want my brain cells bashed out of me."

"No, of course not. You haven't got a single one to spare on such an endeavor," Quinn hastened to say.

Blake nodded. "That's right."

Clearly, the jab had gone over his head. He added *slow-witted* to his grandson's attributes, as well as a note to ask Rose whether she was sure he was indeed their descendent. Maybe there had been some mix-up in the hospital.

"I was thinking if you wanted to make a career move . . . we always need young men like you: strong, smart." Quinn backed away a little. "But then again, you've probably got a great job already. I mean, look at you . . ." He made a gesture toward his clothes. "So, this probably won't interest you. Even though we pay well, but then . . . "

"Then what?" Blake prompted, his curiosity awakened.

"It's a dangerous job. Actually, I can't really call it a job. It's more like an adventure. Every day, you know. Only a select few are made for that line of work . . . "

Quinn turned half away. "Forget I asked."

Before he could walk away, he felt Blake's hand on his shoulder, holding him back. Bingo.

He caught Rose's confused stare, watching them from afar, before he faced his grandson again.

"What's it about? I might be just what you're looking for," Blake said eagerly.

Quinn gave him an assessing look. "Well, we won't know immediately. There are tests, you know." On a whim, he added, "Like Men in Black, just without the aliens."

Blake's jaw dropped. "Cool! I'm in, man. What do I do?"

Quinn pulled out one of Scanguards' cards from his pocket and handed it to him. "Be there tomorrow night at 9 p.m. That's when the selection program starts. Ask for Quinn."

"Quinn," he repeated, staring at the card.

"And your name is?"

Blake stretched out his hand. "Bond. Blake Bond."

Quinn did a double take. Rose had neglected to tell him Blake's last name, and had obviously had some fun with him over that little omission. Great, add that name to the ego the kid had, mix it with the twenty brain cells at his disposal and the packed muscles of his body, and there was disaster waiting to happen.

"Bond, huh?"

Blake grinned from one ear to the other. "Yeah, I get that a lot."

"Well, see you tomorrow night . . . Mr. Bond."

Turning, he walked back to Rose. Before he even reached her, he knew she wasn't happy about what had just happened.

"Are you crazy?" she hissed. "You can't just expose yourself to him. We were going to watch over him, not turn him into Rambo."

"And what better way to keep him safe than bring him in and make him think he's working for us. Don't worry, it'll work out perfectly."

Yeah, perfectly blow up in our faces, he mused. But what was done was done.

"He's going to find out who we are."

"And would that be so terrible?" Quinn asked.

Rose glared at him. "Yes, it would be. He's got a right to a normal life."

He took a step closer to her, eliminating any space between them. "He lost that right when Keegan decided to hurt you by harming him. Now, let's go."

Puffing up her chest, she gestured toward Blake who was now talking to a few other clubbers.

"We have to watch him. Keegan could show up anytime, anywhere."

Did she really think he was an amateur? "That's already taken care of. I've had somebody assigned to him from the moment you told me his name and where to find him."

Her shoulders suddenly dropped. "Oh." Then she took a deep breath. "Okay, where to now?"

Quinn bent his head to her ear and sensed her draw closer as if expecting to hear a secret. "Time to collect the first payment."

As Rose's breath caught, a white hot flame of desire shot into his groin. Yes, payment was just what he needed now.

11

She would never survive this. This much was certain.

Rose listened to the sounds of the shower in the en-suite bathroom and felt her body heat rise with every second that passed.

The room Quinn had led her into was a large bedroom, luxuriously furnished with a King sized bed and comfortable looking furniture in the sitting area in front of a fireplace. Yet instead of using the furniture, she paced about the room.

This was not good.

What had she been thinking, accepting his outrageous condition? If she slept with him, she would never be able to keep her emotional distance from him. She would want more, feel that closeness again that they had once shared. And she would want to confess. Tell him what had really happened. Everything. And it would get her killed.

When the floorboards creaked shortly after the water was turned off, she knew her short reprieve was over. Quinn demanded what was due to him, and she had no choice but to do what he wanted.

Slowly she turned and looked toward the door to the bathroom. Shock made her freeze in place. He hadn't bothered wearing a robe. A towel that barely covered his groin was slung low around his hips, the ends tucked in so haphazardly, they threatened to come loose if he moved.

Her mouth went dry at the sight of his chiseled abs and the defined muscles of his chest, arms, and legs.

Her breath caught, and she quickly averted her eyes.

A moment later, the soft trickle of his voice reached her. "Now, now, Rose. You've seen me wearing less than this."

Maybe, but he hadn't looked like that back then. Clearly the year he'd spent on the battlefield with Wellington's troupes had made him leaner, more defined. And stronger. She chanced another look at his thighs, admiring the smooth skin that covered sinew and muscle, creating a physique that would have put any Greek god to shame.

Swallowing away the lump in her throat, she allowed her eyes to travel higher. It did no good to show weakness now. She couldn't let him know how much he affected her. After all, this wasn't about the fabulous sex they would have shortly. It was about power, about who would come out ahead. And if she admitted that the mere sight of him made her weak in the knees, she might as well throw in the towel now.

Collecting all her courage, she raised her head to meet his gaze and forced a nonchalant shrug. "I've seen a lot of men naked."

When she noticed him narrow his eyes, she added, "More than I can count."

A low growl issued from his chest, and for some strange reason, which she didn't want to examine at present, it filled her with satisfaction.

"Don't think you can play me, Rose. Those days are over."

Quinn took a step toward her. Instinct dictated that she retreat, but her mind overrode her body's reaction. Retreat would only make this worse. She wasn't his prey. *He* would be *hers*.

"I wouldn't think of it. This is a business arrangement, nothing else."

And to make it obvious to him, she pulled her top from her jeans and yanked it over her head, tossing it to the nearby couch. The bra she wore was transparent. Had she known that he wanted to collect payment immediately, she would have worn something less enticing.

"I'm assuming you want to fuck now," she said, getting busy with the button on her jeans. She'd always hated that word, *fuck*, but she forced herself to use it, showing him how little this meant to her, even if she couldn't convince herself of it.

Only when his hand captured hers, stopping her from lowering her zipper, did she realize that he had moved. Startled, she lifted her head and collided with his gaze.

"I think you're forgetting one thing: I'm in charge here. I decide when you get undressed and how. Are we clear on that?"

His voice was a low rumble, but she could barely concentrate on it, because he suddenly stood too close. His scent wrapped around her like a blanket, making it impossible for her to breathe. Little electrical charges seemed to dance on his skin and jump to hers, scorching her.

His hand suddenly came up, sliding underneath her mane, capturing the back of her neck in a firm grip. Effortlessly, he pulled her head closer.

"Do we understand each other . . . Rose?"

Her heart skipped a beat. Had she imagined it, or had his last word carried the same kind of tenderness as that night she'd become his wife?

She searched his hazel eyes, looking for an answer to her questions, but he gave nothing away. Whatever had been there only a split-second earlier, was gone. Or maybe it was simply an illusion, a trick her tired mind played on her.

That same mind now urged her to give in, to surrender. Maybe it was best that way. After two hundred years she was tired of running away, of hiding. She had to do this for Blake, because she had promised Charlotte, she told herself.

With a sigh, she brought her body flush against his. "I understand. Go ahead, take what you want."

Quinn's lips crushed hers before her last word was out. He wasn't tender, not the way he'd been that night in London, and she was glad for it. Tenderness would have crushed her courage and crumbled her resolve to guard her heart. Yet his kiss had another effect: it stoked her desire.

His lips plundered, explored, and demanded. They were both hard and soft as they slanted over her mouth, urging her to surrender. Her skin sizzled under the impact, and his masculine breath only fanned the flames in her body.

Forgetting her plan to remain uninvolved, she slung her arms around his neck and parted her lips under the imploring command of his tongue. A rush of heat charged through her, setting her ablaze, robbing her of the ability to think. When his tongue foraged into her, invading her mouth, she felt her brain disintegrate into a gooey mess.

She felt his silky tongue slide against her teeth, coaxing her to respond to him. Without thinking, she did. With the same perfect rhythm they had danced in the ballrooms of London, their tongues now twirled to a music she could sense reverberating through her entire body. The melody carried her away, cradled her in safety, yet hurtled her toward the inevitable.

Underneath her bra, her nipples chafed as he pressed her harder against his rock-hard chest. The ache was unbearable, but relief was nowhere in sight, because Quinn seemed to have no intention of letting go of her mouth yet to devote his energies to her aching breasts.

One hand was still at her nape to assure she didn't escape the devastating talent of his mouth, the other one palmed her backside as he rubbed his groin against her sex. She felt the hard outline of his cock, but the towel still clung to his hips, preventing a closer connection.

With one swift move, she pulled on it and freed him from it.

A startled gasp was his answer. Then his kiss intensified as if he wanted to punish her for what she'd done. Did he really think he could silence her, take the lead in this? She would show him that she would not be the timid playmate he had once had, the one who'd looked up to him with wonder in her eyes. No, she would take what she wanted.

Digging her nails into his backside, she ground her sex against his hard-on.

Quinn ripped his mouth from hers. "Fuck, Rose!" His eyes were red as he glared at her. "I told you—"

"Fuck you, Quinn! You think I'm still the virgin who's going to obediently spread her legs for you? If you wanna fuck, then we'll do it my way!"

Before he could reply, she reached behind her, releasing the clasp of her bra, sliding the irritating garment off her body.

His gaze instantly shot to her breasts.

"And what way is that, Rose?" he ground out, the tips of his fangs peeking from between his lips.

Her mouth salivated at the sight. She'd never before considered the view of extended fangs sexy. But now, the way he glared at her, it suddenly weakened her knees.

"Well, it sure isn't the way you did it back then!"

His eyes narrowed. Well, now she'd done it. He looked furious. He growled low and dark.

"I know what you're doing. It's not working."

She lifted her chin. "What do you think I'm going?"

"Don't play daft! You think by insulting me, can get out of your obligation. How stupid do you think I am? I'm going to have you. Right now. There's no way out."

It wasn't at all what she'd been doing, but there was no point in correcting him. All she'd wanted was to get it over with, with as little emotional involvement as possible. And that meant as quickly as possible, without any drawn-out foreplay.

Before her eyes, his hands turned into claws. In vampire speed, he ripped her jeans to shreds, tossing the destroyed garment to the floor. Her bikini panties followed.

She should feel at least a little scared, yet no such feeling took hold. Instead, her nipples tightened and a steady trickle of moisture made its way to the outer lips of her sex.

Quinn took a steadying breath, hoping Rose didn't notice that he was practically drooling. She was even more beautiful than he remembered her. Her body was more mature, her hips a little rounder than that night he'd taken her virginity. And her breasts were fuller too. Had the pregnancy done that to her? Was that why she was even more feminine now?

Her skin was still alabaster, her hard nipples a dark tan color, and her lips a deep red. He smelled the scent of her arousal and noticed the dew that glistened on the curls that guarded her sex. As his eyes roamed over her naked body, his anger dissipated. His claws turned back to fingers, but his fangs remained extended. The state of his fangs had nothing to do with anger, and everything to do with lust and desire.

Knowing how close he was to grabbing her and pressing her against the wall, fucking her standing up, he balled his hands into fists. No, he wouldn't allow her to control him like this. He would fuck her just like any other woman, and after it was over, he would realize that there was nothing special about it, that sex with her would be just like sex with any other woman.

"Lie down."

Her lips opened as if wanting to protest.

"Now, Rose!"

Maybe she had seen the determination in his eyes, or maybe the fact that he had shredded her pants had finally made it clear to her that he wasn't joking, but she complied with his request and stretched out on the bed.

She looked like a kitten, her beautiful body contrasted against the dark red sheets, her blond hair fanned out around her like a halo. One leg angled, she made an attempt at hiding her exposed sex from him. Despite the coldness she'd displayed, he had to wonder whether this meant anything to her.

She'd made it clear that she'd seen many men naked. It had been her way of telling him that she'd slept with countless men since he'd deflowered her. Flaunting this fact was an attempt at angering him, for sure. It shouldn't matter, yet it did. Knowing that other men had touched her, been inside her, pleasured her, made his blood boil.

His anger was back in an instant. Maybe it was better this way. Maybe the anger he felt inside him would prevent him from making this into more than it was: pure sex. An itch he needed to scratch.

Determined to prove to himself that she meant nothing to him anymore, he lowered himself onto the bed, pushing her legs apart in the process. He noticed how she closed her eyes. He didn't care. If she didn't want to look at him, it didn't matter. She'd gawked at him earlier, and those few seconds when her eyes had roamed his half naked body had given him some satisfaction. If she wanted to deny it now that there were still remnants of desire between them, then he'd allow it.

Smelling her arousal more intensely, now that her legs were spread before him, reminded him of how he'd feasted on her that night, how he'd enjoyed licking her, drinking her nectar. But he wouldn't do it tonight. This wasn't lovemaking. It was simply sex. If only he could convince his body of this fact.

Quinn moved between her thighs, centering himself over her sex. Without a word, he drove his aching cock into her, pushing deep.

Her eyes shot open, her lips parting on a moan.

Oh, fuck, he was so screwed!

Her slick warmth welcomed him home, her interior muscles gripping him like a tight fist, holding him there like a prisoner. With one single thrust, he'd sealed his fate. It couldn't be. It was impossible, but just being inside her, without even moving, without doing anything, he was aware of the power she still had over him. The power she would always have over him.

"Rose," he whispered, unable to stop his lips from moving.

His hand came up, wanting to caress her cheek, but he quickly suppressed the urge. This wasn't lovemaking, he repeated his mantra. No emotions, no feelings should be involved. He had to remain unaffected. Maybe once he'd found release, he would feel differently. Maybe then, he would see her as just another woman.

Determined to destroy whatever power she had over him, he withdrew from her tight sheath, then plunged back in. It shouldn't matter to him what she felt, whether she enjoyed this or didn't, yet he found himself watching her for signs of pleasure. Every time she let a moan or a sigh emerge, his chest swelled with pride and his cock throbbed in anticipation. He sensed how he adjusted his rhythm to her breathing, how he longed for her hands to touch him.

But her hands remained at her sides. Why didn't she touch him? He glanced at them and noticed how her nails were digging into the sheets, slicing them.

His head whipped back to her face, and he saw how she pulled her lower lip between her teeth, clearly trying not to cry out.

Fuck, pride be damned! "Touch me, Rose!" he commanded. "Do it!"

She instantly released her lip, a surprised look on her face. But moments later, her hands let go of the sheets and she placed them on his chest, stroking him.

He expelled a shaky breath, followed by a moan. Wherever she touched him, he was on fire. There was no use in denying it: her hands were magical. They conjured up memories of a life long gone, of secret kisses and stolen moments, of clandestine meetings and frantic touches. Of a forbidden love.

Everything felt like the first time. Her hands were just as soft as then, yet the shy hands of his virgin Rose were replaced by the experienced touch of a woman who knew what a man needed. Her nails dug into him, demanding, he'd increase his tempo and pound harder into her. Back then, he hadn't been able to do that for fear of hurting her, but today he could drive into her as hard as he wanted, and she would welcome him. Her body was as indestructible as his, yet as pliable as ever.

"More!" she demanded, pulling him closer with her legs wrapped around him.

He had no objections. Riding her hard and fast was just what he needed.

The shy virgin from two centuries earlier had vanished. Quinn couldn't say that he regretted that fact, because the woman who now writhed underneath him, whose body gave him such pleasure, was everything he'd ever dreamed of and more. She'd blossomed into the perfect lover.

Passionate and wild, she tantalized him with unscripted moans and sighs. Her body's reactions to his powerful thrusts were immediate and raw. And with every slide into her silken softness, he lost himself one bit more. Every second of their bodies dancing in perfect harmony, brought him closer to ecstasy. Release beckoned, but he pulled back, slowed down. He couldn't allow this to be over yet. It was too good to stop.

So he endured the torture she dealt him: one lash at a time, one slide, one push. And maybe just one kiss. What would be the harm in that?

On the next thrust, he lowered his head to hers, brought his lips down on her mouth and kissed her. It was different this time, not as angry. She greeted him with passion, slid her tongue against his invitingly, asking him to take her. She didn't have to tell him twice. This time when he invaded her mouth, he did so knowing that she wanted him and that it had nothing to do with the bargain they'd struck. He felt it.

The knowledge catapulted him over the edge. Without warning, his balls tightened, the pressure in them becoming unbearable. Fire shot into his cock, exploding from the tip.

Rose gasped into his mouth.

"Oh, God!" he ground out, ripping his lips from hers.

The waves of his orgasm hit him and whipped him like an Atlantic storm tossing a canoe in the surf. Then another wave crashed, and he realized that this one wasn't coming from him. It was Rose. Her muscles convulsed around his iron rod, clamping down on him so he couldn't leave, couldn't withdraw from her moist cavern. Not that he had any intention of doing so.

He continued riding her, his thrusts slowing and adjusting to her spasms. Captured between her thighs, he moved in and out of her, prolonging the pleasure that coursed through his veins.

When he finally rolled off her, he heard her exhale next to him. He turned his body to face her, angling his elbow and resting his head on his palm.

Maybe they could repair what had gone wrong between them. What he'd just experienced with her had been perfect. He couldn't just throw that away.

"Tell me what happened back then," he said softly, stroking his knuckles along her neck.

She evaded his gaze. "We had an agreement. I'll tell you once Blake is out of danger."

At her refusal, his heart beat faster, but he wasn't willing to give up trying. "Why not? Please tell me, Rose. After you got turned, why did you let me believe you were dead?"

Her mouth tightened. "It doesn't matter."

Quinn shot up to sit. "It matters to me. I loved you, Rose! I thought you felt the same back then."

He stared at the empty fireplace, waiting for her answer, knowing what he wanted to hear: a confession of her love. Then whatever else she would tell him wouldn't matter. Whatever reasons she'd had for never coming to see him, he would understand. If only she'd loved him. Even if she didn't love him anymore. He could live with that. At least he would try.

"I told you I'll explain everything later. But Blake is more important right now. He's in danger and—"

He lifted a hand, stopping her. The knowledge that she was hiding something from him solidified in his stomach and formed tiny painful knots. "I understand," he ground out. "You love Blake more than you ever loved me. I hope you two are gonna be very happy together."

Catapulting from the bed, he snatched the towel from the floor.

"Where are you going?"

He didn't turn but stalked to the door, wrapping the towel around his hips in the process. "Where do you think I'm going, Rose? To my room. We might still be married, but we're not a couple anymore. We never truly were."

The words almost choked his airways off and delivered a painful stab into his heart as if somebody were driving a knife into it. God, how much he'd wanted to have her in his arms, listen to her heartbeat as she slept, cradle her, feel her breath ghosting over his skin. And then, at sunset, wake up with her, feel her stir in his arms, her warm body molded to his, her sweet bottom tucked into his groin.

How many days had he dreamt of it? How many times had he wished for the impossible, for a life with Rose? And even now as he slammed the door shut behind him, he knew those dreams hadn't died. He was irrevocably in love with Rose. For two hundred years he'd kept the love for her alive, and tonight, it had been reaffirmed. She was still his, the wife he'd claimed that fateful night, the woman he couldn't forget. The one who'd spoiled him for all others.

His plan of purging his love for Rose had failed.

What was he supposed to do now?

12

Rose hated washing Quinn's scent off, but she knew it was better that way. It was bad enough that her entire body ached pleasantly and that her sex still hummed with aftershocks from . . . well, she couldn't exactly call it lovemaking. It hadn't been that. It had been a coupling, a pleasant one, a passionate one. But what had followed had destroyed the moment and reminded her that they could never get back what they'd once had. So she had slammed the door to her heart shut again and bolted it.

Reluctantly, she dressed and poked her head out into the hallway. It was empty. And if she was lucky it would remain so for another hour, until sunset. She hadn't had a chance to look around the mansion when she'd first entered. Quinn had explained that it was a Bed and Breakfast, and that Scanguards had exclusive use of it.

It was run by a fellow vampire, and according to Quinn, once the B&B was open for business, only vampires would be able to make reservations. Vampires would have to identify themselves with a code word, and all humans would be turned away, claiming there were no vacancies. That explained why the shutters were dark so they wouldn't let any light in, and why the glass panes appeared to have a special UV coating to reduce the amount of light entering the rooms to a minimum. She assumed that even without the shutters closed, a vampire would be safe on a cloudy or foggy day, and from what she'd heard about San Francisco, there were many of those. Apparently the weather here was a bit like in good old London.

As she walked down the elaborately carved staircase, the plush carpet under her feet absorbed the sound of her steps. Good, she wouldn't wake Quinn. The less she saw of him, the better. She hoped he would take his time with getting ready, because as soon as the sun was down, she needed to feed. And she hated it when anybody went with her on those hunting trips. She hated being watched as she turned into an animal, a predator. It disgusted her.

That was what she hated most about being a vampire: feeding from humans.

But it was a necessary evil to survive.

Rose looked around the foyer, trying to orient herself. A small sign saying *Kitchen* pointed toward the back of the house. She followed it.

Even before she pushed the double-hinged swinging door open, she knew the kitchen wasn't empty. Her stomach instantly lurched at the smell of the blood that emanated from the room.

Her eyes flew to the person who stood in front of the open refrigerator, a bottle with red liquid at his lips, his head tilted back as he gulped it down. Drops of blood ran down his chin as he drank greedily. He was young, his hair a messy dark mane. He was barefoot and only wore a pair of jeans, exposing his lean hairless chest. His muscles weren't as defined as Quinn's; nevertheless his chest was something nice to look at.

The vampire's head whipped toward her, his eyes flashing red, his fangs extended as he issued a warning growl. Instinctively she backed away. Interrupting a vampire while feeding could be ugly, even though she wondered why he was drinking from a bottle. Had he drained a human earlier and then stored the excess in the refrigerator for a later snack?

"Excuse me," she whispered and pushed against the door behind her.

With one move he was on her, pinning her against the door frame. She readied herself to counterattack, but he didn't strike her. He merely sniffed, then pulled back instantly.

Suddenly the color of his eyes changed and his fangs receded. His demeanor turned from predator to shy young man in a second.

"I'm sorry," he said. Then he shrugged. "Not used to all this yet, you know."

Rose nodded, not exactly sure what he meant. "No harm done." She stared past him, where the refrigerator door was still open. On the shelves, neatly lined up stood at least a couple of dozen bottles of red liquid. She pointed her hand toward them. "Are those—?"

"You must be Quinn's wife," the man said.

The bottles in the refrigerator were immediately forgotten.

"Quinn's . . . ?" she choked out. She hadn't expected Quinn to tell everybody about their relationship. After all, hadn't he said only hours earlier that they weren't a couple?

He gave her a startled look. "Well, he said . . . I mean . . . oh God, you'd better leave quickly. He said his wife would join us here, but if you're not her, then you should get out of here before she shows up. Who knows what she's like."

The young vampire nervously looked about the room, then toward the window. "Oh, crap, it's still daylight." His eyes darted to the telephone on the counter. "I can call you a blackout van."

Rose raised her hand. "Hold it."

"No, you don't understand. Once his wife is here, I'm sure she's not gonna be pleased to see that he had some . . . uh . . . some . . . other woman over."

"I'm not some—"

He cut her off. "Listen, I could hear you fucking when he brought you back, no offense, so don't deny it. I know he's a playboy. We all accept that, but for as long as his wife is staying, I'll make sure none of you . . . uh, women, mess things up. Is that clear?"

Playboy? Great, that was just peachy! Quinn was known as a womanizer. What else was new?

The vampire reached for the phone.

Rose slammed her hand over his, preventing him from picking it up. "I'm his fucking wife!"

As soon as the words were out, she wanted to clamp her hand over her mouth and take the words back. She might be his wife on paper, but she was nothing to him.

The young vampire winced.

"So you are," a voice came from the door.

Rose stiffened. Oh, shit! Quinn had heard her outburst. It appeared voices carried well in the old house.

"Oliver, may I introduce Rose to you, my wife, who rejected me after I returned from the war as a vampire."

Despite the calmness with which he'd spoken the words, the accusation was clear. Yes, she had rejected him. Out of fear for her and her daughter's safety. She needed no reminder of it.

"There is no need to air our grievances with strangers," she hissed without turning to him.

Quinn's steps advanced on her until he stood next to her. "But Oliver isn't a stranger. He's my protégé, my son if you wish."

Oliver stretched his hand toward her. "It's nice to meet you. Sorry about . . . you know. I didn't mean what I said. He's not—"

"You don't need to make excuses for me, Oliver," Quinn interrupted. "Rose already has a bad opinion of me. I doubt it can get any worse."

She ignored the jab and instead focused on Oliver. She wondered why Quinn had turned him, but she would rather bite her tongue than ask.

"Nice to meet you, Oliver."

He nodded and smiled, and her gaze slipped to his chin where the blood still clung to his skin. It reminded her of what she'd wanted to ask him earlier.

She pointed to the refrigerator. "The bottles. What are they?"

Oliver's forehead furrowed. "Bottles of blood of course. Why do you ask?"

"I mean, how do you get them? Do you fill them up yourself?" The sheer volume suggested otherwise.

"Are you telling me, you don't know about bottled blood?" Quinn asked, making her look at him. He stared at her as if she'd just crawled out from living under a rock for the last two hundred years.

Just like Oliver, he wore jeans. Spots of his T-shirt seemed wet as if he'd pulled it over his head without properly drying off after a shower.

"I . . . well, where do you get it from?"

"We order it through some connections we have at the blood bank. My boss set up a medical supply company years ago, and that's how the blood gets funneled to us," Quinn explained.

"You mean you don't feed directly from humans?"

She noticed how his look suddenly strayed to her neck, making her skin tingle.

"Only occasionally when there's need."

"That's right," Oliver added. "Most of them have fed from me before. You know, during emergencies. But otherwise they're all on bottled blood, most of the Scanguards guys, I mean."

Rose's chin dropped. Why would they have fed off another vampire? That made no sense whatsoever. "But you're a vampire too."

Oliver grinned, showing little dimples in his cheeks. "I was human until a few days ago."

Quinn ruffled his hair. "He's practically a baby."

"Am not!"

When Quinn's laughter echoed through the kitchen, Rose felt a stab in her heart. God, how she'd missed his laughter, his smiles, the twinkle in his eyes. The way he looked at Oliver now, with mischief and affection, was how she remembered him. He looked so young again, so innocent—so human.

"So you feed from bottles," she repeated. "May I try one?"

Oliver went to the refrigerator, pulled a bottle out and shut the door. "Here. It's pretty good."

Hesitantly she took the bottle from him and unscrewed it. She sniffed. It positively smelled of blood, rich human blood. "Is it real?"

Quinn nodded. "Donated by humans, bottled, and refrigerated. We drink it cold, but if you want it warm, you can use the microwave."

She shook her head. If he and his colleagues drank it cold, so would she. It was bad enough that she had never heard of bottled blood. None of the vampire hordes she had consorted with over the years had used bottled blood. All of them had fed directly from humans.

Setting the bottle to her lips, she took a tentative taste. The thick liquid filled her mouth, and her taste buds instantly analyzed it.

Wow!

She took another sip and another. It was good. Truth be told, it was *very* good. And what was even more important: it wasn't messy. She didn't have to pierce someone's skin and dig her fangs into her victim, didn't have to feel the person struggle against her. Didn't need to see the fear in a human's eyes when he or she knew what was coming. And she didn't feel the disgust that she normally felt when she fed. She felt almost . . . normal. Like a real person, one, who was simply drinking a beverage. Cultivated, civilized, utterly normal.

By the time Rose removed the bottle from her lips, it was empty. She hadn't even realized how fast she'd gulped down the delicious fluid. Clandestinely she eyed the refrigerator. Would it be greedy to ask for another one? The bottle had easily contained a pint. Yet, she was still hungry. Had she taken more than a pint from the humans she'd fed from? She honestly couldn't tell. She had always stopped once her hunger was stilled, never realizing how much blood she'd stolen.

The thought made her sick. No wonder her sub-conscience had made her feel disgusted about the act.

"Give her another one, Oliver," Quinn ordered.

Her gaze shot to him, worried that he was able to read in her face what was going on inside her.

"I'm fine. I don't need anything else." But it was a lie, and in his eyes she saw that he knew.

Quinn's insistent wave to Oliver was all it took for her to cave. A moment later, she held a second bottle and drained it just as fast.

A feeling of fullness settled inside her. For the first time in her life, feeding had made her feel satisfied without giving her a guilty conscience.

"Thank you."

Quinn gave her a long look before nodding. "You've never seen bottled blood before."

Not a question, simply a statement, yet she felt compelled to explain herself. "The various vampire clans I was with, they only fed from humans. Nobody ever mentioned this to me."

"Clans? Plural?" Quinn asked, raising an eyebrow in inquiry.

She shrugged. "Yeah, why?"

"It's unusual for a vampire to change clans. Once you're with a group, you normally stick together. Like a family."

She snorted. The groups of vampires she'd met weren't exactly like loving families, more like a band of Mafioso with even less loyalty than said murderous organization. Backstabbing and infighting was a daily order, and the makeup of each group changed faster than the menu in a fancy restaurant.

"There's no such thing with vampires. Everybody is out for themselves."

Quinn ran his eyes over her, making her feel as if she were being inspected. "Nice crowd you hung around with. That explains certain things."

"It explains nothing. I'm not like them. I refuse to be like them!" And had she known about bottled blood, it would have saved her from a lot of emotional pain.

"Maybe it's time you met my family then." He motioned toward Oliver. "We're off to Scanguards. I want you to come with us. Time to start training."

"But I'm *already* a trained bodyguard," Oliver insisted.

"You were a trained *human* bodyguard. That's totally different. Now we'll kick things up a notch."

Then Quinn looked back at her. "Time to bring our grandson in."

And if his voice didn't have a little softness to it when he said *grandson*. Rose stared at him. Maybe he would learn to care about Blake and keep him safe, even once he knew what she'd done. Time would tell.

13

As soon as the sun set over the Pacific Ocean, Quinn kicked down the gas pedal of the Scanguards-owned SUV and shot out of the six-car-garage underneath the B&B.

On the way to the car, he'd filled Oliver in on their assignment and who their charge was. To say that Oliver was surprised would have been an understatement. But he didn't ask any personal questions, and Quinn wasn't in the mood to divulge any more information than he already had. Confessing that he was hurt by Rose's rejection, had been a major slip, one he could only attribute to the sense of shame he felt about what had happened in her bedroom. Not the sex part, of course, but the words they had exchanged afterwards.

It didn't matter now. What was done was done. And maybe it would give her something to chew on. Maybe even soften her so she would tell him what was really going on. Because he neither believed her claim that Keegan wanted to get back at her for leaving him, nor her even more ridiculous declaration that she hadn't come to see him because she was protecting Charlotte from him. Bullshit, if anybody asked him.

Quinn gripped the steering wheel tighter and forced his thoughts to focus on business instead.

He'd already received a text from one of the human bodyguards he'd assigned to Blake. The boy was on his way to Scanguards' brand-new training facility in an old warehouse in the Mission. It had been refurbished and made vampire proof and been equipped with various training rooms and classrooms where vampires as well as human bodyguards trained for their missions. Samson took training seriously, and it showed.

The place was state of the art, but Quinn barely took any notice of it as they arrived. He flashed his Scanguards ID at the security guard manning the entry. Oliver did likewise.

When the burly guard squared his stance in front of Rose, Quinn tapped the man on his arm. "She's with me."

"She'll still have to go through the check," he answered.

Quinn turned the backside of his ID for the guard to see. *Section V, Class A* it said. The man instantly took a step back.

"I'm sorry, sir, I didn't know. Go right in."

Quinn nodded. The guard didn't know him, since Quinn had only once before visited the brand new facility in San Francisco. Had he been back in New York, he wouldn't even have had to show his ID. He noticed how Rose raised an eyebrow, then brushed past him into the building. Once they were inside, she pointed toward the pocket into which he'd shoved his ID.

"What's it mean?"

"Section V stands for the obvious, not that this guard would know. He thinks it stands for VIP." As it might well have. "Class A is the highest clearance at Scanguards. Anybody with a Section V Class A clearance has access to every area within Scanguards."

"Crap, I still have a Section H ID," Oliver mumbled.

"Time to turn that in. Go up to the main security office and have them issue you a new pass."

Curious, his protégé looked at him. "What shall I tell them?"

Quinn smiled back at him. "They've already received their instructions from Samson. So, go. Find us in the lounge when you're done."

As Oliver wandered off, Quinn walked to the large counter on which *Check in* was inscribed in large bold letters. The young woman looked up and smiled when he stopped right in front of it.

"How may I help you?" She eyed his badge and added, "Quinn."

Automatically, he smiled back with a smile he'd used for the last two hundred years: a smile that had melted practically every woman into his arms. Oddly enough, when the human blushed, a sense of unease crept up his spine. He wasn't in the mood to flirt, and that was something that had never before happened to him. Could it be because Rose had followed him and now stood next to him?

"Can you ping me once Blake Bond has arrived, please."

She beamed. "He's already here." She glanced at the screen in front of her. "Visitor Lounge H."

Quinn nodded. "Thanks."

"Anytime," the girl chirped.

With a sideways glance, he motioned Rose to walk with him. "Just let me talk."

"I still think it's a stupid idea."

He couldn't help it, but her objection needed an answer. "And that's exactly why I'll be doing the talking."

Why he had to rile her up, he didn't know, when he should be trying to use his charm on her to soften her up, turn her into soft clay, just like the girl at the *Check in* desk had instantly responded to the subconscious vibes he gave off. He wondered for a moment whether this was something he could switch off, or whether after two hundred years of milking his gift of seduction it was too ingrained in him.

When he glanced at Rose for a brief second as they walked down the corridor, he noticed the tightness of her jaw and shoulders. Well, maybe he *could* turn off his charm after all. At least it appeared he did it automatically the moment he was alone with Rose.

The visitor lounge looked very much like the lobby of a five-star hotel with comfortable seating areas, a fireplace, and soft music. Two women dressed in business attire roamed the room to attend to the needs of the waiting visitors, serving drinks, answering questions, and assuring them that whoever they had come to see would be with them momentarily.

There were two of these lounges in the building. This was the lounge for humans. At the opposite end of the corridor, Visitor Lounge V catered to the needs of visiting vampires, mostly those Samson planned to recruit. There, instead of coffee and tea, blood was served. Access to the lounge was strictly monitored so that no human accidentally stumbled into it.

Scanning the room, Quinn instantly found his grandson. It was hard not to notice him: he was flirting with one of the hostesses. Shamelessly.

Quinn suddenly felt Rose's gaze on him and turned his head to look at her. He knew exactly what she was thinking, almost as if the two hundred years of separation had never happened. His heart softened for a moment.

"Maybe he just needs some direction in his life so he can mature. This could be the best thing that ever happened to him."

A glimmer of hope sparked in her eyes. "I hope you're right."

At this moment she reminded him so much of the girl he'd courted against her father's will, and he had a hard time tearing his gaze from her.

When they finally approached Blake, he jumped up from his seat, clearly eager to find out why he was here.

Shaking hands, he blurted, "Cool digs, man."

Quinn simply nodded, then motioned to Rose. "This is Rose, my associate." No need to give the kid any more information about his relationship to Rose than was absolutely necessary.

Blake's assessing eyes instantly traveled over her body, eliciting a proprietary response from Quinn: he stepped closer to her.

Rose offered her hand, and for Quinn's liking, Blake held it for far too long.

"Nice to meet you," he responded.

"Likewise."

Quinn pointed to the armchairs. "Shall we?"

They sat down, Quinn making sure that he sat close to Rose to prevent any physical contact between her and Blake. Why he took such precaution, he blamed on the fact that his descendent was a shameless flirt. If the boy knew that he was flirting with his 4th great-grandmother he would probably feel disgusted.

The sooner he established the ground rules, the better.

"I'm sure you're curious to hear more about my offer," Quinn started.

Blake instantly moved forward on his chair, his eagerness and curiosity evident.

"Well, then don't let me keep you on tenterhooks. What I'm telling you now doesn't leave this room. Here's the deal: we're a security outfit of the highest caliber. We don't always work within the confines of the law. Hence, we choose very carefully, who we take into our fold. Only the best will make the cut."

He watched Blake's face light up in fascination. "Wow. So, what do I need to do?"

"There are a number of tests. Only a few pass them."

"Just like in Men in Black, right?" Blake asked, looking like a kid about to unwrap his Christmas presents.

Quinn almost regretted having used the MIB reference the night before. "This is reality, not a movie. People die if we don't do our jobs right. That's why we only take the best. Nothing less will do."

He paused for a second, giving Blake a moment to digest his words, and glanced at Rose.

She mouthed a few words to him. *The best of the best of the best.*

Quinn refrained from rolling his eyes. Great, now even Rose was quoting lines from the movie.

"I have to warn you, should you be selected, the training is grueling. Both mentally and physically. Your life will change irrevocably. It's no place for weaklings."

Blake instantly let out an outraged breath. "I'm not a weakling!" Immediately, the muscles in his arms bulged as if to profess his physical prowess.

"I don't think Quinn is saying that," Rose interjected.

"Rose is right," Quinn said quickly before she could say anything else and interfere with his line of buttering the kid up. "To be selected is a privilege. To survive the training intact is an achievement you can be proud of."

Blake nodded enthusiastically. "I can do it."

Quinn turned when he felt another vampire approach. Oliver appeared next to him, grinning and flashing his shiny new badge at him. He homed in on the ID: *Section V, Class A* it said. He hadn't expected anything else. Oliver had been in the inner circle of vampires and been Samson's personal assistant for four years. It was only natural that he would instantly be elevated to the highest echelon within Scanguards.

They exchanged a brief smile. He felt like a proud father in that moment.

"This is Oliver."

"Hey," Blake greeted him.

"Oliver and Rose will bring you to where the tests are conducted. You'll meet other applicants that were selected by my colleagues." He leaned forward in emphasis. "Between you and me, it's always a competition between the seasoned staff here about who can spot the next recruit. So, don't make me lose this bet."

Blake jumped up. "You can count on me!"

Quinn grinned. The kid was gung-ho. Once they had tired him out with some pointless fake tests competing against some Scanguards staff who'd been selected to play the other applicants, he would be ecstatic to be chosen and agree to the conditions Quinn would present him with later.

Quinn looked at Rose. "We'll meet here in a couple of hours."

Rose shot him a surprised look. "You're not coming with us?"

"I have an appointment in IT."

Then he turned and left the room before Rose could protest. What he had to discuss with Thomas wasn't meant for her ears.

14

Thomas looked up from his console and stared at the dark-haired vampire in front of him. Cain had joined Scanguards only a few weeks earlier after providing them with vital information about an insane Nazi-vampire who wanted to create a master race. During the final battle, Thomas had sustained major injuries, but thanks to the care of his mentee Eddie, he'd recovered quickly.

"But we have nothing to go by," he replied to Cain's earlier question.

"I know that. But everybody says you're a genius and can dig up anything."

Thomas rolled his eyes. "If it comes to hacking into a computer system, sure, but to find out who you are? How do you want me to do that? *You* don't even know who you are."

Cain bent over the desk. "I need your help. I need to know who I am. It's been driving me mad not having any memory from when I was human. What if I have family? What if there is somebody who needs me? Somebody who's looking for me? Don't you understand how that feels?"

His eyes begged for understanding.

Thomas dropped his lids halfway, not wanting to see the pain and desperation that was engrained in Cain's every cell. He understood him all too well. He understood the pain of knowing there was somebody who had counted on him. He'd walked away once himself, knowing if he hadn't he would have become a different person: a power hungry, dangerous vampire. Walked away from one who manipulated others because he could, because of the power that coursed through his veins.

Thomas knew he'd inherited that same blood. It carried power—and destruction. Walking away had been the only way to survive.

Maybe Cain had walked away from something similar, and his mind had graced him with memory loss. What a gift.

"What if you don't like what I find?" Thomas challenged. "What if it's something you'd rather not know?"

Cain shook his head. "Whatever it is, I want to know. I want to be whole again. I know there's something . . . I feel it." He pressed his hand to his chest. "Here. I feel it here."

Then he pointed his finger toward the door. "Out there, somewhere, my past is waiting for me. I need to know what I'm up against before it comes biting me in the ass."

Slowly, Thomas nodded. He wished he didn't have to lie to Cain, but he was already in the middle of investigating the other vampire's past. Gabriel had ordered it shortly after Cain had come on board. Yet so far, nothing had turned up.

"Fine. I'll see what I can find out. Email me everything you remember, anything at all, no matter how insignificant. I know you've already given us some of this information when you joined, but I want you to think about it, try to remember what else there might be. Will you do that?"

A grateful smile spread over Cain's handsome face. But oddly enough, despite the other vampire's attractiveness, Thomas felt nothing other than the connection he felt with all Scanguards vampires. It was different with Eddie, the young vampire he mentored and who lived with him. The straight vampire, he tried to remind himself. And he would never make a pass at a straight man, no matter how much he longed for him, how much he craved his touch.

There were lines he never crossed, because he knew that adhering to his high moral ethics was the only way to keep the lust for dominance at bay and to hide from everybody how truly powerful he was.

"Thank you. You have no idea how much this means to me."

Cain grabbed his hand and shook it enthusiastically.

"Yeah, yeah, now get out of here."

Before Cain could open the door, there was a knock.

"Come in."

To his surprise, Quinn stepped in.

"Hey, what's bringing you to my humble office?"

"Just a quick thing."

"See you," Cain said and walked through the door.

"Oh, Cain," Quinn called after him.

"Yeah?"

"You were just assigned to me. Can you wait for me in the V Staff Lounge?"

"Sure thing." Then he pulled the door shut behind him.

"Do you have a minute?" Quinn asked and let himself fall in the chair opposite Thomas's desk without waiting for an answer.

"Not really. Do you need me to check the system to see what other staff is available for your assignment? I'm assuming since it's bringing in a million dollars, we can throw a few more bodies at it."

Quinn quickly waved him off. "I've already checked with Gabriel on who's available. I've got it in hand. Not to worry. But you could do something else for me." He leaned forward, and his eyes darted to the door, then back to him.

Thomas raised a curious eyebrow.

"I need you to find out everything you can about Rose."

Thomas felt his jaw drop. His friend couldn't be serious. "Listen, I don't know what's between you and her, and I'm not asking about it." He raised his hands when Quinn tried to interrupt. "But I'm not violating somebody else's privacy for no reason other than your curiosity."

Quinn jumped up. "It's got nothing to do with my curiosity. Rose is lying to me. She's hiding something from me, and I need to know what it is."

"That's not my problem. If she's hiding something from you, maybe it's none of your business."

"It is my business," Quinn bit out.

"I can't help you. If it's got nothing to do with the assignment, then I don't want to be dragged into some domestic issues between a couple."

"We're NOT a couple!"

"Aren't you? Funny, because somebody told me she's your wife."

Quinn fumed now. "Consider us divorced. She rejected me after I became a vamp—" He stopped himself, obviously realizing that he'd said too much.

"Well, it very much looks to me like you and Rose have issues. And I'm old enough to know not to get in the middle of it."

"Come on, Thomas. What's it to you? You don't even know her. I thought we were friends," Quinn tried to cajole him.

"We are. And that's exactly why I'm not snooping around for you. Because, trust me, it will come to bite you in the ass."

When he noticed Quinn's face fall in disappointment, he sighed. But he didn't cave. "Now get out of here." He glanced at the clock on the wall. "I want to get some work done before going over to the party."

Quinn stopped in his tracks. "What party?"

"Haven's birthday party, of course. Didn't you get the invite?"

He shook his head.

Then Thomas realized why his friend hadn't been invited. "Of course. Those went out last week, and you were supposed to be back in New York already. Guess that's why Yvette didn't send you one. But, hey, you should go anyway. You know they would have invited you."

"I might just do that."

And maybe it would lift his friend's spirit. He didn't look as carefree as he usually did. Apparently Rose's reappearance had thrown a serious wrench into the playboy's lifestyle. Maybe it was for the better, or maybe it would all blow up one day.

***

Rose could see Blake perspire as he turned in his test, just like the five fake applicants. She waved at him, motioning him to join her and Oliver. Dutifully, he came to her.

He ran a shaky hand through his dark hair, a gesture that reminded her of Quinn. Odd, how certain things got passed on from generation to generation, even though neither Blake nor any of his ancestors had ever met Quinn and been exposed to his idiosyncrasies.

"I think I did well. But I'm not sure how the others did. They looked pretty confident too."

Rose smiled. "We'll just have to wait and see. It shouldn't take long." She turned to Oliver. "Right?"

"They'll just run it through the computer and give the result to Quinn. Let's go to the lounge to wait for him," Oliver instructed, winking clandestinely at Rose.

She managed not to chuckle. How a bunch of grown vampires could go through all these gyrations without flinching was just beyond her. Couldn't they simply have pretended to offer him a job? No, they had to go all Mission Impossible on the kid to make him feel special. Like Blake needed another boost for his ego.

They didn't have to wait long in the lounge. Quinn arrived fifteen minutes after they had sat down. The look on his face was serious.

Rose noticed how Blake swallowed hard.

"Oh, shit, that doesn't look good."

Quinn sat down opposite Blake and took a long look at him. "Well, I have good and bad news."

"Oh."

"Good news is you did extremely well in all the tests." Then he paused, clearly for effect. "The bad news is, so did one other guy. Basically, it's a tie."

"Oh, shit," Blake let out. "What now?"

Quinn edged forward on his seat. "Here's the deal. As we speak, my colleague is making an offer to the other guy—"

"Fuck!"

Quinn raised his hand. "Hold it. But I'm making one to you. Whoever accepts all our conditions first gets the job."

"Conditions? Give 'em to me. Don't waste any time." The urgency in Blake's voice was undeniable.

"The trainee will live at a place of our choosing, surrounded by other trainees and trainers. You'll never leave our sight, unless authorized to do so and under supervision. There are others out there who are keen on snatching our recruits from under our noses. We want to prevent that."

Rose rolled her eyes, which Blake couldn't see. How much more crap was Quinn going to dish up?

"You will follow all our instructions to a T. All your needs will be taken care of. Your housing is paid for, all your bills will be paid. Your salary is more than generous."

"How much?" Blake interjected.

"During training you'll make as much as an attorney in his first year. After that . . . " Quinn shrugged. "Enough to qualify for a mortgage on a house in Pacific Heights."

Blake blew out an impressed breath. "Yeah!"

"But you decide now." Quinn looked toward the door. "If my colleague comes in here before I have a decision from you, the deal is off."

"I'll take it!" Blake blurted out.

"Excellent! Wait here." He rushed to the door, closing it behind him.

Only sixty seconds later he came back in, giving a thumbs-up signal. Next to him, a dark-haired vampire entered.

Excitedly, Blake jumped up and down. "Yeah! I got it!" He pulled her into an embrace, squeezed her against his broad chest. "I got it."

Over his shoulder, Rose peered at Quinn, whose mouth had formed into a thin line.

She had to hand it to him. Apparently, his strategy had paid off. Blake would do whatever they wanted him to. It would make protecting him much easier.

"Okay," Quinn said tightly. Then he pointed to the man next to him. "Cain here and Oliver will accompany you to your new quarters. Training will start immediately."

"Right now?" Blake asked, surprised.

"Yes, didn't I say that?"

"Oh, yeah, sure, of course," he said quickly.

"Well, we'll see you later, then," Quinn confirmed and looked at her. "Rose, shall we?" He motioned her to the door.

A few seconds later they were in the corridor, walking toward the exit.

"Where are we going? I thought we were staying with Blake."

"Oliver and Cain can handle him right now. We have to go to a party."

"A party? I have no time to amuse myself at some party right now."

"We're not going to amuse ourselves. I need to rustle up some humans who can join us at the house, just in case Blake decides to go walking about during daylight hours."

He had a point. If Blake managed to leave the house and their protection during daytime, they would have a hard time keeping up with him. Sure, they could use blackout vans to follow him, but that wouldn't provide sufficient protection, and the vans were only useful on the street. Once Blake dashed into a building or an area inaccessible to vans, they would lose him.

"And you're going to find those humans at some party?"

"Not just *some* party; it's strictly a family affair."

Then he put his hand on her forearm, the contact scorching her skin and reminding her of his touch less than twenty-four hours earlier.

"Let's go. It's not far from here."

15

Haven and Yvette's house wasn't huge. In fact, it was a rather cozy cottage on Telegraph Hill. Parking anywhere in the area was impossible. Quinn knew that much from his first and only prior visit to the house. He had therefore left the SUV for Oliver to drive back to the B&B and opted for a taxi.

On the ride, he remained quiet, still wondering what to do now that Thomas had rejected his request to check up on Rose. Sure, he could try and do some digging himself, but it wasn't his expertise, and all he would do was waste precious time he didn't have. There was only one other way to find out what was really going on inside of Rose: he had to seduce it out of her.

It was a proposition that both thrilled and frightened him. Because by seducing her, he was in danger of exposing his heart to her once more. Could he really afford that kind of casualty? Or would this finally mark his ultimate self-destruction?

When the taxi came to a halt, he paid the cabdriver and jumped out of it, automatically holding his hand out to her as he'd done so many times to help her out of a carriage. When her dainty hand slipped into his palm, he closed his fingers around it and pulled gently. She emerged from the taxi. Her heel caught at the uneven pavement, and she hurtled into his arms. He caught her with ease, slinging his other arm around her waist instinctively. Then a memory came back, hitting him broadside.

She lifted her lids and their gazes collided.

"Do you remember our first kiss?" he murmured.

Rose didn't answer, but her eyes confirmed that her memory was just as good as his.

"You tripped over your hem when you stepped from the carriage. I caught you. It was dark. Your chaperone had fallen asleep on the ride and there was nobody else around except the coachman. And he was purposefully looking the other way."

"Because you bribed him," she added, but there was no hint of reprimand in her voice.

"I'm glad I did. I still remember what your lips tasted like. How soft they were. How sweet."

He leaned in. She didn't back away.

"You smelled so manly, and your arms held me so tightly." Her breath caught.

"You knew I would kiss you, and you allowed it to happen." Could they repeat that moment in history? Replay it over and over again?

"Shut the door. I haven't got all night!" the taxi driver's voice came from within the cab, destroying the tender moment.

Immediately, Rose turned away from him, reached for the door and slammed it shut. The taxi's tires screeched as it took off.

When she turned back to him, he noticed that she avoided looking at him. His heart clenched. Disappointed, he walked to the cottage, knowing she would follow.

The door was unlocked. Inside, the voices of his colleagues and friends mixed with dance music. Several dogs yapped and barked. He was prevented from entering farther than the small lobby when two Labrador puppies blocked his way, excitedly barking up at him, unsure whether to welcome him or defend their territory.

"You little idiots!" Haven appeared through the door to the living room and bent down to the two puppies, stroking them. The intruders instantly forgotten, the two rolled onto their backs, offering their bellies to their master's hands. Laughing, Haven complied, then gently shoved the two toward the kitchen. "Go!"

As he got up from his crouching position he wiped his hands on his jeans, his broad form nearly filling the entire width of the narrow corridor. "Sorry, Quinn, they're just not trained yet."

Quinn grinned. "Haven't found a home for those two monsters yet, have you?"

Haven extended his hand for a shake. "Want one?"

"Good God, no! Too much work!"

His host laughed. "Yeah, but imagine what kind of babe magnet those—"

"Happy birthday, Haven!" Quinn interrupted loudly, hoping to stop him from making any further references to his lifestyle.

When Haven furrowed his forehead, Quinn took a step to the side, making space for Rose to emerge from behind him.

"Oops." Haven made an apologetic gesture, then pasted a broad grin on his face. "Why don't you introduce me to your date?"

Before he could do so, Rose already stretched her hand toward Haven, who instantly shook it. "I'm Rose Haverford. A client."

He hesitated, shooting Quinn a questioning look, before he responded to her introduction. "I'm Haven, Yvette's mate. Come in." He motioned toward the living room. "Yvette's in there." He popped his head through the door. "Baby! More guests. Why don't you introduce Rose here to all our friends?"

And with those words he simply gave Rose a little nudge toward the living room.

"Haven, could I have a quick word?" Quinn asked.

His host motioned his head toward the kitchen.

The moment Haven closed the kitchen door behind them, he leaned against it and hooked his thumbs into his belt.

"Since you know better than to bring a client to my house, I'm assuming Rose is your wife that everybody is talking about."

Quinn sighed. It appeared good news traveled fast. At least it would save him from having to explain to everybody and their dog what their common history was.

"It's complicated. Anyway, she just hired us to protect her 4th grandson."

Haven did a double take. "Grandson?" He blew out an appreciative breath. "That's one hot grandma if I've ever seen one."

Torn between outrage about Haven's comment and pride that even a blood-bonded vampire would find his Rose beautiful, he opted for a lighthearted response.

"Don't let Yvette hear that, or she'll rip your head off."

"No shit! She'd have my balls too. Tell you something: if you ever get blood-bonded, it had better be with a woman you can't get enough of, or the whole *love forever thing* is going to get old pretty soon." He chuckled.

Not wanting to talk about himself, Quinn deflected, "So you think you made the right choice?"

Haven shook his head. "I don't *think* so. I *know* I made the right choice."

Then his lips moved silently. *Isn't that right, baby?* Quinn read.

"You know you don't have to move your lips when you talk to Yvette telepathically," Quinn said.

"Oh, was I doing it again? Darn, it's still so new. Just like everything else about being a vampire."

Quinn nodded. "You'll get used to it. We all did. Do you regret it?"

A fierce shake of his head was the answer. "God, no! I don't regret having lost my human life. Being with Yvette more than makes up for it."

Haven pushed off the door. "So, you wanted to talk to me about something?"

"Yes. About Wesley."

His friend's face fell. "Oh, fuck, what's he done now?"

Quickly, Quinn raised his hands. "Nothing."

"You sure? Because whenever somebody wants to talk to me about Wesley then it's because he screwed up again."

"Trust me, your brother is in the clear."

For now. Of course, that could change quickly. The hotheaded human was as volatile as a powder keg sitting next to an open flame.

Haven's shoulders relaxed visibly. "So what's this about then?"

"I could do with his help."

His friend looked surprised. "You're kidding. Are we talking about the same person? My brother, the same guy who will get into trouble every chance he gets?"

Quinn nodded grimly. If he had a choice, he'd pick somebody else to do the job, but unfortunately, the number of humans within their inner core was dwindling fast, particularly with Oliver now being in the vampire camp. And for this job he needed a human. Besides, Wesley had additional skills.

"How is he doing with his attempts at gaining his witchcraft back?"

"Terribly. And just as well." Haven paused and sighed. "Though he took all of Francine's books and potions after her death, pretty much cleaned out her houseboat. He's studying it. I think it really interests him. First time, I've seen him be serious about anything."

"Maybe it'll come in handy one day."

Haven shrugged. "Who knows? Well, at least we can be sure that even if he gains some amount of his witchcraft back, he will never gain the Power of Three."

Quinn nodded. "Thank heavens for that."

Haven had destroyed the Power of Three only a few months earlier by sacrificing his human life. By doing so, he had robbed himself, Wesley, and their sister Kimberly of the most powerful magic in the world. Yet his brother and sister still remained witches—with no significant powers to speak of. And the powers they did possess, they had no idea of how to use. Hence Wesley's quest to study the books of the witch who had once been their ally, then betrayed them in the end.

When Quinn looked back at Haven, he saw that the witch-turned-vampire was thinking back to the same event.

Haven blinked. "So, what do you need him for?"

"It's a simple job really. He'll need to move into the B&B with us, pretend to be another Scanguards trainee, which actually he is—"

Haven interrupted with a huff. "Yeah, he wiggled that concession out of Samson. Total opportunist, my brother." Then he grinned. "The discipline will do him good."

Laughing, Quinn shook his head. "Let's see if he sticks with it. Anyway, I need him to keep an eye on Rose's grandson, Blake."

He still had a hard time calling him *his* grandson.

"We brought him in as a recruit to watch over him. He thinks he's training to be some kind of special ops superhero. Oliver and Cain will be there too, but we need a couple of humans in case he goes walking about during the day."

"You come up with the craziest shit," Haven commented. "Who's stupid enough to buy that setup anyway?"

"Trust me, Blake has already eaten it up, hook, line, and sinker. I've never seen a guy more eager to be taken for a ride."

"Well, looks like he and Wesley will hit it off instantly. They seem to be cut of the same cloth." Haven grinned mischievously.

Quinn frowned. "That's what I'm afraid of. But I don't really have a choice. I can't take any of the human bodyguards working for Scanguards. This is too sensitive a case. It has to stay within the family."

"Hmm. Guess that leaves only him. Let's talk to him."

16

Rose followed Yvette almost in a trance as she dragged her from one person to the next, introducing her to the assembled guests. The music continued to play, and portions of conversations drifted to her. The looks she got were friendly and curious, not suspicious like she had expected. Whenever she met other vampires for the first time, they had always treated her with suspicion. She was used to it. And she had treated the clans she'd been part of for short periods of time with equal caution. She'd never stayed anywhere long enough for any kind of trust or attachment to develop.

That's why what she faced now felt so utterly different. The way the individuals in this group treated each other was something she'd never seen before. There was an air of warmth and camaraderie between them that she was unaccustomed to when dealing with vampires. And not only that: they weren't all vampires. Several humans moved among them freely. They exhibited no signs of distress either, indicating to her that they were here of their free will.

"Oh, you have to meet Delilah and the baby," Yvette chirped next to her and pulled her along. "Where did she go?"

Baby? Rose wondered. Had she heard right? Before she could ask another question, a beautiful dark haired human entered the room from another door, a baby in her arms.

"Oh there you are," Yvette said and walked over to her.

Rose followed and stared at the woman with her baby. She'd never seen a baby in any vampire coven. How could this woman assume that her child would be safe here?

"I put the diaper in the trashcan in the guest bath," she said to Yvette. "Hope that's okay."

"No problem." Then Yvette turned to Rose. "Rose, may I introduce Delilah. She's Samson's mate. Delilah, this is Rose, Quinn's . . . uh . . ."

"Acquaintance," Rose said quickly and shook Delilah's hand.

"Nice to meet you, Rose."

So the owner of Scanguards was mated to a human woman? She'd never seen those things last. In fact, she'd rarely ever met a mated vampire. In most of the clans she knew, few vampires were mated, most lived footloose and fancy-free, without any ties whatsoever. Yet, since arriving at this party, she'd already been introduced to three mated couples. What were the odds of that?

Rose drew in a breath, suddenly picking up a scent she was unfamiliar with. It was both human and vampire, yet different. Stepping closer to Delilah, it intensified.

Instinctively she stretched her hand toward the baby, but before her fingers connected, a strong hand gripped her wrist. Her head whipped around, and she stared at a vampire with short dark hair, whom she hadn't been introduced to yet.

His intense gaze pinned her, the underlying warning evident.

"Samson, my love," Delilah's soothing voice cooed as if to calm him.

He slowly turned his head toward her.

"I think Rose just wanted to say hello to Isabelle," Delilah added.

Hesitantly, Samson released her hand. Rose refrained from rubbing it to ease the discomfort his violent grip had caused.

"I'm sorry," Rose said quickly. "I'm not accustomed to seeing babies at a party."

Samson nodded quickly, the tension in his posture easing. He had clearly perceived her as a threat. "We rarely leave our daughter with others."

Rose couldn't suppress her surprise. No wonder the smell had been so different. This was Samson and Delilah's daughter?

"She's a hybrid?" She'd heard of them, but hadn't believed they actually existed.

Delilah and Samson exchanged proud smiles.

"She's our little angel," Delilah said.

"She is beautiful," Rose responded, remembering what Charlotte had looked like at that age. She felt the familiar tug at her heart she always felt when thinking of her daughter.

The baby suddenly looked at her, then back at its mother.

"She says you're beautiful too," Delilah continued.

Rose shot her a confused look. Parents could act a little strange when it came to their kids. "Uh . . . thanks."

Next to her, Yvette chuckled. "Takes a little getting used to at first."

Rose looked at her. "Getting used to what?"

"Our little Isabelle is telepathic. She can communicate with her parents."

Her mouth dropped open at the revelation. "Oh." A telepathic baby. What else was she in for? Not only was the baby a hybrid, it also had a special gift. From what she knew, gifted vampires were extremely rare.

"And I think she wants Zane now," Delilah added.

Before Rose could even blink, a bald vampire appeared next to them, and the baby reached its tiny arms toward him. He took her, then looked at Rose.

"We haven't met. I'm Zane. And this . . ." He turned and waved at the young woman who approached behind him. "This is Portia, my mate."

The moment Rose took Portia's hand and inhaled, the same mix of human and vampire scent rose into her nostrils. Another hybrid? How many of them were there?

"I'm Rose," she said automatically.

As she greeted Portia, she noticed how Samson whispered something in Delilah's ear, making her blush in response. Then he took her hand, leading her away.

Hadn't Samson just moments earlier said they rarely left their daughter with anybody else? Odd.

She looked back at the baby and noticed how she grinned up at Zane.

"Hey, my pretty Rachel, how about a dance?"

"Rachel? I thought her name was Isabelle?" Rose blurted without thinking.

"You didn't hear wrong. Her first name is Isabelle, but when she's with me, she's Rachel."

Rose felt confusion spread, when Yvette put her hand on her forearm. She snapped her eyes to her hostess.

"Don't mind him. He likes to be cryptic! He's her mentor, you know, the one she bit first? Anyway, you know what that means. In human terms he'd be her godfather, and that's why he was the one who gave her her second name, Rachel."

She nodded, feeling suddenly overwhelmed. There was so much that she didn't know. But she couldn't admit that. Somehow the vampires around her seemed to be so much more civilized and educated than the ones who had crossed her path. They appeared to live decidedly human lives, not like the hidden existence that she had led, always on the move, always worried about who was waiting around the next corner. Was that why she had never met vampires who lived like this? Like humans?

As she glanced around, she noticed bottles of blood on a small side table. Next to it, human food was spread out. It looked almost natural, almost as if the two things belonged together.

When her gaze drifted away from the table, she noticed that Haven and Quinn had entered the room. But Quinn didn't come toward her; instead he steered in the direction of a young couple, Haven directly behind him. Yvette had not yet introduced them, but something was odd about them. With suspicion she eyed them.

"Oh, that's Wesley and Kimberly, my in-laws," Yvette said. "I'll introduce you."

"Later. I don't want to interrupt their conversation." It was only half the truth. In reality, she felt like her head was ready to burst, too many realizations slamming into her all at once.

She found herself in the middle of a tight-knit group, a unit that could only be described as a family. Names bounced around in her head: Amaury and his mate Nina, Samson and Delilah, Yvette and Haven. She'd also been introduced to Gabriel's mate, the beautiful Maya, and now to Zane and his hybrid mate Portia. Then the baby. Now in-laws. She needed some air.

Now on full alert, she inhaled deeply and her nostrils flared.

Battle-ready she shoved her hand into the inside pocket of her light jacket. Her heart beat into her throat, her pulse raced.

Yvette's hand arrested her movement.

"Intruders," Rose tried to warn her and glanced around the room, trying to find out where the scent of witch emanated from.

"What?"

Rose leaned closer to Yvette, still scanning the room. "Witches. I can smell them. We have to defend ourselves."

Yvette's giggles took her by surprise. Had the woman lost her marbles?

Rose stared at her.

"Sorry, I guess nobody told you, but Wesley and Kimberly, my brother- and sister-in-law are witches."

Rose took a quick step back, surprised by the revelation. "You consort with witches?"

"They're harmless. Besides, Haven was a witch before he became a vampire. His siblings would never hurt us." Then she leaned in closer. "Their powers are negligible anyway, even though Wesley seems to think otherwise."

Rose felt her throat constrict. She couldn't take much more of this. Too much was happening, too many of her beliefs suddenly put in question. Weren't witches sworn enemies of every vampire? She felt heat spread in her body.

"Could I freshen up a little?" she pressed out, wiping pearls of sweat from her neck.

Yvette gave her a curious look. Then she pointed toward a door. "Through there, then the first door on the left."

"Thank you."

Her feet carried her outside into the corridor, where the music was less loud and the temperature lower. She felt as if her body was burning up with fever. She'd never known that vampires lived like this. Why had she not known? Why had she never realized that she could have had a different life, that if she hadn't been hiding all these years, she could have had friends like these, maybe even a family of sorts?

Gasping for air, she turned the door handle to the bathroom and swung the door open. Only the light over the sink was switched on, but it illuminated the small room sufficiently for her to realize what she'd walked into.

Samson's fangs were lodged deep in his mate's neck, his fully clothed body grinding against hers in an unmistakable rhythm, Delilah's hands pressing him closer to her as if she didn't want him to stop.

Instantly, Samson released her neck and snapped his head toward Rose, his eyes glaring red, blood dripping from his extended fangs.

Rose jerked the door shut. Shock and disgust collided in her. These vampires weren't any better than the ones she'd been with. No, they just hid it better.

She whirled around, ready to escape this madhouse—and bumped into a solid form.

Her eyes shot up.

Quinn. He wrapped his arms around her, preventing her from going any further.

"He's not any better. He's using her," she choked out.

Quinn held the trembling Rose firmly in his arms, instantly realizing that she was about to bolt. He couldn't understand what had her suddenly in such a frenzy.

"What's wrong, my love?" he asked and stroked his hand over her hair, trying to soothe her, only belatedly realizing how intimately he was addressing her.

"Your vampires aren't any different." She jerked her head toward the bathroom door. "Samson. He's feeding off her. He's got her under his thrall. You said you all drink bottled blood."

It took him only a second to realize what she was talking about. He shook his head. "Lovebirds."

She gave him a puzzled look that made him chuckle.

"Rose, don't you know what's going on between blood-bonded mates? He feeds from her because she's his mate. A vampire bonded to a human has only one source of nourishment: her blood."

"But he's using her. Just like everybody else I've ever known. We're all using them."

Could she really mean this? Did she not understand what it was like for Delilah to have her mate feed off her? "It's the greatest pleasure he can give her."

Her face froze in shock as she pushed back from him. "What?"

"The feeding. The sexual pleasure that comes with it can't be compared to anything else in this world," he said and crossed the distance that she'd created between them.

Her back was to the wall now. Quinn slid his finger under her chin and lifted it. He stroked along her jaw, caressing her smooth skin.

How was it that she didn't know these things?

When she stared at him, a million questions in her eyes, he finally knew how to proceed with her. He would show her what was beautiful about the life of a vampire. He would show her that they all had the capacity to love, that being a creature of the night didn't mean darkness in their souls.

"Sweet Rose. A vampire's bite is like a kiss—passionate, sensual, tender. It's anything you want it to be. Whatever your heart feels, the bite will magnify."

He stroked his knuckles along her neck, noticing how her plump vein throbbed beneath his touch. Temptation made his gut constrict.

"Like a kiss," she murmured. "But how?"

"Has no vampire ever sunk his fangs into you? Taken your sweet blood?"

He inhaled, filling his lungs with her tantalizing scent. Oh, God, how he was craving her blood now. The beating of her heart suddenly traveled to his ears, the sound so loud he thought everybody in the house could hear it.

"Never. I've never allowed anybody to use me like that."

Her voice was trembling. He glanced at her eyes, noticed how dark they'd gotten. Her lips had parted, and her breaths were unsteady.

"Use? It's not like that between people who love each other."

He lowered his head to her neck, his fangs descending in the process. Slowly, he graced her skin with the tips.

He felt the shiver that went through her. It was a perfect mirror to his own reaction. The lust that raced through him was unparalleled. He wanted to take her right here, take her blood while burying himself in her. Show her what true ecstasy was like. And he would be her first, again.

"Oh, God, Rose, to know that nobody has ever—"

"I remember only one bite. It was horrible," she pressed out.

Instantly, he pulled away from her neck. Her turning. It must have left her traumatized. No wonder she wanted nobody to bite her.

He stroked over her cheek. "It's not like that. It should never be like that." Not between them. It would always be an experience to cherish.

Rose closed her eyes as if wanting to dispel the memories. Her body stiffened, the pliable woman in his arms had suddenly vanished.

If only she were able to confide in him, he could help her. But he could see she was distraught. This would have to wait.

"Come, let's go back and see how Blake likes his new place."

Before he could pull her along the corridor, the door of the bathroom opened behind them.

"Quinn, Rose, a word please," Samson demanded.

17

Standing outside on the porch a few moments later, Rose shivered, even though she knew as a vampire the cold night air didn't affect her like it would a human. Nevertheless, a chill went through her bones. Instinctively her back stiffened.

"Apologies," Samson said after pulling the door shut behind him. A sheepish look crossed his face. "Delilah and I have had little time to ourselves lately. The baby . . . well, she keeps us on our toes."

He was apologizing to her? Because she had walked in on them? How odd. Did he actually mean it? Rose looked at him suspiciously.

"I guess I forgot to lock the door." He smiled briefly, then his face became serious, and he looked at Quinn. "Did you see the text Thomas just sent?"

"What text?" Quinn replied, pulling his cell phone from his pocket in the same instant. He looked at it. "It was still on vibrate."

He swiped his finger over it and tapped one of the apps. Then his eyes shot back to Samson.

"Crap!"

Samson nodded. "Could be a coincidence of course. There are lots of guys named Blake."

At hearing her grandson's name, Rose went on alert. "What's with Blake? What happened?" Her heart instantly began to race.

Samson turned to her. "We were alerted that a man named Blake was kidnapped down South yesterday. He was released without any ransom demands hours later."

"Down South, where?"

Quinn put his hand on her forearm. "A couple of hours north of Los Angeles. It wasn't our Blake. He's safe."

Then he looked at Samson. "But I don't believe in coincidences."

Neither did she. Nor did the proximity of this incident calm her either. Keegan knew from the letter she'd written that she was following Blake to the West Coast, and not only that. He had even more precise information.

"Where exactly?" she urged the two. "Where did it happen?"

Quinn's forehead furrowed at her insistence. "Down in Santa

Barbara."

Her stomach lurched. "Oh God." She knew what Keegan was doing. "He's searching every town on the West Coast that starts with *San*."

Quinn grabbed both her arms, making her look at him. "What does he know?"

Rose swallowed hard. Why had she ever written that damn letter? "He knows Blake is on the West Coast, living in a city starting with *San*."

"Did he follow you here?"

She shook her head. "Impossible."

"How would you know?"

She tossed him an angry glare. She wasn't an amateur. She'd hidden her entire vampire life and knew how to disappear without a trace. "I use a network."

Quinn narrowed his eyes. "What network?"

For a moment she wondered whether to tell him, whether to disclose this information. Knowing that she wouldn't give him any names or anything else specific, she deemed it safe to tell him how she'd gotten out of Chicago.

"There's a network of brothels and escort services I own. It's all wrapped up in trusts. Keegan doesn't know. Nobody does."

Quinn stared at her in disbelief. "You own brothels?"

She shrugged. She had to make money somehow. "I treat them well. The women who work there are safer than if they were on the street somewhere. And they're loyal."

She noticed how Samson leaned against the railing on the deck, his arms crossed over his chest, listening with interest. He didn't seem to judge her.

"They helped you leave Chicago undetected?" Quinn continued his questioning.

"Yes. They act as decoys, dressing like me, wearing wigs, makeup. They travel under my name to various places to lead whoever is following me on a wild goose chase."

Seemingly satisfied with her answer, Quinn nodded. "Then how does Keegan know you're here?"

"He saw a letter."

"What letter? Was there a postmark on it? I thought Blake didn't know you."

She shook her head. "He doesn't. It wasn't a letter Blake wrote. I wrote it."

"Who was it sent to?"

"It was never sent. Keegan interrupted me while I was writing it. It doesn't matter, but he knows. He knows to search every city on the West Coast that starts with *San*. We have to do something."

For a moment Quinn didn't say anything, his eyes simply searching hers. Then he let go of her arms.

"I guess we're going into the offensive earlier than I'd planned."

"Offensive?" Rose echoed.

Quinn and Samson exchanged a look.

Samson smiled at her. "I think what Quinn is trying to say is that we're going to smoke Keegan out before he can find Blake."

"But we can't draw attention to us, or he'll find us even faster." Panic ran through her veins. "You can't do that!"

"It was the plan all along," Quinn said. "You didn't think we'd simply hide Blake away forever? It's only a temporary solution. Granted, I would have liked to get him settled first, explain the ground rules and get a handle on this, before going after Keegan, but knowing what Keegan knows, we have to act now."

"You were planning this from the start? Why didn't you tell me? I have a right to know." She let out an angry breath. She was the one who had hired *them*. She made the rules when it came to protecting Blake.

Quinn's eyes narrowed. "I had a right to know a lot of things too." His chest suddenly heaved and his eyes turned darker, a sign that he was annoyed with her. "You should have told us from the start what Keegan knew. By keeping things from us you're putting Blake in danger. Don't you realize that?"

She clamped her jaw shut.

"I thought you loved our grandson," he added more quietly.

Our? Had he really said *our*? The word did something to her: it softened her heart. She and Quinn had so much in common. Could their flesh and blood, Blake, become the bridge to mending what had gone wrong? Would he be able to forgive her once he found out what she'd done?

"Rose?"

Quinn's voice drifted to her, making her look at him.

"Tell us everything about Keegan. The more we know, the better our chances of finding him before he finds us."

"Quinn is right," Samson added. "We need every bit of information you can remember: where he has properties, who he consorts with, what he does, who his enemies and friends are. Everything, even if you think it's unimportant."

Slowly, she nodded. They were right. She had to tell them, but there was one thing she couldn't tell them: that he was really after her because she had stolen something priceless from him. And she knew he would do anything to get it back, just as she would do anything to keep it from him.

"Agreed."

"Good," Samson said. "Let me check if Thomas is here yet. He needs to be in on this conversation." He opened the door to the house and disappeared inside.

There was silence for a few moments. She avoided looking at Quinn until he suddenly spoke.

"How did you get into owning brothels?"

Rose thrust her chin up, ready to defend her choices, when she noticed that there was no sign of accusation in his eyes, just curiosity.

"It was the only thing that was open to me at the time. The only . . . profession a woman could have back then."

She allowed her gaze to drift past him, not wanting to see him judge her. But he didn't grant her that concession. His fingers underneath her chin tipped her head up, forcing her to look at him.

"But why? As a vampire you were stronger than anybody else. You could have done anything you wanted."

She shook her head. "I couldn't get any help from my parents when they realized what I was. And I didn't want to force them by using mind control. Do you understand that?"

After she'd realized that, she'd urged them to fake her death because they would not survive the scandal she would bring on them. They had done it.

"At first, I stole and cheated to survive. Mind control helped me, my vampire strength made sure nobody was able to hurt me."

"I'm so sorry you had to go through this, Rose."

"After a while, once I'd stopped pitying myself, I realized how lucky I was compared to many other women out on the streets. I saw how many of them were mistreated. So I started protecting them. I was so much stronger than those men they sold their bodies to. They realized it and were afraid of me."

His hand stroked gently over her hair, and she yearned to lean into him.

"I stole from them so I could make a better life for myself and the women around me. They were so grateful, you should have seen them. Their eyes lit up when I told them they wouldn't have to sleep with every violent man anymore. I told them they could reject those who hurt them, and I would take care of them. I made sure those men never dared come back. My brothels only allow civilized men in. We reject the violent ones, the perverts who take pleasure in hurting women."

"My brave Rose," he whispered, pulling her closer. "Always strong, always looking out for everybody but herself."

Tears stung in her eyes, but she didn't allow herself to cry. She couldn't show weakness, not when he praised her for being brave.

"I survived; we all did. I expanded nationwide; I built up a network of brothels. All with the same rules, the same kind of security for the women. I figured if they had to sell their bodies, they might as well do it in a safe environment. Some are run by vampires like me, women who protect other women. I even have a place here in San Francisco. Around the corner from the Ritz Carlton. It's a classy establishment. Nothing seedy, not like the places farther down the hill. The women are taken care of. They're safe."

She hesitated. "Some of them wanted to be like me ... but I couldn't do that to them. I couldn't condemn them to a life like mine."

Quinn's arms came around her, pulling her against his chest. "You should have come to me. I could have shown you how beautiful this life can be. I can still show you. It's not too late."

She lifted her head, looking at him. "Isn't it?"

"It's never too late for—"

The door opened behind them. "Thomas is here. Let's talk," Samson announced.

Hastily, Rose pulled out of Quinn's embrace, wondering what he had wanted to say. Too late for love? Was that what he'd meant?

18

The house was buzzing like a beehive despite the late hour.

Quinn had been able to convince Amaury and Nina to move into the B&B with them to provide extra protection. Since Nina was human and not a stranger to fighting with vampires, she would be the perfect addition to the daytime protection Wesley would provide. However, accepting Nina's services also meant having to put up with her overbearing mate Amaury. Not that he didn't love the guy to death, but the way he hovered over Nina was positively nauseating. Having to watch those lovebirds day in and day out would be grueling.

Cain and Oliver had already gotten Blake settled, putting him on the top floor between their respective rooms. Wesley was in the process of lugging his bags upstairs to take up residence as well.

"Let me take one," Quinn offered and grabbed one of Wesley's bags, slinging the strap over his shoulder as he walked up the stairs alongside him.

"Hey this is great." Wesley let his eyes roam. "What a cool house."

"It'll do for our purposes."

Wesley shook his head. "Could you guys get any more jaded?"

Jaded? He'd never seen it that way, but having lived as long a life as he had, there was little that could really impress him. "This house could have fit three times into my estate up north."

"Up north?"

"Derbyshire. A few hours north of London." Quinn wondered why he suddenly thought of his place. He rarely ever went there. In fact, it shouldn't even belong to him anymore. He'd promised it to Wallace, his sire, for saving his life, yet he'd never come to claim it and had simply disappeared instead.

"You have like a castle?"

Quinn chuckled. "I prefer to think of it as a heap of old stones in dire need of repair." Neglecting the property for decades hadn't improved the drafty building in the least. "And it's definitely not a castle. There's no moat, no drawbridge, and no wall around it. It's just a country estate."

"You Englishmen are funny."

Wesley stopped in front of a door and set down his suitcase.

"This one, right?"

Quinn nodded, then pointed to the other doors along the corridor. "Cain is next to you, then Blake, then Oliver. Amaury and Nina are one floor farther down, same as Rose and my rooms."

Wesley opened the door and entered, lifting the suitcase inside. Quinn followed.

"So, it's true then what the others are saying."

Quinn raised an eyebrow. He asked the question even though he was pretty sure what everybody was talking about. "What are they saying?"

"That you and her ... man, she's quite a stunner. What a figure. And those boobs, not huge, but wow, that cleavage—"

Quinn had heard enough. He shoved Wesley against the nearest wall, flashing his fangs at him.

"You little punk, I want you to listen, and I'm only gonna say this once."

He paused to take a much needed breath of air, trying to tamp down his anger. It didn't work. Jealousy had him in a tight grip. Wesley stared at him, his eyes widened in fear, perspiration building on his brow. Yeah, despite the fact that he was hanging out with vampires now, he was still afraid of them. Just as well.

"I will not tolerate any disrespect toward my wife. Another word like that, a wrong look at her, and I'll have your hide, and not even your brother will be able to save you then. Do you understand that? Rose is mine. She's always been mine, and she'll always be mine. I will kill any man who touches her."

Wesley's nod came instantly. But whatever he wanted to say was cut short by a sound from the door.

Quinn swiveled on his heels to face the intruder.

Rose stood in the door frame, frozen. She'd heard every word of his possessive claim.

Shit.

Quickly, she tore her gaze away. "I just wanted to talk about the bottles in the fridge." Her voice was shaky at first, then normalized. "You're not leaving them there while Blake is here, right?"

"No, I asked Nina to move them."

"I'll help her then." Rose turned and left.

"Rose . . ." he murmured and shoved a hand through his hair, but she didn't turn back.

Behind him, Wesley pulled away from the wall.

"Sorry, Quinn. I didn't mean to be disrespectful. Won't happen again."

His voice sounded deflated, and the exuberance he'd heard in him earlier was gone. Suddenly, Quinn felt like an ass, robbing him of the excitement this assignment presented for him.

"No hard feelings," he assured him and looked at him.

***

Rose rushed down the stairs and headed for the kitchen. Overhearing Quinn talk about her in such a passionate tone had sent a thrill through her entire body. He still considered her his, and while she'd always hated any possessive overtones from men, it was different with Quinn. Knowing that Quinn wanted to possess her like this and would kill any man who touched her, was a bigger turn on than she'd ever imagined. The thought electrified her, stirred her in a way nothing else ever had.

She felt flushed when she reached the kitchen and was grateful for the fact that vampires couldn't blush. At least it would save her from having to explain to anybody she encountered, why she felt so out of sorts.

Pushing the door open, she stepped into the kitchen. There was Nina, rather than dutifully emptying the refrigerator of the incriminating bottles of blood, sitting on the kitchen table, locked in a passionate embrace with one of the biggest vampires she'd ever seen: Amaury. Nina's legs were wrapped around her mate's waist, their lips fused together so firmly that Rose had to wonder whether the jaws of life were necessary to pry the lovers apart.

Suddenly the door closed behind her, the sound alerting the two. Amaury whirled his head around, the expression on his face catapulting Rose back against the door.

Good God, she'd never seen such lust-filled eyes. Were all these vampires totally love crazed? First Samson, now Amaury. As if they couldn't get enough of their mates! As if they truly loved them. Was this even possible? Could vampires love like that? Could they have tender feelings like that? Feelings that were honest?

"Excuse the uh . . ." Amaury grinned from one ear to the other.

" . . . show of affection. But my wife here totally overpowered me. You can blame her."

Nina let out an annoyed huff and slapped her hand against his shoulder, which had no effect whatsoever on her huge mate.

"Look who's calling the kettle black!" She clicked her tongue then smiled at Rose. "Don't mind him. He's just some big oversized Neanderthal I made the mistake of tying up one night."

She jumped off the table and rolled her eyes. "Now he's following me everywhere."

Amaury snatched her hand and pressed a kiss on it. "You can tie me up any day."

Uncomfortable about their continued affectionate banter, Rose put her hand on the door handle. "I'd better leave."

Amaury raised his hand. "No, stay. I'm out of here to help Quinn with a few things. I'll leave you girls alone."

He brushed past her and left the kitchen.

Nina's laugh followed him. "Do you need anything? I was just going to organize the kitchen."

"Let me help you with that. We need to move the . . . uh . . . bottles, you know."

Rose figured it was better not to mention the word blood anywhere in the house, particularly since everybody constantly seemed to walk in on each other and overhear things they shouldn't.

"I was just about to do that when Amaury interrupted." She walked to the refrigerator and opened it.

The natural poise with which Nina moved and spoke impressed her. Her mate was so much bigger and stronger than she, yet she'd handled him as if she were the one in charge.

"It doesn't bother you?"

Nina pointed at the bottles. "The blood? No, I've never been squeamish."

Rose smiled. "I meant being with someone who's clearly so much . . ." She hesitated.

"Bigger?" Nina shook her head.

More powerful, Rose had meant to say, but bigger worked too.

"He would never hurt me. He would give his own life to save mine if he had to. Not that I would accept it, frankly. I'd kick his big butt if he tried that again. But you get the picture."

"Again?"

Nina waved her off. "Don't remind me. He almost got himself killed saving me from some crazy v—" She quickly glanced at the door before continuing. "Anyway, I know he would do it again in a heartbeat."

The clans Rose had lived with had never put such stock in their human lovers, certainly not when it came to the point of protecting a human against one's own species. That choice was always clear: vampires came before humans. Humans were expendable. While she didn't subscribe to this mantra herself, she'd seen enough to realize that this attitude was widespread.

"I suppose someone like him is rare."

Nina shrugged and placed a couple of bottles onto a tray. Rose reached into the refrigerator and followed her example.

"That's the only way I know them. I think all of Scanguards' men are like that. Yvette, too. They're tough, but when it comes to their mates, they're like little tame kittens or cuddly bears like Amaury." She leaned closer. "Just don't tell them that we've figured them out, or you'll get a show of testosterone."

Rose laughed. She liked Nina. She hadn't gotten a chance to exchange more than a couple of words at the party when she'd been introduced, but now that she was able to chat with her, she realized more and more that Nina would never let herself be used by anybody, least of all her mate. Which made Rose wonder about one thing: did she enjoy Amaury's bite?

But she couldn't ask her that. It was too personal, and it was none of her business. But since Quinn had told her at the party that a bite represented the greatest sexual pleasure a vampire could give his partner, she was intrigued.

Rose had never allowed anybody to bite her and quickly severed any ties to any vampire who'd even made the attempt. Whenever she had to feed off a human, she had put herself into a state akin to a trance, where she would not truly realize what she was doing. She'd separated her mind as much as she could from what her body was doing. She had never enjoyed it.

But now, remembering what she'd seen Samson and Delilah do, and knowing that Amaury and Nina did the same, she couldn't help but wonder how two human women could remain so happy when at the same time, their mates hungered for their blood on a daily basis. What were Delilah and Nina getting out of this?

"Something wrong?" Nina suddenly asked.

Quickly, Rose pasted a smile on her face. "No, nothing."

"You haven't met many like them, have you? I mean—" She lowered her voice. "—vampires who are mated to humans."

"Don't take this the wrong way, but how can it work? There's no balance of power in such a relationship. We're so much stronger than humans. How can you not feel that you're in an inferior position?"

Nina chuckled softly. "Because love is a great equalizer."

"But when he bites you . . . sorry, forget it. I didn't mean to get personal."

Rose placed another bottle on the tray and closed the refrigerator door. "Where shall we put those?"

"Rose."

She looked back at Nina. "Yes?"

"I love his bite. I crave it. I don't think I could ever live without it."

"I wish I knew what that meant," Rose murmured more to herself than as a response to Nina.

When she turned away from Nina, she caught a movement at the door. Quinn stood there, looking at her, his eyes shimmering golden, his lips lightly parted. She stopped breathing, and for a moment she was transported back to their wedding night. He'd looked at her like that when he'd made her his wife. With such love, such passion.

She knew she could trust him with her body. But could she trust him with her past?

19

Quinn turned on his heels before he could follow his first impulse: to take Rose into his arms and sink his fangs into her lovely neck, to show her what his bite would do to her. It made no difference that she wasn't human. His bite would have the same effect Amaury's bite had on Nina.

He was glad when he ran into Blake as soon as he turned a corner. At least having to deal with his grandson would keep his mind off Rose's enticing neck.

"You're just the man I'm looking for," Quinn said, and steered him away from the kitchen, knowing it hadn't been made *human-proof* yet.

Blake grinned. "Hey, cool digs."

"Come, I want to introduce you to one of your trainers." Then he raised his voice. "Amaury, where are you?"

"Looking for you," his voice came from the living room, before he popped his head out into the hallway. "Are we going over the rules?"

"Thought we'd start with that," Quinn said, entering the room.

Blake followed him like a well-trained puppy. "Rules?"

Quinn exchanged a quick smirk with Amaury, before turning to him. "You'll have rules coming out of your ears by the time we're done here. But, first things first. This is Amaury LeSang. You've lucked out. He's our best trainer."

Eagerly, Blake shook his hand. "Bond. Blake Bond."

Noticing how Amaury's lips twisted, Quinn instantly shot him a warning look to compel him to remain serious. Encouraging Blake's 007 routine would only make matters worse. It was best to ignore it. His ego was big enough; now it was time to take him down a notch and make him realize that he had a lot to learn. Why that idea pleased him, Quinn didn't really want to examine. Maybe in some small way, Blake reminded him of himself as a young man when he'd thought he could conquer the world, when he'd thought even going to war would not change him. He'd thought he'd be prepared for everything that was thrown at him. Well, he hadn't been prepared for death.

Pushing back the rising memories, he motioned to the sitting area.

"We have a lot to discuss. There are ground rules every trainee has to comply with. Break one, and you're out. Orders will be followed. Think of this as boot camp. Once you pass this, you're ready to join the general trainees."

"Huh?" Blake asked as he dropped onto the sofa. "This is not the real training yet?"

"It is," Amaury cut in. "It's where you get taught the basics, you and one other trainee. Only once you have those down is it safe to let you join the other trainees."

Blake's eyes lit up. "So, you're saying this is dangerous?" The thought seemed to excite him.

"Absolutely."

Quinn shot Amaury a scolding look. Great, now he would have to come up with some seemingly dangerous element of training just to keep the kid interested.

"Like what?"

"We'll go into that later," Quinn deflected. "Rule one: you won't leave this house unless it's in the company of one of the trainers or another trainee. You have to understand that there are other outfits out there that love poaching our recruits, and they will go as far as practically kidnapping a trainee just to throw a wrench into our operations."

A deep frown built on Blake's forehead. "Kidnap? You've gotta be joking. Why would somebody do that?"

"Because we're too valuable," Wesley's voice came from the door.

He entered with long strides, an air of confidence around him. It appeared that the dressing down he'd received only minutes earlier had pearled off him like he was made of Teflon.

"I'm Wesley." He stretched his hand out, and Blake jumped up to shake it.

Quinn nodded at him. "Wesley is the other trainee."

"Hey," Blake greeted him.

"Take a seat. To address your question, Blake, I'm afraid Wesley is right. You are too valuable. We're making a large investment in you, and we're prepared to protect this investment. In order to help us with our task, we require our recruits to be in top physical condition . . ."

After leaving Blake to a rigorous physical exercise program in the gym in the basement, under the supervision of Oliver, Quinn nodded to Amaury.

"I'm going on a perimeter check."

Quinn welcomed the cool night air as he stepped outside into the dark. He wasn't wearing a jacket, but the cold didn't bother him.

Unsuccessfully, he tried to shake off the unease that kept creeping up on him. While he knew bringing Blake in was the best way to protect him in the short term, he also realized that in the long run, the only way to keep him safe was to eliminate the threat. If only he knew what Keegan really wanted.

His schooled eyes surveyed his surroundings as he walked along the sidewalk. The light of the streetlamps lining the quiet residential street threw dark shadows of his form onto the pavement.

He missed nothing: not the young man who stood hovering over his dog as the animal did its business, nor the car that tried to squeeze into a parking spot that was entirely too short for it.

With a sigh, he turned left at the end of the block. In the distance, several cars could be heard passing. There was light in the neighboring houses, but nobody was outside. His gaze drifted up to the windows and the roofs. No movement. Then his eyes roamed the gardens, his vampire night vision easily penetrating the dark shadows the bushes and trees created.

This was routine for him, and he or Amaury would perform this check several times a night. His actions were so automatic, so familiar to him, that his mind drifted back to Rose.

Why had everything gone so wrong?

He could still taste the bitterness in his mouth when she'd rejected him after he'd come back from the war a changed man. Her frightened look had shredded his heart, so much so that he was ready to die there and then.

London 1814

Quinn didn't bother with the carriage, leaving his coachman waiting. As the heavy door fell shut behind him, the knocker echoing the sound, he fell into a frantic run as if a slayer were chasing him with a wooden stake. He couldn't get far enough away from Rose and the pain she had inflicted on him by rejecting him.

The words pierced through his heart like tiny spikes. *Get away from me!*

The woman he loved more than his own life was afraid of him. Too afraid to recognize that he was still the same man as before. That what was in his heart hadn't changed. She believed him to be a monster and had recoiled from him.

Despite the fast sprint through half of London, he arrived at his house showing barely any exhaustion. Pushing the front door open, he marched inside, heading for the parlor, his mind focused on one single thing: to eliminate the pain.

As he reached for the crystal decanter that contained the amber liquid that had helped him so many times before, he took it and poured a glass to its rim. But when he lifted it to his lips, the scent of it stung his nostrils. Instinctively he tossed the glass to the floor where it shattered.

Anger churned in him: he couldn't even get drunk to forget his sorrow! He couldn't do what any sane man in his position would do, to obliterate any memory of her, to drown it in alcohol.

Frustrated, he growled and took hold of the small side table that held the liquor he'd enjoyed as a human. Without another thought, he flung the table and its contents to the other end of the room. With a loud bang it crashed against the wall, the glasses, bottles and their contents scattering across the rugs, the wood splintering. The stench of alcohol filled the room instantly, only fueling his anger.

His eyes surveyed the scene, homing in on the pieces of wood that had only seconds ago been a beautiful table. Before he knew what he was doing, his feet catapulted him toward the chaos. Crouching down, he reached for a piece of wood. It tapered to a sharp point at one end. The perfect weapon, the perfect way to die.

Yes, it would be better that way. He should have never survived. He should have died on the battlefield instead, and spared both him and Rose this tragedy. She would have remembered him in a more favorable light than she would now. But he couldn't change that.

He lifted the makeshift stake. But as much as he tried to move it toward his chest, his hand wouldn't follow his command. Almost as if his survival instinct was stronger. God, how pathetic was that? He couldn't even kill himself!

Angrily, he jerked his hand toward his chest once more and was stopped in the process. An iron hand clamped around his wrist.

"Careful with that."

Quinn snapped his head to Wallace.

He lashed a furious glare at his sire. How dare he stop him? "It's my life! My business, my choice."

"No! It is not! How can you want to throw this life away? The power that I gave you, how dare you waste it? As if it were worth nothing? Do you have no concept of what you are, what makes you great?" He pointed toward the door. "There are thousands out there who want to be like you, who want to remain young and powerful, who crave immortality. And you, you're prepared to throw it into the gutter! To toss it out like last week's whore."

Wallace twisted the stake from his hand and hurled it to the other end of the room. Wrenching his arm free from Wallace's grip, Quinn bared his fangs.

He needed no lecture from a man who clearly had no idea what he was going through.

"I can't live like this!" He avoided looking at his maker.

Wallace put a calming hand on his shoulder. "What happened?"

Quinn took a breath, but when he released it, it came out as a sob. "She doesn't love me anymore . . . because of what I am." He lifted his eyes. "I'm a monster to her. A monster she's afraid of."

Putting it into words made it even worse. As a human, he'd never felt as much pain as he felt now. Not even when he'd been injured on the battlefield, had his body been in such agony.

"I can't live like this. Don't you understand? I did this for Rose. Without her, there's no point in going on." Eternity without her would be one endless night of torture.

Wallace pulled him against his chest. "Son, you will get over this. Your heart will be broken many times until you learn to protect it. The humans around you that you love will die. You'll lose them one by one. But there'll be others who will take their place."

Quinn yanked himself free of Wallace's embrace. "Nobody can take Rose's place!"

"You love her so much?"

"More than my life." Without her he felt nothing. Only pain and coldness.

"We've all said that when we were young. We all had a woman who we thought was above all others. Special." His eyes suddenly drifted away as if remembering somebody. "So beautiful that it aches to even think of her. And to see her wither away. To see her grow old. Such pain. Yet over time, it all fades. We continue living. We survive. Pain is only temporary. We are powerful. No heartache shall ever bring us down."

"Powerful? To do what? To live in the dark? Without love, without sunshine?"

Wallace narrowed his eyes. "You want love? Buy it from a whore. That's the kind of love you need. It'll make you forget."

"You think you can throw whores at me so I'll forget Rose? How dare you! You don't understand me at all! You want to help me? Then help me! Help me make her love me again. Or get out of my sight!"

Wallace gave him a dark look. For a long moment, he simply stood there like a statue.

"Very well."

Then he turned and left.

It was the last time he ever saw his sire. He had clearly taken his words to heart and disappeared. Just when he'd needed guidance the most. He had nobody in his life now. To fill the emptiness in his heart, he'd done exactly what Wallace had advised in his anger: he'd purchased love from whores.

Quinn suddenly shivered as he turned the last corner to enter the block on which the B&B stood. For two hundred years he'd tried to forget Rose by drowning out any feelings in senseless debauchery. And for two hundred years he'd failed. He wanted Rose back, not just in his bed—that was the easy part—he wanted to be back in her heart.

Determined to try anything in his power, he straightened his shoulders and walked up the short path to the entrance door, when he froze, an offending scent penetrating his nostrils: spray paint.

There, on the white front door of the B&B, somebody had spray-painted a message. Quinn's gut clenched. He'd suspected that Rose hadn't told him the truth about why Keegan wanted to harm Blake, but to have it confirmed tore at him nevertheless.

Give me back what you've stolen.

20

"What the fuck is he talking about? And this time I want the truth!"

Quinn glared at her and pointed to the door, which he'd slammed shut only a second earlier.

Instinctively, Rose took a step back, however, there was no escaping him or his anger. But that wasn't the worst of it. Keegan knew where she was, where Blake was. Had she led him here despite the precautions she'd taken?

"Oh, God, he's found us."

"He was bound to sooner or later. Unfortunately it was a little sooner than I anticipated. But that's beside the point. What did you steal from him, Rose? What was it? Money?"

She shook her head. "I have plenty of money."

Nervously, she shifted from one foot to the other. What would she tell him? Could she trust him with the truth? Or would he too want the power that came with the item she'd taken from Keegan?

When he gripped her shoulders with both hands and pressed her against the wall, the little wheels in her head started spinning out of control.

"Now, Rose! Before I toss you and Blake out on your ass to let you fend for yourselves. I don't need this shit! You waltz back into my life after two hundred years and think you can play me for a fool. I'm not a fool, Rose." His lips peeled back from his teeth, exposing his extended fangs. "I'm dangerous."

Her breath hitched, her heartbeat escalating at the same time. She sensed the vein at her neck pulsating violently, noticed how his look slid there for a second before drawing back to glare at her eyes. She had no choice, she knew that now. Only the truth would pacify him.

"Keegan killed another vampire and took a flash drive from him. I stole it from Keegan." The words tumbled from her lips like marbles from a turned over jar.

"What's on the flash drive?"

For an instant, she squeezed her eyes shut, praying that Quinn was still the same honorable man he'd been when human.

"It contains a list of names and addresses . . ." She swallowed hard then looked straight at him. " . . . of all vampires in North America and a large number of those abroad."

With a surprised gasp, Quinn released her, stepping back as if he'd touched silver and felt the stinging burn of it.

"Rose . . . that's madness. That can't be true."

That was what she'd thought too when she'd found out about the list.

"That's why I had to steal it. It can't be allowed in Keegan's hands. He'll use it to gain control. He'll be able to eliminate those who oppose him. He'll be too powerful."

"What do you think he intends to do with it?"

"He'll turn vampires to his side, create an army."

Quinn clicked his tongue. "That's not as easy as you might think. Nobody is that convincing!"

"Keegan is." A cold shiver ran down her spine as she remembered an incident while with Keegan. "I saw him use mind control on a vampire once."

Quinn stared at her. "No vampire is foolish enough to employ mind control on another of his species. Whoever is attacked with mind control will instinctively defend himself. It's inborn; there's no way to fight that instinct. And it's always a fight to the death. Nobody's ever been known to break it off before its inevitable conclusion. There's no way Keegan can use it to impose his will on another vampire. The other one would fight him, and if Keegan is stronger, he'll kill his opponent rather than control him."

"Keegan was able to control him without killing him. He was drained after it, almost had a breakdown, but he can do it. If he has managed since to perfect what he was capable of with difficulty then, he will be able to control vampires and have them do his bidding."

"Shit!" Quinn cursed and ran a hand through his hair. "What makes you think this is the only copy of it? If he had it in his possession for any length of time, he's probably already made a backup copy."

"Impossible. The drive is encrypted. You can't copy it; you can't even print it. Somebody wanted to make sure this remained the only copy."

"Where is it now?" The urgency in Quinn's voice was undeniable.

"It's safe."

"Where?"

She shook her head. "Quinn, please don't ask. It's better for you not to know."

It was safer if he didn't know, safer for *him*. At least Keegan couldn't torture it out of him.

"Better? You still don't trust me!"

"That's not what this is about."

"It's exactly what this is about. You didn't trust me back then to keep you safe, and you don't trust me now. Isn't that the truth, Rose?" He shook his head as if trying to shake off a bad memory.

Then he stared back at her. "You have to destroy it. Nobody can ever be allowed to have this kind of information at their fingertips."

At his words, she felt relief flood her. He didn't want the flash drive for himself. He didn't want the power that came with it. The Quinn she knew was still in there somewhere. Honor still drove him as it had back when he was human.

Without realizing it, she reached out her hand to stroke his cheek. "My—"

He recoiled from her touch.

My love, she'd wanted to say, but the words got stuck in her throat. His eyes looked at her, hurt sitting deep within them. There was so much she had to repair, so much she had to do penance for. She didn't want to hurt him any longer. And she didn't want to lie any longer.

"Samson needs to know about this," Quinn suddenly said and turned away, pulling out his cell phone. When the call connected he only said a few words. "We need you at the house, now. It's important."

Then he turned back to her. "If we'd known what this was all about, we could have gone in full force from the beginning and smoked him out before he had a chance to find us. Now he's got the upper hand."

***

Quinn waited in the office for Samson. It took his boss only ten minutes to arrive. Quinn heard Amaury greet him at the door, then the two of them entered the office. Amaury gave him a grave look. It appeared he had overheard the heated conversation he'd had with Rose. Just as well.

Quinn summarized the situation in two sentences, bringing Samson up to speed within seconds.

"That changes everything," Samson announced. "Where is it now?"

"She won't tell me."

"We'll have to find it and destroy it."

"I told her that." But she had simply looked at him as if he didn't understand. Her touch had confused him even more.

"She's not going to do it, is she?" Samson asked.

Amaury moved closer. "You can't blame her. It's her insurance policy. As long as Keegan believes Rose is the only one who knows where the flash drive is, he won't kill her. If he assumes that she told one of us, what's stopping him from getting rid of her and getting the information out of us?"

Reluctantly, Quinn had to admit to himself that his friend had a point, even if it didn't make the fact that Rose didn't trust him any more palatable.

"Still, we're ultimately more equipped to safeguard this information rather than having a civilian do it. We have to know where she keeps it hidden." Samson paced. "I wish we would have never been dragged into this mess, but there's no way we can back out now. Besides, she's family."

Quinn shot a look at his boss, whose last word had jolted him. How had they accepted Rose so easily?

Samson shrugged. "She's your wife. That makes her family, no matter what the situation between the two of you might be." Then he motioned to the door. "And Blake is your flesh and blood. We can't turn away from that."

"You have no obligation toward her or Blake. Only I do," Quinn protested. "I can't put all of you in danger, because my wife has made a bad call."

It felt odd to call her that again, but at the same time, he knew he couldn't back down from acknowledging what she was to him, what she would always be: his wife.

Amaury rolled his eyes. "Oh, put a sock in it, Quinn. You would do the same for any of us. So, let's cut to the chase. There's only one way to get Keegan off Rose's back."

"Remove what he's after and you remove the threat," Samson said.

"No, destroying the flash drive alone won't be sufficient," Quinn interrupted. "The only way to eliminate the threat for good, is to eliminate Keegan. Even if we destroy the data he wants, he'll seek revenge. Rose and Blake will never be safe as long as he's alive."

Amaury nodded. "Exactly."

"I want to know more about this Keegan before we come to a decision," Samson cautioned.

"But we can't wait!" Quinn protested.

"There's no need to wait. You do what you need to do to protect Rose and Blake, and the rest of us target Keegan. Thomas is already working on finding everything he can about him. It shouldn't take long."

Quinn knew his boss's high ethics and realized that he wouldn't give permission to kill him unless it was the only possibility. There was no use in trying to convince him otherwise. But he hoped that whatever Thomas dug up would justify taking Keegan out for good. Any man who posed a threat to Rose had to be eliminated. Particularly one who'd laid his dirty paws on her.

Samson turned to the door, then changed his mind and turned back to Quinn. "And another thing: you and Rose . . ."

The hairs on Quinn's nape rose, instantly alert.

"Maybe if the two of you resolved whatever issues you have, she might tell you where to find the flash drive. It would help us out a great deal."

"Easier said than done," he murmured under his breath.

But his boss had heard him nevertheless. "Maybe you should try harder. I didn't win Delilah over by twiddling my thumbs. Neither will your anger get you any further with Rose. I thought you were a master in seduction, or am I mistaken?"

With a smirk, Samson left the room.

Amaury grinned. "If you want to, I can give you a few pointers."

"Get out of my sight!"

He needed no advice on how to seduce his wife. Seducing Rose had never been the problem. Her body still responded to him, he knew that for certain. But would her heart answer to his again? Would she open it once more and let him in? Would she trust him once more?

Despite the misgivings he had about her lying to him, to a certain extend he could understand her caution. After all, they hadn't seen each other in two hundred years, and he was practically a stranger to her. But that was something he wanted to change.

21

Instead of heading home, Samson drove to Thomas's house. Eddie opened the door instantly, inviting him into the spacious living room where Thomas sat in a corner, which had been fitted out as an office.

Eddie shut the door behind him. "Hey, what's up?"

"We have a situation. I have a job for the two of you."

Eddie's boyish face lit up. "Cool. What do you need?"

Thomas rose from his chair and joined them. "Short party, huh?"

"I doubt Haven minded that we all had to leave early. I'm sure he's got better things to do than entertaining the likes of us."

Samson grinned. He had better things to do too. Delilah was waiting for him at home. Isabelle was finally asleep, and he hoped would remain that way for a few hours to give him and Delilah some time alone together.

He caught a flash of sadness in Thomas's eyes before he hid it again, reminding him that his friend hadn't had a steady partner in a long time. For a moment he wondered whether it was all that good for Thomas to have the object of his affections living with him, yet unattainable. Maybe it would be better for Eddie to move out. But Samson would be the last man to suggest such a thing. If the two of them liked this arrangement, it wasn't for him to question it.

"Well, anyway," he started, and filled them in about the happenings at the B&B. When he finished, he laid out what he needed the two to do for him.

"Is there a way of sweeping an area for this flash drive?"

Thomas raised an eyebrow. "I'm assuming you don't want anybody to know you're looking for it?"

"You could say that."

"And when we've found it, what then?" There was something akin to suspicion in his tone now.

Samson shook his head and chuckled to himself. "Thomas, how long have we known each other?"

"Do you ever truly know anybody, even after a hundred years?" Thomas replied with another question.

"Sometimes it's a matter of trust, don't you think?" Then he looked at Eddie. "Has Thomas ever told you how we met?"

Eddie looked at him with keen interest in his eyes. "Thomas doesn't like to talk about his past."

"Well, I'm not one to spill the beans. Maybe one day you can coax it out of him." Then he trained his look back on Thomas who'd been quiet the entire time. "So what do you say, considering our history, do you trust me to do the right thing?"

Their gazes locked.

"There's a device I tinkered with. Considering that a flash drive has no power of its own, none of the conventional bug sweepers would work. But I've been working on a programmable device that allows me to search for any combination of metals. So if I enter the components in some of the most common flash drives into it, theoretically, it should be able to search for it. But it's only a prototype."

Samson smiled. "Then let's put it to the test. Start at the B&B. And if it's not there, you and Eddie will go and visit all of Rose's brothels from here to Chicago and find that damn flash drive."

"Brothels?" Thomas repeated. "You've got to be kidding me. Quinn's wife is a *Madame*? I'm sure there's a story there."

***

London 1814

Rose knew she had to get away. Sooner or later, Quinn would return and do unspeakable things to her. She was certain of that. Because he wasn't her sweet Quinn anymore, he was a monster now, a vampire! A bloodthirsty animal. The red glare in his eyes had chilled her to the bone, but when she'd seen his fangs, the weapons with which he could kill her in an instant, her heart had stopped only to restart moments later at triple the pace.

She'd never felt so frightened in her entire life. And not just for herself. If he ever found out about his daughter, he would take her too. His possessive words before he'd left her chamber still echoed in her ears.

You're mine, Rose.

A cold shiver ran down her spine. No, she didn't belong to a monster, and neither did her daughter. She would go to the country, and later, when she'd calmed down, she would plead with her father to let her stay at the estate closest to where he'd placed her child. She knew now, since a marriage with Quinn was impossible, that she had no chance of ever getting her daughter back.

A sob tore from her chest at the terrible thought. She could never be her child's mother now. But maybe, if she begged her father long enough, he would relent and let her stay close to Charlotte so she could at least watch how her daughter grew up to be a young woman. She would never have the kind of privileged upbringing that Rose had enjoyed, but at least she could make sure that the girl lacked nothing.

With her parents having just left for a soiree, Rose summoned her maid and ordered her to alert the coachman to ready the carriage. She would be hours away before her parents even knew she was gone. She would deal with their wrath later. Leaving London during the height of the season was an affront they would not take lightly. It mattered not. If they knew what she was running from, they would understand, but she couldn't tell them. They would never believe her.

But she'd seen what she'd seen: Quinn was a vampire.

Within an hour she was on her way. But she didn't even reach the outskirts of London before her travels were interrupted. The horses let out frightened whinnies and reared up. Her driver stopped the carriage instantly, pulling back the horses and trying to calm them, but they were scared out of their wits.

Rose poked her head out of the carriage. "What seems to be the problem, William?"

Instead of an answer, her driver suddenly screamed. The carriage rattled as if somebody had jumped onto it. A struggle ensued. But within seconds it was over. Quiet spread through the night again.

"William?" Panic coursed through her veins, where her blood had turned to ice.

Her trusted servant didn't respond. Oh God, no! She craned her neck trying to see what had happened.

"Now that we're alone, let's talk."

The stranger's voice came from behind her. She whirled around, but he'd already opened the carriage door and squeezed inside. His clothes were simple, but his face was all she could look at. His eyes glared red the way she'd seen Quinn's eyes glare, and pointy fangs protruded from his mouth. Blood trickled from them.

She screamed.

All it earned her was his mocking laughter.

"Nobody will hear you. Your driver is dead. Damn tasty too. Who would have thought an old man like him has such sweet blood? But then, you can never tell what's inside until you open a present, can you?"

Shrinking back from him, her hand reached for the door on the other side, but the vampire's hand clamped around her wrist like a vice in a motion too fast for her eyes to follow.

"Let me go!"

His eyes bored into her. "I can't do that."

"Who are you? What do you want? Money?"

"Apologies, my lady. I neglected to introduced myself. I am Wallace."

Wallace? Where had she heard that name before?

"I'm Quinn's maker. His sire, the vampire who made him what he is today. I saved his life on the battlefield."

Rose gasped. "Oh God, no!" Quinn had sent him after her to hurt her.

"I saved his life on the battlefield so he could come back to you." Suddenly his voice turned to ice. "And what do you do? You reject his love. You toss him out on the street. You think you're better than him?"

Wallace lashed an angry glare at her.

"You're not any better than Quinn, not once I'm done with you."

Her breath caught in her throat.

"Yes, you know what's coming, don't you? I'll make you in his image."

"No," she whispered, her voice deserting her.

"You'll be like him. You'll be equals then. There will be no more reason to reject him. He will finally get what he wants."

A terrible thought spread in her heart. "Did he ask you to do that?"

"Quinn? He's too distraught to think. You brought this on yourself! It's my gift to him."

Why his words gave her momentary relief, she didn't have time to contemplate, because Wallace grabbed her and pulled her closer. Despite her struggles, she couldn't get away from him. Kicking and screaming did nothing to dissuade him from his mission.

His head came closer, ever closer to her throat until his lips connected with the skin on her neck. A moment later she felt his fangs. Then a violent pain. She fought against him, the pain in her neck intensifying, spreading over her entire body as his fangs dug deeper.

When darkness encroached she fought against that too, but her struggle was useless, her body too weak to hold off the inevitable. He was turning her into a monster, and she had no way of stopping him.

Darkness came and went. The pain anchored in her heart, spreading like black mold. It engulfed her entire being, overtook her senses so all she could think of was the throbbing hurt of a life lost. She would never be the same again.

Even as she was reborn that same night, the pain never vanished.

When Rose took her first breath as a vampire and opened her eyes to a new world, she found herself in a shabby room. From the noise she heard coming from downstairs, she knew she was in some tavern.

Everything seemed sharper, her vision, her hearing, her sense of smell. Particularly the latter. But all she could think of as she reared up from her position on the hard bed was the thirst that controlled her like the strings of a marionette. She needed to drink, to still the thirst that drove her wild.

"Finally awake."

Wallace's voice was the last thing in the world she wanted to hear. But he was here, sitting in front of the fireplace. At his feet, she noticed a bundle. Her eyes homed in on it, as did her nose. It smelled delicious.

Without thinking, she rose in one fluid motion and charged toward it.

"Thought you'd be hungry." The rickety chair he sat on creaked as he bent down.

She was faster and reached for the bundle. The girl was maybe sixteen and judging by her clothing she was most likely a scullery maid.

"She's tasty. I had a sip before." Wallace gave her a suggestive look. "Have at it. I know you're thirsty. I can see it in your eyes."

Rose recoiled from him and the human who was now stirring. Her jaw suddenly ached. Her hand came up to touch her mouth, and she felt sharp teeth peeking past her lips. Fangs! She had fangs! The finality of this fact hit her. There was no denying it. She was a monster now, one that killed to survive.

"No!" she screamed.

The girl on the floor reared her head, her frightened eyes staring up at her. Rose tried to pull back, but the human's blood smelled enticing, better than anything she'd ever smelled. Though she was filled with disgust at herself, her body didn't obey her mind. As if pulled by invisible ropes, Rose felt herself pulled toward the girl. Closer and closer.

She fought to resist. But her body's needs were stronger.

As she sank down and pulled the struggling girl toward her, hunger overcame her. It drove her, controlled her. Only when her fangs sank in the human's neck and drew the precious liquid from her, did her need ebb, making way for repulsion and loathing.

Rose withdrew from the girl as soon as she had the strength to command her body again, but it was too late. She'd drained her. As tears filled her eyes, fury surged through her. Without thinking, she charged at Wallace. The chair crashed beneath him as they both landed on the floor, fighting.

She was aware of her sudden strength, the immense power that ran through her veins. Her hatred for Wallace and what he'd done to her only fueled this power, pumped it up, stoked the fire in her belly higher.

"I hate you!" she yelled.

He tried to subdue her, grabbing her arms, but she twisted from his grip, her hands searching for any weapon she could find. When her fingers encountered the texture of wood, she wrapped her palm around it. Without looking she knew what it was: one of the broken legs of the chair.

With more force than she thought her body could muster, she plunged the makeshift stake into his chest.

A sound at the door coincided with her driving the stake through Wallace's heart. As he disintegrated into dust, the door shut, making her snap her head toward it, ready to dispatch whoever else was threatening her.

A man leaned casually against the door. She didn't know why, but instinctively she recognized him as a vampire.

"Saved me from having to kill him. Had a bill to settle with him," he drawled.

Still gripping her stake tightly, she jumped up.

"Who are you?"

One side of his mouth lifted. "Let's just say, we have the same enemies."

Rose glanced at the floor where the dust settled. In front of the fireplace, the dead girl lay like a ragdoll. Nausea suddenly overcame her, but except for dry heaving, she produced nothing.

"Ah, your first kill," the stranger commented. "It'll get easier."

She shook her head. Never. She never wanted to kill again. What she needed now was someone to hold her.

"Quinn, oh God, Quinn," she murmured. She had to find him. He would help her.

"You know his protégé?"

Rose raised her head, looking back at the vampire without really seeing him. "I need him now." Lifting her eyes, she begged, "Help me, Quinn, please help me."

A moment later, strong arms prevented her from falling. They shook her back to consciousness. "You can't go to his protégé."

"No, I need Quinn. I need him now."

"You don't understand!" The vampire's voice became more insistent. "If he finds out you killed his sire, he will kill you."

"No! Quinn loves me!" He had professed so only a short time ago.

"He has no choice. It's the duty of a protégé to kill his sire's killer, no matter who this person is. It's an instinct, as ingrained as the lust for blood. Once he knows what you did, he won't be able to resist the urge. The pull will be too strong. It's a duty bred into us."

"But he loves me . . ." she whispered.

"It won't matter. If you stay here and let him find you, you're as good as dead."

Her heart clenched. Had she been on her own, she would have let it happen, let Quinn find and kill her. But there was Charlotte. She still had to protect Charlotte.

"Help me," she begged the stranger.

Rose blinked the tears away. She stood outside of Quinn's bedroom door on the second floor of the B&B, battling with herself. He deserved to know why she hadn't come to him all these years and why she had faked her own death. It had been the only way to make sure he wouldn't look for her.

She was done lying to him, hiding from him. And now that Quinn knew what was at stake if Keegan got his hands on the flash drive, she was certain he would continue protecting Blake even if he had to take his revenge on her for killing Wallace. Blake wouldn't need her anymore. He would be taken care of.

Her heart beat into her throat, which was dry as sandpaper. Her pulse raced uncontrollably, and her palms were damp. A pearl of sweat made its way down her neck and into her cleavage.

Rose tried to raise her hand to knock at his door, but her body didn't obey her mind. As much as she wanted to, she couldn't move. She stood there like a frozen statue, her feet rooted to the floor, her body stiff with fear.

Yet, strangely enough, the sensation that filled her wasn't fear of losing her life if she told him the truth about what she'd done, but of losing his love. It overrode everything else. The thought that wherever she was going, be it heaven or hell or any place in between, she would be going there without his love, was unbearable.

She was a coward and a wimp—simply not strong enough to do this—even less now than right after Wallace's death. Because even after two hundred years, she loved Quinn with the same intensity as the night she'd given him her virginity. If anything, the years apart had cemented that love.

Disappointed in herself, she turned on her heels, and her heart stopped.

Only a few feet from her, Quinn stood watching her. Now he advanced on her, putting himself within arm's length.

His hazel eyes shimmered golden as he ran them over her in slow motion. Then he locked eyes with her.

"I missed you, my love," he murmured.

No, if she told him the truth now, she would never see that look of love in his eyes again.

22

Quinn stroked his fingers over her cheek. He'd watched her as she'd stood in front of his door, clearly torn whether to enter or not. It told him everything he needed to know. Rose wanted a second chance. As did he.

He'd been angry with her only hours earlier when he'd found Keegan's message and discovered her deception. But the longer he thought about it the more he understood why she'd hidden that fact from him. He hadn't behaved like the man she knew back then. He'd coerced her into sleeping with him as payment for his services, and this display of power had given her the wrong impression. She'd had to assume that he had changed, so how could she trust that he would do the right thing and not try to steal the data from her to use it for his own purposes? He had given her no reason to trust him.

It would change now. He would set his pride aside, forget the last two hundred years and woo her again, just as he'd done in the ballrooms of London. Only this time his wooing would include passionate lovemaking of a more intense kind than he'd been allowed back then, when she'd been an innocent.

"I'm so sorry for the things I said to you," he murmured.

"Quinn, I—"

He slid a finger over her lips. "Shh, my love. Hear me out. Whatever happened between us, I want us to forget about it. I want a fresh start. A clean slate. I know I've been acting like an ass. I was angry and hurt. But I'm also grateful, grateful that you're alive. And that's the only thing that counts. For whatever reason, I've got you back, and I'm not going to let this chance pass me by. Rose, please forgive me for whatever I've done. Just let me love you again."

Seconds of silence passed.

"I've never stopped loving you," she replied, her voice heavy with unshed tears. "But the things I've done . . ."

Her eyelids dropped to half-mast.

Sliding his fingers under her chin, he made her look at him. Was she alluding to the fact that she ran brothels? In his eyes she'd done an honorable thing by protecting those women even if others wouldn't see it that way.

"I love you no matter what."

Rose was still pure. To him she was still the young woman he'd left behind to go to war.

Reaching past her, he opened the door to his room and nudged her inside, following her closely. Once inside, he locked the door, making sure nobody could simply walk in and interrupt them.

Rose's gaze snapped to the lock, then back to him; a second later it landed on the bed.

Quinn followed her gaze before looking back at her. "I'm not going to force you to do anything this time. Whatever happens here will be because we both want it. You can walk away anytime, you can say no to anything."

" . . . or I can say yes to anything."

The suggestive look she graced him with shot through his body like a bullet. It was how he remembered her: playful and receptive.

"Will I have to wait much longer for a kiss, or would it be too forward for a lady to steal one?"

Her coquettish smile melted his heart.

"I would never make a lady wait." No sooner had the words left his lips, than he pulled her into his arms. "But I always make a lady come."

Crushing his mouth to hers, he unleashed the passion he'd kept bottled up for two centuries.

With one arm around her waist, he pulled her into the hard planes of his body, as he buried the other hand in her golden tresses, angling her head for a closer connection. Her lips were inviting, her tongue tantalizing him with gentle strokes, urging him to delve deeper into her delicious mouth.

The soft press of her breasts against his chest shot a thrill through his groin, the knowledge that she was here out of her own free will and not because he was forcing her, only intensifying the feeling. Rose wanted him. Everything she did attested to it: her hands that caressed his nape, making him shiver, her pelvis grinding against him, letting him sense her heat, her fangs that had lowered fractionally and now presented an altogether different temptation.

Unable to resist, he stroked his tongue over the tip of one of her fangs, making her jolt instantly. The unexpected movement made her fang pierce his tongue, just deep enough to draw blood, which seeped from it instantly.

Rose yanked her head back, interrupting their kiss, a horrified expression on her face.

"Oh, God, I'm sorry. I didn't mean to."

Despite the apologetic words, her eyes were transfixed on his mouth, her nostrils flaring in the process.

Pulling her back to him, he parted his lips, letting her see the drops of blood he could taste on his tongue. "I'm not. Sorry, that is."

His lips hovered over hers as he allowed her to inhale the scent of his blood. Too soon, the tiny wound would heal by itself, shutting off the flow of blood, but before that happened, he wanted one thing from her.

"Taste me."

Her eyes widened, interest and horror colliding within them in a battle of equally matched opponents. It was unclear which side would win. But Quinn had never been one to play by the rules when it came to women. He knew how to press his advantage, how to turn the tables in his favor.

Sliding his hand down to the round curves of her backside, he gently urged her closer to him, wanting to make her aware of the effect she had on him.

"Do you feel that, Rose? Just the thought of you tasting my blood makes me harder than granite."

Her next intake of breath brought with it a moan that reverberated deep inside his chest. A moment later, her lips were on him, her tongue foraging ahead, swiping over his to collect the blood that was waiting there for her. When she swallowed, his heart beat into his throat, waiting anxiously for her reaction.

All of a sudden, her heart beat against his in an excited rhythm, as deep and melodic as a drum, yet as rapid as a jackhammer.

"Quinn," she whimpered, releasing his mouth for a split-second.

Had he not been so busy recapturing her lips, he would have smiled. Knowing that she loved his taste, that she'd taken a small drop of his blood gave him hope: they would work things out between them, remove whatever obstacles remained. This time, they would make it work.

His need for her spiraling, he let his hands wander over her body. As he palmed one breast through the fabric of her top, her sounds of pleasure vibrated against his lips, making them tingle pleasantly.

He growled, impatient now to touch her naked skin. As if she knew what he wanted, she dropped her hands to the seam of her shirt, pulling it upwards.

"No, please," he whispered. "Let me do that."

He couldn't think of a greater joy than to unwrap her, to lay her bare like a present on Christmas Day.

Obediently, she let go of her shirt, placing her hands on his chest. Her nimble fingers instantly went to the buttons of his shirt, popping one after the other open.

"Tit for tat," she said.

Chuckling, he tugged at her top, pulling it up and making her interrupt her own activity as he pulled it over her head. While he tossed it on the floor, his eyes were already drinking in what he'd laid bare. Her lace bra was practically see-through, leaving nothing to his imagination.

In awe he lowered his head, bringing his lips to the nipple he could clearly see through the wafer-thin fabric. Snaking out his tongue, he lapped over it, tasting the rosebud. Yes, this was what he'd missed all his life: a taste of Rose.

Rose's hands working his buttons instantly stilled and instead gripped the lapels of his shirt as if holding on for dear life.

Continuing his sensual assault on her nipple, his hands went for the bra straps, sliding them quickly over her shoulders, allowing him to push the fabric away from her breasts. When his lips and tongue met her flesh, he sucked greedily, the nipple in his mouth having long ago turned hard.

Not wanting to neglect her other breast, Quinn switched sides, licking and sucking the other nipple in the same way while kneading her flesh with his hand. The aroma of her skin intensified, filling his nostrils with the sweet smell of aroused woman. Her skin tasted of rose petals, engulfing him in an English garden filled with hundreds of rose bushes.

Knowing there were more places on her body he needed to taste, he continued to undress her, his hands making quick work of the button and zipper of her pants, then shoving them over her hips. Pulling them down her legs, he dropped farther down, leaving her breasts, and instead bringing his head to the apex of her thighs. As she stepped out of her pants, having discarded her high heeled sandals moments earlier, he steadied her with his hands on the back of her thighs.

Rose swayed for an instant, but he pulled her toward him, pressing his face into her center, where her panties hid her sex. As delicate as the wings of a butterfly, the fabric clung to her, hiding his view, yet her scent escaped.

At the next intake of breath, he filled his lungs with her delectable aroma, feeling how it did things to him no other woman had ever managed: his heart softened, the walls around it cracking for the first time in two centuries.

Her fingers dug into his shoulders. "Stop."

He raised his head to look at her, surprised at her command. Had she changed her mind? When he met her look, he noticed her smile.

"I want you naked too."

Quinn rose, his fingers jerking the last button of his shirt open in the process, then shrugging the garment off his shoulders.

"Better," she approved, then she motioned to his jeans. "Now your pants."

Stepping out of his shoes, he brought his hands to the button of his jeans, opening them, then fingered for the zipper. Her hand slid over his, taking the task from him. Deliberately, slowly, she lowered the zipper while she stroked alongside it with the palm of her other hand, caressing the hard ridge that curved against his groin.

Quinn let a hiss escape his mouth. "Fuck, Rose, do that again, and this'll be over before it began."

She clicked her tongue, then smoothed her hand over him again. "And here I thought you were the experienced playboy who had more stamina than anybody."

He slowly shook his head while he clamped his jaw shut, fighting the onslaught of emotions that her tender hand unleashed on him.

"With you, I'm only a green boy. It's like the first time again."

She pulled his pants to mid-thigh, then brought her hand back to him, sliding it into his boxers. When she captured him in her palm, his heart stopped beating. It was like the first time again, just as magical and new.

"Is that why you're already weeping for me?" She rubbed her finger over the head of his cock, spreading the bead of moisture that had seeped from his slit.

"Yes." He closed his eyes, allowing himself to enjoy her touch to the fullest. "That's why pulling out didn't work back then."

She lifted her head. As their gazes connected, he saw a sad smile on her lips.

"Let's not talk of the past."

With his hand stroking her jaw, he pulled her closer, nodding. "Let's live in the present," he agreed, and sank his lips onto hers.

Her hand squeezed him in agreement, and her lips yielded to his touch.

Within seconds, he'd rid himself of his pants. Rose took care of his boxers. When her bra and panties finally joined his clothes on the floor, he drew her back into his embrace, their bodies sizzling wherever they touched.

Lifting her into his arms, he carried her to the bed and laid her on it as if placing a precious item on a surface to be displayed. He ran his eyes over her, letting the moment sink in.

"You're beautiful."

Her eyelashes fluttered; her lips were parted and moist from his kiss. "That's what I always thought of you."

The way her eyes admired him, hungrily scanning his body, made him even harder than he already was. If she continued doing this, he would burst without another touch from her.

Quinn lowered himself onto the bed, joining her, his body sliding over hers. Her arms came around him instantly, her legs widening to accommodate him. As if they'd done this a hundred times, they fit together perfectly.

His hard length settled in between her spread legs, nudging against her moist center, but he held back, not wanting to rush this perfect moment. They had all day. The sun had come up and most everybody in the house was asleep or at least had withdrawn to their respective rooms. For several hours, there was nothing he needed to do other than to take care of Rose, to show her how beautiful life could be.

To love her.

Rose ground against him, her pelvis tilting, asking for his invasion.

Gently, he brushed a strand of her long hair from her cheek. "Patience, my love. We have all the time in the world."

"But I want you now." She looked up at him, impatience and longing in her eyes, suddenly looking the same way she had looked on their wedding night.

Quinn felt a soft smile play around his lips. "You already have me."

His words couldn't have been truer. His heart belonged to her. It had been that way since he'd first fallen in love with her. It was no different now. Or maybe it was: his love was more intense now, the hold she had on his heart stronger.

Grinding against her, he slid his cock over her sex, pressing down, searching for her most sensitive point. He knew that he'd found it when she moaned softly.

"Right there, huh, Rose?" he asked.

She choked out a single word. "Yes."

Quinn raised his hips, adjusted his angle, then drove into her inviting cave, drenching himself in the warm wetness of it. The tightness was intoxicating, robbing him of his ability to breathe.

A relieved sigh was her answer. But no sooner had the sigh died on her lips, than he pulled back out and slid his erection over her clit. Now moist with her juices, it was a perfect slide of flesh on flesh. The rubbing motion spread the scent of aroused woman in the room, making him feel drunk with it, if vampires could feel anything akin to that state. He was aware only of Rose and her sensual movements, of her irregular breaths that escalated to pants, of her moans and sighs that echoed in the room.

Sinking his lips onto her neck, he kissed the graceful column of it. A sheen of perspiration had built on her skin, the taste and scent of it more delicious than anything he'd ever known. He blew against her perspiring skin, eliciting a shiver from her.

His body responded in kind, a shudder racing down his spine, shooting into his cock. His balls tingled, pulling up tightly, his shaft filling with more blood, stretching him to capacity.

"Can't wait any longer," he pressed out a split-second before he plunged into her.

The action shoved her inches higher toward the headboard, her back arching, her head pressing harder into the pillow. She thrust her breasts out, the hard nipples begging to be sucked. So ripe, ready to be harvested. Quinn's fangs elongated at the sight.

Pulling back from her tight sheath, he thrust back inside, with each slide reaching deeper. Their bodies danced with each other in perfect rhythm. Rose's legs wrapped around his hips, driving him harder into her. Imprisoned between her strong thighs, he felt complete.

With every thrust, Quinn felt the pressure build in his balls and knew that he was getting close to his breaking point. But he pushed back the need for release, not wanting this to end. At the same time, his fangs itched, urging him to demand another kind of release, to fill another kind of need.

His gaze slid back to her neck. The vein underneath her skin throbbed, the steady rhythm calling to him like a beacon leading him home. Slowly, he dropped his head back to her neck, slowing his strokes. Peeling back his lips, he allowed his fangs to graze her delicate skin. The contact sent a bolt through his body, nearly electrocuting him. He jerked his head back, looking at her.

"Rose, I want . . . I want . . . I need your blood."

Rose's half closed eyes shot open.

He wanted to bite her? At Quinn's words, an unfamiliar sensation went through her. Despite the disgust she'd always felt at the idea of anybody ever biting her again, the two-hundred-year-old memory of her violent turning still fresh in her mind, something inside her wanted to surrender.

As she stared at his extended fangs, her heart beat a little faster, but it wasn't out of fear, because in concert with her heart, her clit throbbed. Almost uncontrollably. So violently in fact, that she knew she was about to come. It was impossible that the idea of Quinn wanting to bite her would have such an impact on her. If anything, it should repel her, make her push him off her, toss him out of bed.

Yet all she could do was continue respond to the rhythm of his hips as his cock plunged into her without pausing.

What would it be like if he bit her, if he drank her blood? Would it be the same pain she'd gone through once before? Would she fight him?

Her hand trembled when she reached for his face and extended a finger toward his mouth. Quinn stopped his movements, went entirely still, his erection remaining lodged deep inside her. He opened his mouth wider, allowing her better access.

Cautiously, she touched one fang with the pad of her index finger.

Quinn's eyes squeezed shut, a moan issuing from his throat. "Oh, God!"

When he opened his eyes an instant later, the golden shimmer had faded into a dark red, the sign that he was all vampire now, controlled by his animal instincts.

The sight should have made her pull back, but instead it filled her with excitement. She had done that to him by touching his fang.

Stroking over his elongated canine once more, she took in the smooth texture of his tooth, the sharpness of its tip. Such a deadly instrument. Was it true what he'd said to her at the party? That his bite could deliver pleasure?

"I'm scared," she whispered.

He closed his eyes, clearly trying to get himself under control. "I won't do it if you say no."

Even though she recognized the sincerity in his voice, she sensed his disappointment. It made her own heart ache with emptiness. As if she'd lost something all over again.

Determined not to push him away, she pressed the fleshy part of her finger against his fang, allowing it to pierce her skin.

Quinn's eyes flew open, his nostrils flaring as he took in the scent of her blood.

"Rose, you don't have to . . ."

She pulled her finger from him, then smeared the drops of blood that dripped from it over the vein on her neck. Breathing heavily, excitement colliding with the remnants of her fear, she locked eyes with him.

"I want to give you everything you need."

Lust and love poured from his eyes in equal measures.

"I'll be gentle."

She nodded, bracing herself for the pain. If this was what he wanted, she would give it to him. She couldn't disappoint him.

First his lips brushed over her neck, then his tongue licked the blood off her skin. She heard him inhale as he swallowed.

"Oh, Rose, I've never tasted anything better in my life."

The words drove tears into her eyes, and she had difficulty holding them back. She stiffened when his fangs scraped against her skin.

"I love you," he murmured, then his fangs pressed deeper, piercing her skin, driving into her flesh.

At first, it felt like somebody had pricked her finger with a toothpick. There was no pain. Relief flooded her instantly. He hadn't lied to her. This was not the brutal bite with which she had been brought into the world of vampires; this was a gentle kiss, a loving caress.

As her body relaxed in his embrace, she suddenly felt the pull on her vein. Bolts of energy raced through her body, shooting through her veins like hot lava, making her body burn from the inside. But this was no angry, destroying fire; this was life-giving, passionate, and consuming.

"Yes," she whispered, pulling him closer.

She felt how Quinn resumed plunging his cock in and out of her, his movements measured, with every withdrawal making her yearn for him, with every thrust back inside, rubbing over her clit. His bite was a passionate kiss just like he'd promised earlier, but he'd neglected to mention just where she would feel that kiss. His fangs in her neck made her feel as if he were licking her clit with his tongue while his cock was filling her. Anatomically impossible, yet the sensation was the same. Nothing had ever felt this way.

Why had she been so afraid of this for so long?

As she let herself fall in his arms, allowing his caresses to sweep her away on a cloud of utter bliss, she knew that she would never be able to live without him. Now that she understood what he could make her body feel, the sensations he could awaken in her, she could never turn back.

When his thrusts became faster, she felt him pull his fangs from her neck and lick over the tiny incisions. Then he looked at her, perspiration running down his chest in little rivulets.

"I can't even tell you what this means to me . . . Rose, I don't know how to ever thank you for this gift."

She felt tears threaten to overwhelm her, but forced them back. She'd never carried her emotions this close to the surface.

"I know a way you can thank me. Make me come."

He let out a groan. "Oh, Rose, I don't deserve you."

Then he sank his lips onto hers. She could taste her own blood on his tongue, but it didn't disgust her. Not anymore.

Quinn's body moved with hers, his hips grinding, withdrawing, then slamming back against her, his cock never ceasing its relentless rhythm. He filled her with his hardness, reaching deep into her, touching places that released sensations she'd scarcely known she was capable of feeling.

Tilting her pelvis, she responded to his movements, finding the right angle at which each of Quinn's thrusts sent a tantalizing, tingling sensation through her clit, hurtling her toward the inevitable. As their bodies moved in a rhythm as old as time, she felt him tense in her arms.

"Now, Rose, now!"

As he flooded her channel with his seed, she felt the approach of her own orgasm. Like a wave far out in the ocean, it built and built until it reached the shore line and broke on the beach, tearing down anything in its path.

Rose sensed Quinn's spasms coincide with her own. His heavy panting echoed hers.

She'd never felt so connected to anybody. Not even their wedding night had been like this. The bite had made her feel a deeper connection to him, even though she had not been the one to do the biting. Would it be even more intense if she bit him? The thought jolted her. Yet, she couldn't deny that it excited her at the same time.

Quinn nuzzled his face against the crook of her neck as his body stilled and he slowly pulled out of her. Rolling off her, he drew her back into his arms, pressing her against his heated body.

"This was amazing," he said.

"Better than anything."

He pressed a kiss on her temple. "Rose?"

She turned her face to look at him, alerted. Would he press her for information about her past now? "Yes?"

"Did you love Keegan?"

Relieved, she let out a breath, then dropped her lids. "Can a vampire love?"

His finger under her chin urged her to look at him. She noticed how he shook his head.

"You loved our daughter. There is love, even for a vampire. You can love, just as you loved as a human."

Feeling her eyes moisten, she nodded quickly. "I loved her, yes. But that's different. She was my flesh and blood. But another man . . . I never loved anybody."

"You said you loved me, or was that only in the throes of passion?" His voice remained light as if he already knew the answer to his question.

Yes, she had said that, hadn't she? And she meant it.

Rose lost herself in the golden hue of his eyes, unable to say a word.

"So you do love me."

She could only nod before the tears started streaming down her face. If only things were that easy. If only she could tell him everything, then this would have been the happiest moment in her life.

"Don't cry, my love. Because I love you too. And we've been given a new chance."

His lips slanted over her mouth, quieting the sobs that tore from her chest. But his kiss could not quiet the guilt that spread in her for continuing to deceive him and accept the love she didn't deserve.

23

It was already late afternoon, and despite the fact that he'd slept a good eight hours, Blake felt exhausted. They had really worked him in the gym overnight. He would never admit it though, not to Wesley, who seemed totally full of himself, nor to any of the trainers. He would make it through this training if it killed him. Not that he was all that clear about what exactly he was training for. Quinn had been kind of vague about it.

But right now, it didn't matter, because he'd just discovered that in addition to the extremely beautiful Rose there was another female trainer. She had simply introduced herself as Nina. The woman was drop-dead gorgeous with a sassy attitude to match. Oh, yeah! That was how he liked his women: ample boobs, dick sucking lips, and strong legs. He could tell that Nina had all of that and more to boot.

On top of it she was a natural blonde, her hair only reaching to about chin length. A bit tomboyish, but sexy and feminine at the same time.

Blake allowed his eyes to roam over her hot body while she projected the dullest PowerPoint presentation he'd ever been made to sit through onto the white wall in front of him.

He could tell that the room wasn't really meant for this purpose. At one point it had probably been a small dining room, and for a moment he wondered why classroom instruction wasn't held at the facility where he'd passed his test.

At least he was the only student. Wesley had made himself scarce after grabbing a coffee in the kitchen, and Nina hadn't stopped him. Maybe she didn't mind being alone with him. After all, she had given him an assessing look when he'd shaken her hand. There was no harm in trying his luck.

Nina was about his age, in fact, now that he thought of it, all the people at the house looked rather young, even the trainers. Even Quinn couldn't be any older than twenty-five. How had they all gotten to be trainers at such an early age? Well, at least that probably meant that the company wasn't stodgy, and it was possible to get promoted quickly. Which was just up his alley. The faster he could rise to the top and let other people do the grunt work the better.

"Oh darn," Nina suddenly cursed.

She shook the wireless controller that allowed her to advance the slides. She pressed the button again and again, but the slide didn't move.

Blake jumped up from his chair and approached her. "Let me see. Could just be a loose connection."

He reached for the remote in her hand, moving a step closer than necessary. He was a good head taller than she, and from his vantage point he had a clear view at her cleavage. Her T-shirt stretched over her boobs, and he noticed that she wasn't wearing a bra.

Beads of sweat suddenly formed on his forehead.

"Here, maybe it's the battery." Nina's voice drifted to him.

Absentmindedly, he took the remote from her hand and turned it over, sliding the back covering off. But his focus was still on her breasts, making his fingers slip.

The batteries fell to the floor, the sound echoing loudly in the small room. Quickly, he crouched down to snatch them up before they had a chance to roll underneath the table.

When he reared up again, he bounced against Nina, his shoulder brushing her breast. The action wedged her between him and the table.

He lashed his practiced grin at her. "Oops, how clumsy of me."

"I'd advise you to take a step back before you get in trouble," she said, her eyes narrowing.

"Trouble can be fun sometimes." He let his eyes travel lower. Oh yeah, a lot of fun.

"Second time I tell you, it'll hurt."

He pulled one corner of his mouth up into a smirk. "What is it, some sort of rule that trainees and trainers can't get friendly? I won't tell if you won't."

"Agreed then." She smiled sweetly. "Then you won't tell anybody about this."

Her hands came up and forcefully pushed him back. Surprised by her sudden movement, he stumbled and fell against one of the chairs, taking it down with him. Before he could get up, the door burst open and like a blur, somebody entered. His eyes couldn't process the movement fast enough.

Only once the person stopped in front of him and pulled him up by the front of his shirt, did he recognize him: Amaury.

Blake couldn't move. He could only stare—at the glaring red eyes and the teeth that were protruding from his mouth.

"Shit!"

"Baby, I had it under control," Nina said calmly from behind him.

Amaury ignored her, his chest heaving, his head leaning in. "You touch her one more time, you're a dead man. She's mine!"

Fuck! Why had nobody told him that those two were an item? Not that this was his biggest problem right now.

Nina pushed into view, arms crossed over her chest, scowling at her man. "There was no need for that."

Amaury tossed her a quick look. "There was need." His voice sounded more like the growl of an animal than that of a man.

"What are you?" Blake croaked.

Staring at his pointy teeth, he already knew the answer, but couldn't process it. Vampires didn't exist. Shit, had he gotten drunk last night and was now hallucinating?

"What's going on?" another voice came from the door, before the person came into view: Cain, one of the trainers.

He wore pajama bottoms, and now that Blake looked down at Amaury, he realized that he too was only half dressed. He wore a pair of jeans and nothing else. Amaury's gaze swung back to his colleague.

"Nothing to worry about."

Cain, dark hair messy, and clearly still somewhat sleepy, appeared to disagree. "Hate to point it out, but are you aware that your fangs are showing? I thought the kid wasn't supposed to know."

"Uh, *merde*!"Amaury let out. Then he shot Nina a somewhat apologetic look. "Sorry, *chérie*."

Nina just shook her head. "You really thought I couldn't handle a little punk like him? Puh-lease!"

Then Amaury turned back to him, set him on his two feet, which for the first time since Blake could remember, wobbled, and gingerly brushed his disheveled shirt straight as if that would make things better.

Hell, it didn't change anything about the fact that that man was a vampire!

Blake jumped back, eager to get out of the guy's reach, but unfortunately, this . . . thing . . . Amaury, was between him and the door. Could he make it to the window, open it and jump out? He tossed

a quick look in that direction. The blinds were drawn. Nina had done
that earlier to make it easier to see the PowerPoint presentation.

Maybe if he could pull the blinds up fast enough, the sun would kill
the bastard. He lunged for the cord, but a split-second later, Amaury had
him by the collar again and held him back.

"What's going on here?"

At the sound of Quinn's thundering voice, Blake let out a sigh of
relief. He whirled around.

"He's a vampire! Amaury's a vampire. You gotta help me."

Quinn rolled his eyes and stared at Amaury. "That's just great. I
brought you here to help, not to mess things up."

"He accosted Nina."

"He was trying to flirt with me!" Nina corrected him. "He didn't
succeed, but my big macho man here had to burst into the room in
vampire speed and flash his fangs at our guest."

Amaury narrowed his eyes at her. "You and I will have a word in
private in a minute."

Nina didn't back down from the threat. Instead, a red flush crept up
her cheeks.

Blake did a double take. What the fuck? This was all just too
freaking weird! He had to get out of here. Using Amaury's temporary
distraction, he ran for the door.

Cain cut him off, holding him back, slinging his arm around him. As
Blake struggled to free himself, his opponent didn't even take an extra
breath.

"What do you want to do with him now?" he asked Quinn.

Suddenly the door opened and Rose entered, wearing a short robe.
Blake couldn't stop his eyes from trailing down her long legs. Yeah,
shit, that kind of thinking was what had gotten him into trouble in the
first place.

Rose glared at Cain. "Let him go."

Cain looked at Quinn, asking for approval. "If I let go of him, he's
gonna run."

"Why?" Rose's tone was sharp.

"He saw Amaury in his vampire form," Quinn explained.

"Oh, my god! How can you do this to him? You have to wipe his
memory. Now."

Blake twisted and turned under Cain's hold. They wanted to wipe his memory? How on earth were they gonna do that? He knew what he'd seen, and there was no way in hell he'd ever forget that. They could inject him with whatever drug they wanted, but this memory would stay with him.

"No! Let me go. You can't keep me here, you can't do this to me. I'm an American citizen, I have rights," Blake yelled.

"Join the club," Cain said dryly. "We're Americans too. Same rights."

Quinn glanced at him, then back at Rose. "Maybe he should know. He has a right to know what's going on."

Rose vehemently shook her head. "No. He can't know. He has a right to a normal life."

It took seconds until Quinn finally nodded. "As you wish." He motioned to Amaury. "Do it."

Panic thundering through his veins, Blake thrashed about, kicking Cain, but the man wasn't even swaying an inch, as if he was built as strong and indestructible as a tank.

"Shit!"

"It won't hurt," Amaury assured and locked eyes with him.

For whatever odd reason, Blake couldn't pull his gaze from the vampire. Fascinated, he stared into his blue eyes. He'd never seen anything that blue. Even the ocean couldn't compete with the beautiful color.

In the background he heard words, but as soon as they entered his head, they vanished again. Around him everything felt like cotton candy, soft and warm. His eyelids felt heavy, falling over his eyes. For a moment everything went dark and quiet.

When he opened his eyes again, he needed a second to find his bearings.

"Darn fire alarm," Quinn said, yawning. "But not to worry. It was just a fuse blowing. We're good."

Blake nodded and looked into the round. All the trainers were assembled. The door opened and Wesley and Oliver trotted in.

"What's going on?" Wesley asked.

"Didn't you hear the fire bell go off?" Quinn asked.

Wesley's chin dropped. "Huh?"

For the first time, Blake sympathized with Wesley: he hadn't heard the fire alarm either. Maybe he'd been too engrossed watching his pretty trainer as she presented the most boring slides about the history of security anybody could assemble.

"Well, since we're all awake now, we might as well get ready for our next training assignment," Quinn announced.

Blake listened up. He hoped whatever it was, it was more interesting than the PowerPoint presentation. "What kind of training?"

"It's a game of evasion."

24

Rose had pulled him aside, dragging him to the office with her. Now she stood close enough so she only had to whisper to him. Definitely a position Quinn liked. The closer she was, the better.

"He's much safer here," Rose insisted.

Quinn shook his head, disagreeing with her. "Keegan knows where we are. If I were he, I'd mount an attack tonight. He can't afford to give us any time to prepare. I'm surprised he even gave us a warning."

Rose huffed. "He likes to prove his superiority by doing shit like that. He thinks it'll scare us and make us surrender."

"Charming guy. In any case, we won't surrender. But we won't be sitting ducks either. We're getting Blake out of here during the day."

She put her hand on his arm. "But we can't be with him during the day." She jerked her head toward the door. "Wesley can't protect him on his own. He's human. And as tough as Nina seems to be, I doubt she can either. He needs us." Her look was pleading.

Quinn took her hand and squeezed it. "Let me worry about that. I have a plan. But we can't wait until nightfall to get him out of here. That's when Keegan will be able to move and go on the attack. We have a much better chance during daytime. This is our turf."

"But don't you think he's having somebody watch the house?"

Quinn grinned. "I would be disappointed if he didn't."

Rose gave him a confused look. "But, then . . ."

He pulled her hand to his mouth and planted a kiss on it. "Don't worry, I've been in this business for a long time. I know what I'm doing." Then he looked into her eyes, holding her gaze. "He's our flesh and blood. I'll make sure no harm will come to him."

Rose's eyes softened. "You know that's only the second time you've called him *our*."

"Yes, and it won't be the last." Then he tugged at her hand. "Come, let's go over the plan with everybody."

When they walked into the living room moments later, everybody was assembled, now fully dressed: Amaury, Cain, Oliver, Nina, Wesley, and Blake. Quinn motioned for Rose to sit, but remained standing himself. They all looked at him with expectant gazes. He hadn't even had a chance to share his plan with Amaury yet.

"We've been given our first test," he announced for Blake's benefit. "It's a simple hide and seek operation. The goal is to get one of our trainees out of this house without our opposing team finding out where we're taking him. The second trainee will be the decoy. As with every test, we're allowed to use all tools at our disposal."

He looked at the assembled. "Now, as for the roles . . ."

"I want to be the decoy," Blake blurted.

"I'm afraid, roles have already been assigned. Wesley has been chosen as the decoy."

Blake's disappointed gaze drifted to Wesley, who merely shrugged, indicating that he didn't know any more than Blake.

"Blake, you'll be the person to be hidden from our opposing team. The hiding place will be a safe house in Twin Peaks. Our opponents don't know of its existence. To help us with moving our trainee, headquarters has authorized two additional agents," Quinn continued his deception.

While the plan was essentially what he laid out, there was neither a safe house, nor any additional agents. No, the two people who were supposed to arrive within minutes couldn't be further away from being agents or bodyguards of Scanguards. Nevertheless, he continued his charade so that Blake would play along without giving them any trouble.

"I was lucky to secure two of the best." He looked at Blake and Wesley. "Don't be fooled when you see them. They're both lethal and the best in their field. Questions?"

Amaury straightened. "What do you want me to do?"

"You'll help secure the property once Blake has left."

Blake raised his hand. "How are you planning to move me out of here without anybody noticing?" He made a movement with his hand, indicating the size of his body. "I'm not exactly easy to overlook."

"Good question." But Quinn had already thought about this and found a way. "You'll find out in time."

"When are we starting?" Wesley asked.

"As soon as our two agents have arrived."

Rose got up from her armchair. "In the meantime, we'd better get those two looking like twins." She pointed her finger toward Wesley and Blake.

Blake scowled. "No chance in hell. I'm taller than him and broader. He looks nothing like me."

"Maybe not close up, but with the right kind of adjustments and the same clothing, you'll look like you've come from the same womb," Rose insisted.

Quinn nodded in agreement. Rose had told him about how the prostitutes she employed had helped her disguise herself and how they'd become decoys for her. It had given him the idea of how to get Blake out of the way of the impending attack.

"I'll believe it when I see it," Blake said skeptically.

"Upstairs, get changed," Quinn ordered. "Rose, do you need me?"

She shook her head. "Trust me, I've done this for a long time."

Rose ushered Blake and Wesley out of the room. When Wesley walked passed him, Quinn lowered his voice for only him to hear. "And keep your hands off Rose. Make sure Blake does the same. I'm holding you responsible."

"I got the message the first time."

When he heard them walk up the stairs, he looked back at his friends.

"Nice performance," Amaury smirked.

Cain shoved a hand through his hair. "I still don't understand why you don't just tell him. He seems robust enough to get over it quickly. Hell, I bet he'd even find it cool."

"Yeah, that's what I'm worried about. But joke aside, Rose doesn't want him to know." If it were his choice, he would tell Blake what was really going on. But he had to respect Rose's wishes. He was her grandson too.

"What do you need us to do now?" Oliver asked.

Quinn looked at him, noticing instantly that he seemed tense when he only knew the kid as relaxed. He shifted uncomfortably from one foot to the next, almost as if moving farther away from Nina. His nostrils trembled.

Concern for his protégé made him furrow his forehead. He'd not spent much time with Oliver since they'd moved into the B&B two nights earlier. And by the looks of it, this fact wouldn't change in the next few hours either.

"You okay?" he asked Oliver.

His protégé straightened visibly. "Sure."

"Good. I'll have you three secure the house. Make sure no entry points are left open. Check all windows and doors; then give me your assessment of where they'll try to attack. Find our weakest point."

"How about me?" Nina asked.

"I don't have an immediate need for you. However, once Blake and Wesley are gone, I'll need you to do a perimeter check. It's daylight, so whoever is out there watching us, is human. Stay away from any dark vans in case any vampires are hiding in them and might pull you in."

He looked at Amaury. "You okay with that?"

Amaury nodded, then glanced at his mate. "Just don't do anything rash. Just a perimeter check. You find something suspicious, you come right back. Don't take care of it yourself."

Nina waved him off. "I know the drill. So, if you don't need me right now, I might as well help Rose, getting those boys all decked out."

She took only one step before Amaury grabbed her from behind and pulled her back.

"Oh, no, you won't!"

Quinn watched with amusement as Nina struggled in Amaury's grip.

"What's your problem?"

"My problem?" Amaury growled. "My problem is that Blake made a pass at you not an hour ago. Do you really think I'm so stupid as to let him get close to you again?"

Amaury glanced at Quinn. "Your grandson is a womanizer, and you would do the same if you were in my shoes. No offense."

"None taken." Unfortunately, Amaury was right: Blake was so much like him, or rather, like he'd been over the last two hundred years. All because he wanted to forget Rose. So what was Blake's excuse?

"You big oaf!" Nina griped.

"You wouldn't have it any other way!"

Nina pouted her lips. "As if!"

Instead of an answer, Amaury pulled her closer and sank his lips onto hers, shutting her up with a kiss.

While Cain chuckled, Oliver looked tense again.

Shit, he had to get his protégé out of here, away from whatever temptation there was.

"Oliver, I want you to start with the garage and basement. Now."

The kid almost bolted from the room.

Then Quinn turned back to Amaury, who was still kissing his wife. "Amaury!" he shouted. "We are still here. And there's work to be done."

His friend released Nina instantly, shrugging and tossing him a sheepish look. "Sure."

Then he let a seductive look slide over his wife. "Later."

Nina simply boxed him in the shoulder and left the room, shaking her head. "I'll be in the kitchen."

Amaury's eyes followed the tantalizing sway of her hips, then he twisted his lips into a smile. "Oh, yeah, she wants me."

Quinn rolled his eyes, noticing that Cain was doing the same. "She's your mate. Of course she wants you."

"Yeah, but right now, she *really* wants me."

"She'll have to wait, because I *really* want you to start securing the house," Quinn answered in dry tones.

When Cain laughed out loud, Amaury shot him a pissed off glare. "Wait until it hits you, then you won't be laughing at the rest of us anymore."

"Out, both, now!" Quinn ordered.

Even before the two had left the room, Quinn's sensitive ears picked up the sound of the garage door in the back of the house opening. Since the house was build on a slight incline, the backside of the house was lower than the front. The garage was accessible at street level from the back of the house, yet inaccessible from the front, where it lay underground.

"They're here," he murmured to himself and headed for the stairs to the basement and garage.

By the time he reached the garage, the car had already pulled in, and the garage door was closed again. Quinn walked up to the convertible, a red BMW. The top was down, and thanks to the unusually sunny weather, that fact would not look suspicious to anybody watching them. Quinn counted on it. It was important that Keegan's people saw who entered and left the house. A convertible made sure of that.

He rushed to the driver's side, opening the door before Delilah had a chance to open it herself. She gave him a grateful smile and accepted his hand.

"Thanks for coming so quickly."

"Goes without saying."

Portia exited from the passenger side. "At least that gives us something useful to do."

He smiled at Zane's mate who despite her young age acted more mature than he'd seen two-hundred-year-old vampires behave.

He was about to turn away from the car when he saw a movement on the backseat. His mouth dropped open. "You brought the baby?"

Delilah lifted her daughter out of the car seat. "I talked Samson into it. Nobody will suspect us if we're traveling with a baby. She's the perfect distraction." She planted a soft kiss on Isabelle's head. "Aren't you?"

Quinn lifted his hands in capitulation. "If Samson is okay with that . . . ."

"Not to worry," Portia added, exchanging a wicked grin with Delilah. "He'll get over it. I'm riding along for protection. Even if the other side sets anybody on our tail and tries to attack us, they can only use humans during daytime. They won't know what hit them when they try to attack us. They're not gonna know that I'm part vampire."

"And Zane agreed to that?" Quinn asked doubtfully.

"He did," a muffled voice came from the direction of the trunk. *"And now he'd like to get out of this prison."*

"Oops, sorry, baby," Portia said hastily and hurried to the trunk, opening it.

Zane peeled his long figure out from the tight interior, stretching as soon as he stood.

"I wasn't expecting you."

"I figured you could use an extra pair of hands."

"Always appreciated."

Suddenly, Delilah seemed to remember something and dug into her pocket. "Here's the phone you asked for. Thomas rigged it. The only person who can text or call back to this phone is the one you contact with it. Otherwise, it's untraceable."

"Thanks." Quinn took it and stuffed it into his pocket.

Pleased that things were running right on schedule, Quinn led the new arrivals upstairs, filling them in on their tasks while they waited for

Wesley and Blake to get ready.

They didn't have to wait long.

Rose had done an amazing job, making the two look indeed very similar from afar. Even at close range the similarities were striking. The clothing was the easy part. They both wore jeans and red T-shirts.

"You look a lot taller, Wes," Quinn commented, wondering how Rose had achieved that.

He grinned, lifting his jeans by a few inches, exposing the boots he wore. "Rose stapled some rubber underneath it, adding a couple of inches."

"Looks good," he said approvingly.

"And I'm wearing padding," Wes added.

"Are those the agents?" Blake interrupted, pointing at Delilah, Portia, and Zane. "I thought there were only going to be two."

Quinn winked at Blake. "Sometimes you have to know when to cheat a little."

"Cool!"

"These are Delilah, Portia, and Zane."

Blake nodded in greeting, eying the baby in Delilah's arms suspiciously. Taking a step closer to Quinn, he leaned in and lowered his voice. "They brought a baby?"

"To distract the other side. Watch and learn," Quinn answered quickly. "As I said before, they are the best at what they do."

Which in Delilah's case meant producing a beautiful child. But Blake didn't need to know that. As for Portia, she was the best thing that could have ever happened to Zane, the vampire he considered his closest friend, who had battled with the demons of his past and finally won. He'd emerged a different man: finally free of the shackles of his mental prison. He was still one of the most lethal vampires he'd ever known, yet some of the volatility that had ruled Zane's life had been replaced by the peace his mate gave him.

"Okay, into positions. Blake, you and Portia will go out on the porch, make sure you wander around out there, so whoever is watching can see you."

Quinn couldn't help but see the grin on Blake's face as he let his eyes run over Portia's body. Nor did he miss Zane's corresponding scowl.

"And Blake," he added. "We're watching you."

He hoped that would be a sufficient hint to make sure the kid would keep his hands to himself and behave. If not, Zane would be on Blake's ass like a bee on honey. And whatever Zane dealt out would hurt more than a bee sting.

As Portia motioned Blake to the doors that led to the terrace, Quinn and his fellow vampires quickly stepped into the hallway, away from the rays of the sun about to stream into the room.

"If he weren't related to you, I wouldn't let Portia near him," Zane started. "But don't be fooled. If he touches her, the deal is off."

Quinn refrained from shaking his head. "Why is it that you guys constantly have to remind me that you'll defend your mates against any man? First Amaury, now you. Don't you think I already know that?"

"Just a friendly reminder." Zane tried a courteous smile, but it looked wooden. Friendly was just not his way.

"He'll behave," Quinn answered automatically, turning to look at Rose. As he sought her eyes, she smiled at him; however, doubt remained in her eyes.

"You sure this'll work?" she whispered to him.

"Him behaving? Don't worry."

"No, fooling Keegan."

He stroked his hand over her jaw, forgetting for a moment that they weren't alone. "Trust me."

From inside the living room, he heard Delilah's voice call Blake back into the room. "Blake, honey, you should wear a baseball hat or you'll get a sunburn."

Footsteps announced that Blake was coming back into the room.

Quinn could see through the gap of the door they'd left ajar that he entered. A minute later, Delilah said loudly, "There, that's better."

It was Wesley's cue to take Blake's place on the terrace, a San Francisco Giants baseball cap partially obscuring his face. As he walked out to join Portia, Delilah and Blake stepped into the hallway.

"Good. Follow me," Quinn ordered, leading them downstairs into the garage.

He pointed at the convertible. "In you go."

When Blake headed for the front seat, Quinn stopped him quickly. "The trunk."

"What?"

"We can't smuggle you out of here if they can see you."

"But can't I just lie on the backseat with a blanket over me?"

Quinn chuckled and exchanged a look with Delilah. "You're watching entirely too many bad movies. That trick doesn't work in the real world."

He crossed the distance to the car and opened the trunk. "Make yourself comfortable."

"There's no space," Blake complained.

"Bigger men than you have fit in here."

"Yeah, cut up in pieces maybe," his grandson grumbled.

"If you don't want this job, you just have to let me know, and you're out."

A shocked expression spread on Blake's face. "No, I want it. I do." To prove his statement, he lifted his leg and stepped into the trunk, crouching down, then finding a position in which he could lie down relatively comfortably.

"See, told you you'd fit. Don't talk while you're in there." Quinn let the hood snap in. "And don't worry, there's plenty of air in there."

Then he looked back at Delilah who'd strapped Isabelle back into her car seat, before he lifted his eyes toward the staircase.

"Portia?" he called out.

"Coming." She rushed down the stairs, coming into view a moment later.

"Everything okay?" he asked.

"Wesley is sitting on the porch, pretending to read a newspaper. He knows to stay out there for half an hour after we've left."

"Thanks."

Portia took her seat while Delilah squeezed behind the steering wheel and started the engine. Quickly, Quinn turned to the stairs and climbed them, hearing the garage door opening as he reached the top.

"The package is on its way," he announced to Zane and Rose, who were still standing in the hallway. "We'll give them a half hour. Then Wesley will come in from the porch and the game begins."

Zane raised an eyebrow. "You don't honestly think Keegan will fall for our little trick, do you?"

Quinn grinned. "Of course not. He'll assume we're trying to pull a fast one."

"Then why are we doing it?"

"Because he'll think we can't possibly be stupid enough to pull an old trick like that. He'll assume that Blake is still here. Keegan was going to pull something anyway. We might as well control the *where* and *when* and make sure he attacks tonight."

Zane twisted one side of his mouth upwards. "Just wondering. How are you going to do that?"

He pulled the disposable phone Delilah had brought him earlier from his pocket and handed it to Rose. "Rose is going to invite him."

25

After sunset, Rose punched a message into the cell and reread the text, which was meant as an answer to Keegan's give-me-back-what-you've-stolen-paintjob.

Over my dead body. Rose.

She sensed Quinn looking over her shoulder.

"It's not exactly an invitation," he murmured. "But I think he'll get the message. Send it."

Pushing the *send* button, she turned to him, shoving the phone into her front jeans pocket. "He'll be fuming when he gets this."

"Angry men make for irrational fighters. It'll be to our advantage. So, while the others are keeping watch, come with me." He tugged at her hand.

She felt heat rise into her cheeks. "Quinn, not now. There's no time for that."

His eyes shimmered golden when he looked at her. A wicked smile curled around his sensual lips. When he leaned closer, her knees started to wobble. After their amazing time in bed together, she felt more feminine than ever—and more vulnerable. And she couldn't get enough of him.

"As much as I would love to drag you back to bed, I agree with you, there's no time." He winked. "I was going to arm you with a few weapons instead."

Embarrassed that she'd misread his intention, she tried to cover up. "Of course, I knew that."

His eyes were glued to her lips, his smile confirming that he knew what she had really been thinking of. "Of course."

She let Quinn lead her upstairs to his room. When he opened the closet and dragged out a large metal crate, Rose realized instantly that arming her wouldn't mean simply pressing a wooden stake into her hand.

The crate contained hand guns, knives, stakes, silver chains, throwing stars, and lots of other equipment she couldn't instantly identify.

Quinn bent over the case, rummaging through it, then pulled out something and turned to her. "Here, you've got to wear gloves so the silver won't injure you."

As she took the leather gloves he handed her, she watched him pull on gloves of his own. Then he dug back into the box, pulled out the weapons, and laid on them on the bed.

"I don't know how to use any of these. I'm used to defending myself with a stake," she told him and pointed to her favorite weapon.

Quinn shook his head. "You won't get anywhere close enough to be able to use it. Not if I can help it," he grumbled. "You'll be staying away from the action. You'll take the gun. And it's merely for self-defense."

She glanced at the weapon. "That's not a very big gun."

"It's a .22 caliber gun with silver bullets. Anything larger than that, and you risk the bullet passing through your target. The bullets from a small gun like this will lodge in your victim and do the most damage—burning him from the inside. But as I said, you're only keeping this for self-defense."

Rose squared her stance. "This is my fight. You don't honestly think I would step back and hide somewhere safe just because you say so, do you?"

With her hands at her hips, she underscored her position.

Quinn leaned closer. "I'm a trained fighter, you're not. No discussion."

"How do you think I survived the last two hundred years? I'm not a withering debutante anymore. I'm stronger than you think. And you seem to have a problem with that."

His eyes narrowed. "Are you suggesting that I underestimate you?"

She took a deep breath. "I'm suggesting that you, *my lord*," she mocked, "still see me as a helpless woman who will faint at the slightest sight of trouble. I'm not that person anymore. Don't be fooled by the packaging."

"Rose," he said, a warning growl in his voice. "I can overpower you in two seconds flat, and close combat isn't even my specialty. Trust me—"

He didn't get any further. Rose pressed her lips onto his. As she felt him respond to her kiss, she reached toward the bed. Gripping her weapon of choice, feeling the smooth wood settling in her palm, she twisted from his embrace, whirled behind him, and within a split-second had him in a tight grip, the stake pointing to his heart.

"Close combat is *my* specialty," she whispered in his ear. "The closer, the better."

His chest rose against the tip of the stake.

"Because you tricked me. Is that how you're planning to defeat Keegan? Is it, Rose?" He turned his head to look at her. "Then be prepared for a massacre, because if that man gets to touch you one more time, I'm going to rip his fucking heart out while it's still beating."

His jealousy was palpable. She'd never seen his eyes this wild, his facial expression this tense, not even when he'd been angry with her after realizing that she'd lied to him.

Her grip loosened.

An instant later she found herself on her back with Quinn pressing her into the mattress, his hand now holding the stake against her chest. Her breath hitched, her thoughts instantly traveling back in time to the night she'd killed his sire. If he found out, was this how he would finish her off? Killing her one day as she lay beneath him, his hot body the last sensation she would ever feel?

"I might have misled you by saying close combat wasn't my specialty." A wicked smile appeared on his face. "My bad."

Quinn tossed the stake to the side, making her take a relieved breath. He noticed it, a surprised look on his face. He glanced at the stake, then back at her. "I was only making a point. You know I would never hurt you."

She hesitated before she answered him. "I know that."

But she also knew that once he knew the truth, things would change and his promise of never hurting her would vanish into thin air.

He tilted his head. "Then why do you look so worried?"

She pushed against him, wanting to free herself, and avoided his gaze. "Why wouldn't I look worried? Keegan is about to attack us."

Quinn searched her eyes, but for whatever reason she had shut him out. Something was bothering her, and he was pretty sure it wasn't the fact that Keegan was about to burst into their safe house. He'd hoped that after Rose had let him drink her blood, she would finally open up to him completely, but he realized now that she was still holding back. As if she were afraid of something.

Disappointed that she still didn't fully trust him, he rolled off her.

"Let's get ready then."

In detached efficiency, he explained the weapons to her, showed her how to use the gun and even let her keep a stake, even though he hoped that she would not have to use it. Shooting from a safe distance was all he wanted her to do.

Quinn kept the throwing stars for himself, tucked a gun into the waistband of his pants, and armed himself with a flail, a medieval ball and chain weapon vampires had adapted for their own purposes. Two chains of pure silver hung from a stick, two balls at each end so when the flail was thrown with skill, the chain and balls would wrap around a person's neck. The silver would burn into the opposing vampire's skin, disabling him for long enough to finish him off in close combat.

"How did you get into this line of work? I mean, working for Scanguards," Rose suddenly asked. "You didn't need the money, not after your brother died shortly after . . ."

She stopped herself as if she'd said something she shouldn't have.

He shot her a surprised look. "You knew about that?"

And why shouldn't she? The headstone on Rose's grave might have been dated before his brother's death, but she had never lain in that grave.

"A hunting accident. It was tragic. He had no heir, so I inherited the title. How ironic. Had it happened two years earlier, I would have been the Marquess of Thornton. Your father would have consented to my suit."

"You would have never had to go to war."

There was so much regret in her voice, it clamped around his heart like an icy cold hand.

He sighed. "We can't turn back time. And I can't begrudge my brother those two years of life. I would never be able to live with myself if I even wished it for a second. I've accepted what happened. And I mourned him."

"Is that why you refused the title and made a deal with the new heir to allow your brother's widow to remain at the estate?"

"You give me too much credit, Rose. I refused the title because I needed to live a life away from the eyes of society."

Yet the real truth was that he was still mourning Rose. And to see the same kind of pain reflected in the eyes of his brother's widow made him want to soothe that pain in whichever way was possible, knowing he couldn't soothe his own. Throwing her out of her home that housed so many happy memories would have only added to her grief. Besides, the title and its holdings meant nothing to him anymore.

So he simply became Quinn Ralston, no title, with only a small property to his name—which of course, by today's standards, represented considerable wealth.

"I met Amaury at a bar brawl on the Lower East Side of Manhattan just a few days after my ship had docked at New York harbor. He made his job sound like a great adventure. So I signed on. I haven't looked back since." He paused. "But then, you know all that, don't you?" he fished.

Slowly, she nodded. "I knew where you were, but I didn't pry into your life, if that's what you mean."

The confirmation that she would have had no trouble contacting him whenever she wanted hurt. But he didn't allow himself to make a comment about it, because if he did, it would only widen the gap between them that still existed.

The vibration of his cell phone saved him from having to come up with an appropriate response. He pulled it out and read the text message.

"There's activity outside."

Quinn crossed the distance to the door and flipped the light switch, drowning the room in darkness. Then he stalked to the window, aware that Rose was at his side. From the corner of his eye, he noticed her gloved hand tucking a silver chain into her jacket pocket.

He peeled the dark curtain aside by an inch and looked outside. All appeared quiet.

"Do you see them?" Rose asked from behind him.

He shrugged and let the curtain fall closed again, stepping away from the window. "Maybe at the front of the house. Stay close to me."

By the time he and Rose reached the corridor and ran along it toward the front of the house, Quinn already heard the curses of his colleagues. Why they were cursing was evident when he reached a window overlooking the front garden and sidewalk: several youngsters were setting off illegal fireworks right in front of the house, joking and laughing as they did so. Beer cans in their hands, they gave off the impression that they were drunk.

Quinn recognized a diversion when he saw one. "Looks like Keegan hired a few kids to throw us off our game."

"Or is using mind control on them," Rose added drily.

Considering the few things he'd heard about their opponent so far, he was inclined to agree with her.

Turning toward the staircase he called down, "They'll be attacking from the back."

"Already figured that," came Zane's response from a floor lower. "You joining in on the fight or are you planning on cozying up to your girl instead?"

While Zane's remark would have warranted a fist fight at any other time, Quinn let the words slide by him and headed for the stairs instead.

"We're taking the tradesmen entrance."

"Somebody has to keep an eye on the front," Rose cautioned as they rushed down the stairs, meeting Zane on the first floor. "Keegan is too crafty to go for a simple diversion like that. I know him too well. And he knows that."

How well Rose knew Keegan wasn't exactly something Quinn wanted to contemplate right now. The very thought of them having been lovers turned his insides out.

"Wesley is watching the front," Zane confirmed. "Don't worry, if he thinks he can fool us with a few fireworks, he'll have to get up earlier."

Quinn noticed how Rose's forehead creased.

"He's smarter than he lets on. And very devious," Rose added.

"We can handle whatever he throws at us," Quinn answered.

He squeezed her forearm in reassurance and hoped the coming events wouldn't brand him a liar.

26

It took only ten minutes of waiting at their designated posts within the mansion before all hell broke loose.

The sirens of a fire engine alerted Quinn that something was about to happen. He cursed. It figured that some concerned neighbor had called 911 after the ruckus the teens out on the street were producing. The fire danger their actions represented had clearly worried the concerned homeowners. Quinn couldn't blame them, but going out there and stopping them himself wasn't an option. It would only give Keegan another front on which to attack. After all, he had most likely instigated the entire incident.

"I'll check on the fire engine," Rose whispered next to him.

Before he could stop her, she was gone. "Don't—"

Ah, hell, why did he bother? Rose had her own mind and would do what she wanted anyway. There was no way of holding her back. And maybe it was better to let her do what she wanted. Maybe if he let her feel that he wouldn't be the kind of overpowering husband he might have turned into two hundred years ago—had they ever had the chance to live as husband and wife—then maybe she would finally learn to trust him.

Besides, he loved that she was strong and independent. The new Rose was even more exciting than the old one.

Quinn sighed, and the smell of smoke suddenly tickled his nose. It was odd that it was getting stronger now that the fire department had arrived to put an end to the fireworks on the street. He had no time to investigate it any further.

A loud banging on the front door coupled with an insistent male voice echoed through the hallway. "San Francisco Fire Department, open the door!"

Torn between wanting to stay at his post and knowing somebody had to deal with the authorities, Quinn threw a cautious look out the small window next to the tradesmen entrance. Everything looked quiet. He tested the door knob. The door was locked and bolted.

"Open the door!" the voice insisted, now louder.

In vampire speed, he reached the front door a second later. Looking through the spy hole, he recognized the uniform of a fireman.

"Coming!" he called out. Quickly he pulled his shirt from his pants, letting it fall over the gun he'd tucked into his waistband. With some luck everybody would be too busy with their own work to notice the weapon.

He opened the door a few inches. "Officer, what—?" But he didn't get any further.

"You have a fire on your roof. You need to evacuate the building. Now."

The uniformed fireman pushed the door open wider, making Quinn suddenly aware of the flail that was sticking out from his back pocket. He reached behind him, using the door as a cover and pulled it from his pocket, dropping it into the only thing he could reach without moving: an empty vase on the sideboard.

The fireman motioned to the other men in uniform who came up the steps, wearing oxygen masks, carrying axes and oxygen tanks on their backs.

"We need access to the roof."

"What's going on?" Amaury called out from the kitchen area where he'd been guarding the back entrance.

Quinn lifted his head toward the stairs, sniffing. He smelled the faint smell of smoldering wood more intensely now. When turning back to the fireman, he realized that the man was right. The smell of smoke he'd perceived earlier hadn't come from outside. It was coming from upstairs.

"Shit!"

"How many people are staying here?" the fire captain asked while he waved his colleagues into the house and pointed to the stairs leading up.

Quinn counted in his head. "Nine including me. But nobody is upstairs. We're all on the first floor. I'm sure it's not necessary to evacuate."

Was this what Keegan had planned—to set fire to the place so they had to leave the house, thinking once they were out in the open, he could easily snatch Blake? Good thing that Blake was safe at Thomas's house.

"It's for your own safety. Everybody has to leave. Now!" Then he raised his voice. "Evacuate the building! All occupants, evacuate now!"

More firemen rushed past them and headed upstairs.

Looking out the door, Quinn noticed how the ladder of the fire engine was being raised, a fireman holding the fire hose being lifted with it. Neighbors had started to gather to watch the proceedings. Typical! Everybody liked a good spectacle.

Quinn had no choice. There were too many witnesses to deal with if he refused the fire captain's orders. But maybe that same fact would help them in the end: there were too many witnesses gathering for Keegan to really do any damage.

"Everybody, evacuate," Quinn called into the house, letting his colleagues know that the fireman's orders were to be followed.

When Zane appeared in the hallway, his colleague's warning glare landed on him. "Is that necessary?" he asked from between clenched teeth.

Where on his lean body he'd hidden the silver knife, the throwing stars and the stake he liked to fight with was anybody's guess. Even knowing Zane was armed didn't help Quinn figure out where he might have hidden the weapons.

Quinn approached his friend and whispered back, "Too many people out there. If I use mind control on him, we'll draw too much suspicion on us from the other firefighters and all the gawkers. There are already too many witnesses watching what's going on. And besides, there's nothing Keegan can do out there without drawing attention to himself. In a few minutes we'll have news teams breathing down own necks."

"I wish I knew what he looked like," Zane griped.

"We'll catch him." His eyes followed the humans who stormed upstairs.

One by one, his colleagues reached the foyer, each of them clearly reluctant to leave the house. Luckily, they all had either tucked their weapons away inside their clothing or hidden them in the house. It would be hard to explain why they were sitting around in a dark house in the middle of the night armed to the teeth.

"All civilians evacuate the building," the fire captain repeated and pointed to the door.

Quinn exchanged a look with Amaury and Zane, instilling caution in them as they exited. When he stepped out into the night, the lights of the fire engine illuminated the front yard with another one pointed at the roof. His eyes quickly adjusted and scanned the assembled crowd. He used his vampire senses to ascertain if any vampire had infiltrated the crowd and was biding his time to attack should the occasion arise. He noticed how his friends did the same.

The police had arrived in the meantime and were taking the three youths into custody. As he'd suspected, they were human and from their stunned looks on their faces they appeared unaware of what they had been doing. Quinn made a mental note to talk to Samson so he could use his influence with the mayor, a vampire hybrid, to smooth things over for those kids.

Turning back to the mansion while his friends continued to keep an eye on the crowd, he glanced up at the roof. The fire was contained to a small area, flames working their way through the shingles. The engine's ladder was already at a sufficient height to attack the fire. When the water started to shoot from the fire hose, Quinn lowered his head and looked back at his friends. They had spread out, each of them positioning themselves at strategic locations from which to counterattack should Keegan make a move.

Nina stayed close to Amaury, Rose was backing up Wesley, while Zane and Amaury stood battle-ready at the periphery. Relieved he turned his head back toward the entrance, when realization hit him.

Shit! Oliver and Cain were missing.

He scanned the crowd once more, his eyes racing from one face to the next, but Oliver and Cain were nowhere to be seen.

Something was wrong. Concern for his protégé and his colleague made him spring into action. He walked up the steps to the front door. One fireman stood guard, blocking the entrance.

"Step back, sir, you can't go in there."

But this time Quinn wasn't going to obey any commands. He allowed his power to flow and sent his thoughts into the man's mind, until he stepped aside and let him enter.

The foyer and staircase were illuminated, but nobody had switched on any lights in any of the other rooms. Quinn used his night vision and sense of smell to guide him through the house. The two had to be somewhere in there. Rounding another corner, he picked up the scent of vampire. He followed it down the corridor, cautiously looking around him, walking softly so he couldn't be heard.

Not that any human would have heard him over the din in the house that the firemen were producing. But he was still aware that Keegan had to have caused all this and therefore couldn't be far away.

Before he reached the kitchen, he heard a noise coming from the laundry room. Quinn slid along the wall, then tested the door. It was ajar. Heavy breathing originated from inside the small room. He filled his lungs with the scent and let out a sigh of relief.

Pushing the door open, he entered.

"What's wrong?"

The glaring red color in Oliver's eyes was impossible to miss, as were the claws that were holding him back from charging out the door: Cain had slung his arms around him, immobilizing him.

"He wants their blood," Cain pressed out. "The humans out there . . . the scent is too much for him."

Oliver looked like a wild animal, his fangs protruding from his mouth. Sharp claws were where his fingers had been, and his eyes glared with aggression.

"Shit!"

As he rushed to help Cain, Quinn felt guilt blast through him. He hadn't spent much time with his protégé to help him through the change. He should have been by his side, leading him outside and staying with him to help him control his urges.

"Oliver, I'm so sorry. It'll be okay. You'll get through this."

He grabbed Oliver's arms and held him in a vice grip, then motioned to Cain. "Get bottled blood from the pantry. He has to feed right now."

Cain nodded. "You got it." He rushed out the door.

Quinn looked into Oliver's eyes, hoping to connect with him, to get his attention. But it appeared that his protégé didn't even see him.

"Oliver, talk to me. It's me, Quinn, your sire."

He shook him lightly, then harder. No reaction. He felt the strength with which the kid was fighting him to get out of his hold, but as an older vampire, Quinn was stronger.

"Everything will be good in a minute. Trust me. You'll feel better in a little while. I'm sorry I wasn't here for you."

The door burst open and Cain rushed in, two bottles of blood in his hands. Setting one on the washer, he unscrewed the other.

"Feed him," Quinn ordered.

Cain led the bottle to Oliver's lips and started pouring the red liquid into his mouth. At the first swallow, Quinn felt the tension in his body release.

It took only seconds for Oliver to down the bottle.

"Give him the second one too. We've gotta be sure that he's sated." Considering how wild Oliver had looked, Quinn wondered if a third bottle might be needed to subdue the kid's lust for human blood.

Slowly, he felt Oliver's muscles relax under his grip. He stopped fighting. Quinn watched as his claws turned back into fingers and the red glare in his eyes dissipated.

"He looks better already," Cain remarked and removed the second empty bottle from Oliver's lips.

Suddenly, Oliver seemed to realize where he was and what had happened. A rueful look crossed his face.

"I'm sorry. I didn't . . . I couldn't . . . I wanted . . ." He broke off and dropped his lids, clearly ashamed of his actions.

Quinn released his arms and pulled him into an embrace, patting his head. "It's happened to all of us before. I should have been there for you. I should have known that the crowd of humans outside the front door would create too strong a scent for you to resist. It's not your fault."

Oliver lifted his head. "I disappointed you."

"What happened is natural. And it will continue to happen until we've got it under control. But I know you're strong. Stronger than those urges. You can do it."

"I hope so," Oliver mused then turned his head to Cain. "Thanks for helping me."

Cain shrugged. "Hey, whatever it takes."

Quinn released his protégé from his arms. "Let's get you upstairs."

"But I thought we had to evacuate," Oliver protested.

"Screw that. The fire is pretty much under control from what I saw. You're staying inside. We'll smuggle you past the firemen to your room, and if they see us, we'll wipe their memories."

Cain peeked out the door into the corridor. "All clear."

They quietly snuck out of the laundry room and rounded the next corner. Quinn arrested his movement and pulled back, stretching his arm to the back to stop his friends from going any farther.

A fireman came down the stairs, but instead of heading out the door, he turned a corner, going in the opposite direction. Unlike the other firemen Quinn had seen earlier, this one wasn't wearing an oxygen tank on this back.

Just as he turned toward the door to the basement and garage, Quinn caught a glimpse of him. He read the nametag on his uniform. *Cheng* it said. His eyes shot up to the guy's face. The man was clearly Caucasian, not Asian as the name would suggest. Within a split-second he noticed something else: the man's aura. It wasn't human, nor was his scent, which now drifted toward Quinn. The man was a vampire.

And there was only one reason a strange vampire would be in this house: he had to be one of Keegan's men. Quinn was pretty sure that it wasn't Keegan himself since Rose had mentioned that he had dark hair and this man's hair, sticking out from beneath his helmet, was clearly blond. He briefly wondered how the vampire had been able to infiltrate into the group of firefighters, but figured that he would have had to employ mind control for them not to realize that he wasn't Cheng.

Quinn turned to his friends and put his finger on his lips, then made a motion for them to remain where they were. As soon as the intruder had opened the door to the basement and disappeared, Quinn stalked after him.

Quietly, he opened the door and set a foot on the stairs leading to the basement. It was dark, but he needed no light to know where the other vampire was heading. Even Quinn could smell it now: the scent of human sweat. Blake had worked out down here in the last twenty-four hours, and his scent still clung to the area. It appeared that the intruder was following the human scent to find if Blake was hidden down here.

Quinn made sure to avoid the stair that creaked and reached the bottom of the stairs without being noticed. Despite the commotion in the rest of the house, it was quiet in the garage. Barely a sound drifted to him as he followed Keegan's man toward the door to the gym. He kept back behind a wall and readied himself to attack.

Automatically his hand went to his back pocket to reach for the flail he'd placed there earlier in the evening and realized too late that he'd gotten rid of it when the fire captain had entered the home.

Quinn suppressed a curse. He couldn't use his gun with the silver bullets to bring down the enemy vampire. First, the shot could possibly attract some of the firemen, and secondly, he didn't want to kill the guy. He wanted him alive so he could be questioned. He wasn't as good a shot as Thomas, and the danger of hitting a vital organ or major artery and having him bleed out quickly or, worse, combust instantly was too great.

Which only left him with one weapon: the throwing stars he carried in his jacket pocket. Before he could pull them out, the vampire opened the door to the gym and disappeared inside.

Shit! Throwing stars were useless in close combat, and now there was no other choice but to enter the gym, which was no larger than fifteen by fifteen feet, and engage the bastard in a fist fight. Not something he was particularly looking forward to.

He placed his hand on the doorknob and inhaled. The scent of vampire and a sound from behind him assaulted him at once, and he whirled around. His heart came to a standstill, and his fist, which had been ready to strike, stopped in mid movement.

Rose, he mouthed.

She leaned toward him, whispering into his ear, "Thought you might need some help."

He rolled his eyes. "You shouldn't have followed me," he murmured into her ear. "One of Keegan's men is in there."

She moved away from him, pulling a long chain from her jacket pocket and grinned.

Let's get him. Her lips moved, but no words came out.

Quinn nodded and took the chain from her, wrapping one end over each gloved hand. When he heard steps in the gym, he knew the guy was moving toward the door, having searched the gym and found nothing.

He heard the sound of numbers being punched into a phone, then the vampire's low voice. "He's gone ... No, I'm sure he was here ... Yes, sir."

The person on the other end could only be Keegan. Maybe the fact that this vampire was reporting back to him that Blake was nowhere to be found would turn out to be a good thing.

Quinn motioned Rose to step behind the door while he took the other side when he heard their enemy move again. When the door opened and the vampire came out, Quinn pounced. The vampire's fire helmet fell to the floor as Quinn slung the chain around his neck from behind. He forced him to the ground by kicking his knee into the guy's back, wrapping the silver tighter around his exposed neck.

"Welcome to the Pacific Heights B&B," Quinn hissed. "I hope you'll enjoy your stay."

27

A couple of hours after the fire department responded to the call, they had cleaned up and were on their way back to their station. The neighbors had started to return to their homes as soon as it was clear that the fire was small and had only caused minimal damage to the roof. The firemen had boarded up the area and cautioned Quinn and his colleagues not to let anybody go up to the attic until it was repaired. But they had lifted the evacuation order and declared the home safe.

Everybody was back inside, but the night wasn't over yet.

Amaury and Wesley were keeping watch on the house, and Cain was with Oliver, who had protested, saying he didn't need a babysitter. Quinn had begged to differ.

"By now Keegan must know that we've got his guy," Quinn said, looking at Rose.

They both stood just outside the gym while Zane guarded the prisoner who'd been tied up with silver chains.

Rose snorted. "He probably thinks that we killed him. It's what he would do. Maybe we should."

"He's more valuable to us alive."

"If you think that Keegan will trade for him, I have to disappoint you. I've seen him kill his own men for minor infractions. Hell, he staked one of his bodyguards just for making a comment about his dick."

Quinn gave her a questioning look. "He what?"

Rose waved him off. "Long story. But I'm saying he won't lift a finger to get his assassin back. Keegan only thinks of himself. It doesn't matter how many people will lose their lives in the pursuit of his goal."

"I have no plans about trading our prisoner. I want to find out what he knows."

"He won't talk. He knows that if he talks he's a dead man. You might as well kill him now, because if you leave him alive, Keegan will finish him off. He knows it too."

Quinn frowned. "Charming man, this Keegan. But we'll get some intel, one way or another."

Rose's pretty face pulled into a doubting grimace. "Good luck with torturing him."

Quinn grinned. "You obviously haven't seen Zane's methods. Come, let's check on them."

He was about to open the door to the gym, when he turned abruptly, remembering something else he wanted to tell her.

"Oh, and Rose, thanks for helping out earlier, but I could have done it on my own. You should have stayed with the others where you were safe."

"Ungrateful bastard," she hissed.

"I said thanks, didn't I?"

She let out an exasperated breath. "A thank you followed by a *but* doesn't count."

"How about this then? Does that count?"

Before she could answer, he pulled her into his arms and captured her mouth. It took only seconds for her to soften, her pliable body molding itself to his.

He briefly lifted his lips from hers only to whisper another *thank you*, then went on to ravage her mouth. As tempting as it was to continue, he knew this wasn't the time or place. Reluctantly, he released her lips and gazed at her. Her lids had dropped to half mast and her mouth looked red and moist and utterly sensual.

"I love the way you look when you've just been kissed."

Her eyes shot open, but she couldn't hide the vulnerability that resided in them. That he could still do this to her—make her look like a debutante after her first kiss—floored him. His heart beat so loudly in his chest that he thought it might burst.

"Come."

Quinn opened the door to the gym and pulled her into the room.

Inside, Zane was hard at work, doing what he did best: convincing an unwilling subject to talk. However, his friend looked a little more frustrated than usual.

"Problems?" Quinn asked.

Zane shrugged. "Just a little stubbornness I'm going to have to beat out of him first."

"He won't talk," Rose predicted. "Keegan has that effect on his men. They're too afraid of him."

"Nobody has ever resisted me," Zane claimed and lashed an angry glare at his prisoner. "Neither will you when I'm done with you."

The captured vampire lifted his head from his chest and grunted. "Never."

From what Quinn could see, Zane had already inflicted painful injuries to the vampire's face, torso and extremities. Yet nothing seemed to have worked. Not wanting to lose out on this opportunity to acquire useful information, Quinn pulled out his cell.

"We can do this another way. There's always Gabriel."

Quinn dialed a number and waited for the call to connect.

"Yeah?"

"Hey, Gabriel. Keegan's people made an attempt tonight. But they didn't get far. However, we got a prisoner in the bargain. He won't talk though. Can you come over and help us out?"

"Sure. Be there in ten."

He disconnected the call and shoved the cell back in his front pocket.

"And how is Gabriel going to help when Zane can't get anything out of him?" Rose leaned closer and lowered her voice to a whisper. "Between you and me, Zane looks a lot scarier than Gabriel."

But Zane had heard her nevertheless. "And I don't just look it. But Gabriel gets to cheat."

Quinn grinned. "I wouldn't call his gift cheating."

"What gift?" Rose asked.

"He reads memories."

And truth be told, at this moment Quinn envied his boss for it, because if he could access memories the way Gabriel could, he would have a much easier time, figuring out Rose and why she had stayed away from him for two centuries. But then, would he really want to see all she'd been through, see the men she'd been with? He shook his head, trying to rid himself of the thought.

"He what? I don't understand."

Quinn pointed at the prisoner who now stared at him, interest flickering in his irises. "Gabriel can dive into his memory and see what he's seen. He'll be able to tell us where Keegan is hiding. Once we have the information, we're going in." Then he stared straight at the captured vampire, addressing him directly. "Nobody can resist Gabriel's gift. And there's nothing you can do about it."

Realization spread in his eyes, and Quinn could firmly see this mind working. Rose was right: he was afraid of Keegan more than he feared torture. His arms bound behind him, his legs shackled to one of the machines, he struggled against his restraints. But they didn't give an inch.

Then he glared back at them. "There is."

Before Quinn understood what he meant, he saw the prisoner work his mouth as if he was chewing something, or trying to move something around in his mouth.

"Ah, shit!" Zane yelled and jumped him, trying to force his mouth open. "Suicide pill," he said by way of explanation as he continued to try and pry the vampire's clamped jaws apart.

Quinn rushed to him to help, but it was too late. He heard a tiny cracking sound as if something had popped. An instant later, the captive's body turned hot, and both he and Zane backed away from him.

The hostile vampire burst into flames from the inside, incinerating within seconds.

"Fuck!"

Quinn could only echo his colleague's curse. Behind him, Rose gasped uncontrollably.

"Oh my god! What happened?" she asked, stunned.

"In World War II they handed out cyanide capsules to high ranking officers so they could kill them themselves if they got captured," Zane explained. "While cyanide doesn't work on vampires, silver does. He must have had a silver nitrate capsule hidden in his mouth."

Quinn could only agree. "Silver nitrate, if ingested, causes spontaneous combustion."

"So much for getting anything useful out of him," Zane added.

"Back to the drawing board," Quinn conceded.

***

Thomas didn't have to look over his shoulder to know that Eddie was standing over him as he was sitting at his computer. In the far corner of his living room, Portia and Delilah were keeping Blake busy with a game of Wii while the baby slept peacefully on the couch, oblivious to the noise the adults were making.

"Still nothing?" Eddie asked and pulled a chair closer to sit next to him.

Thomas gave him a sideways glance, willing his eyes not to linger too long on the young vampire's broad shoulders and narrow hips. All it would result in was a bolt of lust coursing through his body, scorching him from the inside. And he was determined not to go down that road, knowing it was a dead end.

"It's like this Keegan is a ghost. I can't find anything on him, not even with all the info Rose gave us. All we have is where he last resided, but Rose already knew that. Before that, there's nothing. And from my contacts in Chicago I know that he's already cleaned out that place and disappeared," Thomas elaborated.

Eddie frowned. "It's not like you to find nothing. You're the best."

He smiled at his mentee's enthusiastic exclamation.

"I wish. But even I can't find anything. No birth certificate, not even a fake one, no social security number, no driver's license, no photos of him, no property in his name, no trusts that lead to him, nothing. It's impossible that a man with his apparent power can remain invisible like this. But there's no trace of him. Keegan doesn't exist."

Eddie gave him a puzzled look. "You mean Rose invented him?"

Thomas shook his head. "No. Keegan invented himself."

And that bothered him. Because only a man who had something very important to hide would go to the pains of erasing every trace of himself and turn into a ghost.

"But why?"

"Because he needs to hide who he really is."

It was the only explanation that made sense to Thomas. And for a tiny moment he felt a kindred spirit with this man, because just like him, Thomas had made sure his own origins would never be discovered. He'd all but destroyed any evidence of who he was.

The insistent ring of his phone pulled him from his thoughts. Automatically he reached for it.

Glancing at caller ID, he answered. "Yes, Quinn?"

"We need to get Blake back here."

"Already?" He lowered his voice to make sure Blake, who was still playing Wii, wouldn't hear him. "Has Keegan already attacked?"

"He has, but he didn't succeed."

"Don't you think it's safer if he stays here? The B&B has been compromised."

"He isn't safe anywhere. Keegan is combing the city for him. Rose would rather have him here where we have the manpower to protect him than at your place. No offense."

Thomas shrugged. "None taken. So, what's the plan?"

"We're consolidating all resources at the B&B. We want you and Eddie to bring him in and then stay here."

Eddie gave him a thumbs-up as he heard the news, clearly ready for some action. And it suited Thomas fine too, considering they still hadn't executed Samson's orders to make a sweep for the flash drive containing the list of vampires.

"We're on our way."

He disconnected the phone and swiveled in his chair. "Blake."

The human turned his head. "Yeah?"

"Training exercise is over. We're heading back to the base."

"Did we win?" he asked eagerly.

Thomas grinned. "Yeah, we won."

If only one battle. The war was still ahead of them. But there was no need to worry the kid.

28

Rose sighed in relief when she heard the SUV that carried Blake enter the garage. She felt like hugging him when he walked into the foyer, but refrained from such a show of emotion. Knowing her grandson, he would have misconstrued the situation and thought she was coming onto him.

Thomas and Eddie were right behind him. She had met Eddie very briefly at Haven's party, but had had more contact with Thomas when she had given him information on Keegan. Adding two more vampires to the guards at the B&B filled her with confidence. Not that she had any illusions that they could trick Keegan into thinking for very long that Blake wasn't at the B&B. He had to suspect that they were bringing him back. It didn't matter. Protecting Blake at the B&B was ultimately safer than keeping him hidden at Thomas's house. By now Keegan had to know about Scanguards and was probably already trying to hack into their systems to find out where Blake could be hidden.

"So we won, huh?" Blake grinned from one ear to the other and looked at Quinn and her.

"Good work," Quinn praised. "You must be starving. Why don't you join Nina and Wesley in the kitchen? I think they cooked a late supper."

"Great! I can eat a whole cow!" Blake claimed and patted his belly.

"And then you might want to get some shuteye. It's well past midnight, and you've got a long day ahead of you."

"Sounds good."

Blake trotted off toward the kitchen. As soon as he was out of earshot, Thomas pointed toward the stairs.

"Eddie and I will get situated. Which rooms are available?"

Only now did Rose notice the small backpack Thomas had slung over his shoulder.

"There's only one room empty on the second floor, next to mine. If you guys don't mind sharing?" Quinn answered.

Rose caught an odd expression on Thomas's face, as if he would rather stay by himself. Knowing that Quinn would most likely not use his room anyway, she figured there was no need to make the two guys uncomfortable.

She tugged at Quinn's arm and leaned closer. "Why don't you give up your room?" she murmured.

Immediately Quinn stared at her. "Why would I—?"

He stopped, his gaze suddenly dropping to her mouth where her tongue darted out to moisten her suddenly dry lips.

"You won't need it."

Realization darkened his eyes, lust suddenly blazing from them. Without breaking eye contact, he gave Thomas new instructions.

"Take rooms 23 and 24. I'll move my stuff into Rose's room later."

"Great!" Thomas answered, relief evident in his voice as he headed up the stairs, Eddie on his heels.

A moment later, Quinn pulled her into his arms. "How can I thank you for the invitation?"

Need bubbled up in her. She bit her lip. "It's not as much an invitation as it is a demand."

His mouth twisted into a smile. "How so?"

"As a wife, I have certain rights. One of them is to be bedded by my husband."

She noticed his Adam's apple move as he swallowed. Then his hand on her back slipped lower, palming her backside and pressing her closer.

"Your husband has certain rights too, as well as duties. As luck would have it, they coincide with yours."

"Well, then I'm a lucky lady." She rubbed herself against him, feeling the ridge in his pants swell and harden.

Quinn's eyes shimmered golden as he expelled a hasty breath. Rose smiled, relishing the power she had over him. To turn him into a man controlled by his desire made her feel strong and desirable. How had she ever managed to live without him for so long?

"Are you busy right now?" she husked.

His lips moved closer, hovering over hers. "I've got all the time in the world."

Sliding her hands down to his buttocks, she dragged his hips against hers, enjoying the hard outline of his flesh rubbing against her stomach.

Everything else was forgotten. Quinn's presence, his arms around her, the evidence of his desire pressing against her belly, sent her back to her wedding night. She'd been scared; yet at the same time, she'd been curious. And when he'd revealed his male glory to her, she had salivated. She'd never seen anything more exciting. And it remained true until today. Quinn was still the only man who could make her feel like a real woman. It didn't matter that she now had the body of a vampire.

"Take me now," she whispered and slanted her lips over his mouth.

Somebody clicked his tongue, making Rose snap her head to the side and step out of Quinn's embrace.

Zane leaned against the door to the living room, arms crossed over his chest, eyes rolling.

"Get a room."

Quinn gave him a sideways grin. "Good advice." Without being the least bit embarrassed, he took her hand and turned toward the door.

Rose avoided Zane's assessing gaze as she walked past him, feeling more than a little flushed. The fact that Quinn's colleague knew exactly what they were about to do shouldn't bother her, after all, she was no blushing debutante anymore. However, it made her nervous.

"Maybe we'd better go over our plan of action before Keegan attacks again," she said quickly, trying to slip her hand from Quinn's. But he held on, as if he'd foreseen her action.

One side of Zane's mouth pulled up slightly. He seemed to enjoy her discomfort. "I can cover you for a half hour."

Winking at her, Quinn addressed his friend. "Make that an hour. And thanks. Appreciate it."

Less than a minute later she found herself outside the door to her room on the second floor, Quinn's hands all over her, his mouth kissing her greedily.

"God, woman, if you keep playing me like that, I'll lose all respect of my colleagues." Despite the complaint, there was no reprimand in his voice.

"Do you care?"

"Right now? Right now, all I care about is getting inside you."

The feral look in his eyes sent a lightning bolt through her core, making her body hum with excitement. His hands were already on her jeans, reaching for the top button, when she turned the door knob and pushed the door inwards.

They tumbled into the room. Quinn slammed the door shut with his foot and pressed her against it, when a movement caught her eye.

"What the f—?"

Pushing Quinn away from her, she glared at the two intruders: Thomas and Eddie. Their guilty conscience was pasted as thickly on their faces as makeup on an old whore. Thomas held a device in his hand that looked like a wand of some sort.

"What are you doing here?" Rose tried to keep the rage under control that started boiling up in her.

Thomas and Eddie exchanged terse looks.

"Answer her!" Quinn demanded. "Because I'd like to know too."

"Crap," Eddie cursed.

Thomas straightened his shoulders. "We're sweeping the room for bugs; standard procedure."

Rose narrowed her eyes. She'd never heard such bullshit in her life. "Bugs, my ass! You're looking for the flash drive, aren't you? Go on, admit it!"

"Fuck!" Quinn hissed, making her shift her attention to him.

"Did you know of this? Did you?"

He glared back at her. "No, I didn't! You should know me better than to think I'd go behind your back."

He held her glare for several long tense seconds without wavering. Satisfied that he had told the truth, she nodded.

"If I'd known about it, I would have stopped it," he added and turned to his two colleagues. "I want an explanation. And I want it now. Whose idea was this?"

"Samson ordered it," Thomas admitted grudgingly.

Rose felt suspicion about the owner of Scanguards rise in her. "Why?"

Did he want the list for himself, knowing how valuable it was to anybody who had it in his possession? Did he want the power that came with it? So much for trusting Scanguards and their high ethics. Clearly, no such thing existed in the vampire world.

"He wants to make sure it's destroyed," came Thomas's curt reply.

"I don't believe you!" she cried out. "You all want the same: power, control, supremacy. With the information on the flash drive you'll have all of that and more. Anybody who possesses it will try to use the information for his own purposes—and depending on how strong this person already is . . ." She allowed her unfinished sentence to linger in the air, before continuing. "So don't tell me Samson wanted to destroy it. If he did, he wouldn't have gone behind my back searching for it!"

Thomas's calm demeanor didn't change. "You do him wrong. Samson has no need for power. He's content. Finally content."

Rose caught an odd tone in his voice, almost as if he seemed somewhat envious of his boss. He took a step closer before he continued.

"He doesn't lust for power. He felt that the flash drive would be better protected if it was in Scanguards' hands. You're not trained for this. And it's exactly what you hired us for."

"What I hired you for? I hired you to protect my grandson, not to snoop around in my personal affairs. I've kept the flash drive from Keegan's hands so far, and I'll continue to do so. It's safe. He'll never find out where it is. And it will stay there until Keegan is dead. Only then will I destroy it."

Thomas stared at her, then stumbled back two paces. "And what if we don't get him? Are you prepared to run for eternity?"

Rose thrust up her chin. "If I destroy the data now, I might as well paint a target symbol over my heart and walk outside for him to stake me. The flash drive is the only protection I have against Keegan. He won't kill me as long as he knows I'm the only one who knows where it's hidden."

She felt Quinn reach for her hand and squeeze it.

"She's right, Thomas, and you know it. Once Keegan knows the data is destroyed, what's stopping him from going on a killing rampage? At least now, he's still trying to negotiate. It's giving us the best chance we'll ever have to set a trap for him. He has to come to us because he wants something from us. Once that something is gone, we have no way of reeling him in."

A skeptical look crossed over Thomas's face. Next to him, Eddie shifted from one foot to the other, rubbing the back of his neck at the same time.

"He has a point," Eddie said. "It's better if nobody else knows where the drive is. It's the only thing that will keep her safe."

"What about Blake?" Thomas challenged, looking back at her. "He's still as vulnerable as the day you stole the data."

"I trust Scanguards to keep him safe." She smiled at Quinn, whose eyes radiated with warmth.

He mouthed a silent *thank you* to her.

"Well, at least you've picked the right gang to protect him," Thomas answered drily.

Eddie grinned and slapped his mentor on the shoulder. "Because we're the best at this."

"What about Samson?" Thomas threw in.

"I'll talk to him about this," Quinn answered.

29

Blake blinked as a faint ray of sunshine tickled his nose through the half-closed curtains. He'd been too tired the night before to pull them shut completely and had fallen into bed after gorging himself on the delicious stew Nina had cooked.

He squinted at the radio alarm on the nightstand. It was already midday. Sitting up, he listened for any sounds in the house, but it was quiet. He padded to the window in his pajama bottoms and pulled up the sash to let fresh air into the room. Instantly, the room was even brighter than before.

He pushed the curtains back and looked down into the back yard, the fire escape right outside his window partially blocking his view. As he pulled his head back in, he bumped against the window.

"Ouch!" he complained, rubbing the back of his head.

His eyes caught at the glass, and he suddenly noticed that it seemed much darker than a conventional windowpane. He leaned in to inspect it and noticed what appeared to be a thin plastic film covering the glass. It had a light brown color. Odd! Why would somebody want to darken the room when San Francisco wasn't exactly graced with all-year-round sunny weather? There was no chance of overheating in this foggy city.

He shrugged and held his overly full stomach. The rich food was giving him heartburn. Maybe he should have warned Nina that he was lactose intolerant so she would go easy on the cream she'd poured into the stew. But he would have rather bitten his lip than do so. He didn't want to be looked at as a weakling by his trainers. For all he knew, they would drop him from the program like a hot potato.

And what an odd program this was. Their unconventional hours were only the start. Spending half the day and evening at the safe house in Twin Peaks had been strange to say the least. He'd passed the time playing Wii with the other agents. Were they actually paying him for this? He could hardly believe his luck.

Feeling another bout of heartburn assault him he turned to his bag and rummaged through it, but realized quickly that he'd forgotten to pack antacids in his haste. Oliver and Cain had rushed him when packing his stuff to move to the house, and now he was paying the price for it. Somewhere in this house they had to have some sort of medicine cabinet stocked with the basics.

Without getting dressed, he left his room, wearing only his PJ bottoms, and trotted downstairs.

It was still quiet despite the late hour. Suited him fine; he wasn't a morning person anyway, and if this company preferred to operate later in the day and into the night, he had no objections.

Nobody had really explained the layout of the home all that thoroughly when he'd moved in two days earlier, so he decided to simply open a few doors to see what he could find. Truth be told, he was antsy and raring to do something, preferably take part in another training exercise. And this time, he wanted to be the decoy. He was sure that Wesley had had fun in that role. Now it was his turn.

Pushing the first door along the first floor corridor open, he entered and looked around. It was an office. He glanced around quickly. It was tidy. Trying a few of the drawers, he realized that everything was locked. Shrugging, he left and continued his explorations.

When he reached the next door, he eased it open and peered inside the room. An oversized washer and dryer lined one wall. Since there was no chance of finding antacids in a laundry room, he turned to leave, but something odd caught his eye. He pivoted and took two steps into the room.

His hand reached out and lifted the empty bottle that stood on the dryer. Remnants of red liquid were encrusted on its bottom. The clear glass was imprinted with only two letters: *AB+*.

Blake sniffed and recoiled, instantly being reminded of the many bar fights that lay in his past. The smell was the same as when he'd tasted his own blood when some jerk had broken his nose with a well-aimed punch.

"Yuck!" he ground out.

This couldn't possibly be what it smelled like. No way did blood come in bottles. Sure, if there was a bleeder in the house, then maybe he might keep bags of blood in the fridge for an emergency transfusion, he knew that much from the science channel, but who on earth would keep blood in bottles? No, his sense of smell had to be off. Maybe it was because of that damn heartburn that plagued him.

He set the weird bottle back where he found it and left the room. His best chance at finding a remedy for his stomach troubles was most likely in the kitchen. For sure, that's where they kept any meds like that.

Blake entered the kitchen and was surprised to see Wesley sitting at the kitchen table, his head buried in a book. At the sound of the door closing behind him, the other trainee's head snapped toward him.

"Oh, hey, Blake. Didn't think you'd be up this early."

"Early? Guess you're not used to this odd schedule either, huh? I mean—" He motioned his head to the ceiling. "—can you believe that our trainers sleep practically all day? What kind of company allows that?"

Wesley grinned from one ear to the other. "A pretty cool company." Then he pointed to the kitchen counter. "Want some coffee? I made a fresh pot."

Blake was about to decline, knowing that coffee would make him feel even worse, but thought otherwise of it. He didn't want Wesley to think he was a weakling.

"Sure."

"Milk is in the fridge."

"I drink it black, thanks." No need to add another dose of lactose to his sensitive stomach.

As he poured himself a cup, he opened up one of the cabinets, clandestinely looking for some antacids.

"What do you need?" Wesley asked.

"Uh, sugar," he lied and opened another cabinet, but came up empty once more. Darn, was he the only one in this house who used antacids?

"On the table."

Pasting a smile on his face he turned back to Wesley and joined him at the kitchen table.

"What are you reading?"

"Just some research," Wesley deflected and closed the book, shoving it under a newspaper, before Blake could read the title.

His curiosity aroused, he reached for it and pulled it out before his fellow trainee had a chance to stop him.

"Hey, that's mine!"

Wesley reached for it, but Blake pulled away from the table, then read the book's title.

"*Witchcraft: Get your potions just right?*" He tossed Wesley an incredulous look. "You'd better not have any of the trainers see what crap you're reading. They'll think you're wacko!"

Wesley tore the book from his grip and rose hastily, his chair making a loud noise as it scraped along the kitchen floor. "None of your business, or theirs! And I would suggest that you don't start snooping around. You might not like what you find."

Clearly annoyed, he turned and headed for the door.

"Hey, Wesley, don't be such a hothead. I don't care what you read. I'm not gonna tell the others."

But Wesley was already out the door. Moments later he heard the door to the living room being opened, then closing again. Great, it had taken him about two minutes to piss his only ally off. And he'd wanted to talk to him about how his mission as decoy had gone. Even though they had eaten together the night before, he hadn't had a chance to talk to him in private since Nina had been around. He figured it wasn't cool milking another trainee for information in front of a trainer.

"Uh, screw it," he murmured to himself.

He dumped the coffee into the sink, glad he didn't have to drink it now. Then he went about to open every drawer and cabinet he could find. No inch remained unexplored. No antacids. All he noticed was that for the fact this was such a large house and a large and modern kitchen, it was only sparsely equipped. Considering that at least ten people were currently staying there, he doubted that there were enough knives and forks available for everybody to eat at the same time.

He shrugged. Not his problem.

As the burning in his stomach intensified, he knew he had to take matters into his own hands and go to the nearest drugstore to buy what he needed. One of the rules instantly flashed in his mind: *don't leave the house on your own.*

Since he'd just pissed off Wesley, he would rather bite his tongue than ask him to accompany him. It didn't matter. Nobody was awake yet. They wouldn't even know that he'd left the house. And if he snuck out through one of the side doors, Wesley wouldn't hear him either.

Blake looked down at himself. Crap, he needed to get dressed first and fetch his wallet. But before he could even reach the kitchen door, it burst open and Oliver charged in, dressed in his pajamas, his body advancing toward the locked pantry in a blur of movement.

Blake gasped in surprise, his heart stopping simultaneously. If he'd still been holding the coffee mug, he would have dropped it now.

Having heard his gasp, Oliver whirled around and faced him. Blake wished instantly he hadn't, because the creature that looked at him was more animal than man: eyes glaring red, a wild look about him, his body tense.

Tilting his head, Oliver's eyes assessed him. His nostrils flared, and it reminded him of a bull or a horse. When he sniffed and approached with the graceful movements of a predator, Blade shrunk back from him, quickly looking behind him, wondering where to escape to.

"Oliver, what's wrong?" he stammered.

But his trainer didn't respond. Instead he peeled his lips back and exposed his white teeth, Oliver's gaze not pinned on his face anymore, but sliding down to somewhere on his neck.

"Shit!" Blake yelled.

Oliver's teeth weren't evenly shaped. Two of his canines were longer and pointy. As if he'd put on Halloween props. His teeth looked like fangs.

Setting one foot in front of the other, Oliver appeared as if he was fighting to stay back. But he kept advancing.

"Run," he pressed out between clenched teeth.

Despite the warning, Blake didn't move: he was frozen in shock, paralyzed. His limbs didn't follow his command, his legs were heavy like lead and didn't move.

Something akin to regret flashed in Oliver's eyes, before they turned a darker red.

"I can't . . . tried to resist . . . "

Whatever else he wanted to say died on his lips when he pounced. Blake felt Oliver's hands dig into his shoulders and pull him against his body. He struggled against his grip without success, when he should have easily pushed him off. Oliver was less bulky than himself, less muscular, yet he didn't even break a sweat, keeping him immobile.

Then he felt Oliver's fangs dig into his neck.

Shit, he was going to die!

30

The scream came from downstairs, catapulting Quinn out of bed. Rose, whose warm body had been molded against his, woke simultaneously. Exchanging a worried look, they recognized immediately who had screamed.

"Blake!"

Jumping up, Quinn snatched his pants off the floor and pulled them on, not bothering with underwear or anything else. A split-second later he was out the door, knowing Rose wouldn't be far behind him. He charged down the stairs and past the other guestrooms. Doors opened as he flew past them, voices chasing his rapid descent to the first floor.

The scent of human blood now reached his nostrils.

"Shit!"

Had Keegan managed to gain access to the house? It should be impossible: Wesley and Nina were supposed to be keeping watch during the day to alert them should anybody approach the house.

Panicked, Quinn almost collided with Wesley who came running from the living room.

"Is it Keegan?" Quinn asked without slowing down.

"Nobody got in," Wesley claimed, following him.

Voices and footsteps from the other residents filled the previously quiet house.

Quinn kicked the kitchen door open and barreled in. He rocked to an abrupt halt when his eyes quickly assessed the situation.

"Oliver! Fuck!"

His protégé had his fangs lodged deep in Blake's neck as the latter struggled against the attack, his eyes open and drenched in fear and panic.

Quinn rushed to them and clamped his hands around Oliver's arms, holding him immobile. He couldn't simply pull him away from Blake or he would risk tearing his grandson's neck open.

"Release him! Withdraw your fangs! Now! I command you as your sire!"

A low growl came from Oliver.

"Do it, son," Quinn urged more quietly. "You don't want to hurt him. I know you don't."

Slowly, Oliver's shoulders relaxed, and Quinn felt him shift his head backwards, away from Blake's neck. From the corner of his eye he saw that the kitchen was quickly getting crowded. The scream had woken everybody.

"Oh, God, no!" Rose screamed as she pushed past him and reached for Blake.

As Quinn pulled his protégé away from his grandson, he looked at the damage he'd done. The incisions on Blake's neck were deep and bleeding profusely. Blake instantly pressed his hand against it, but he was swaying.

Pushing Oliver behind him, Quinn barked out an order, "Cain, Amaury, take care of Oliver."

Then he reached for Blake. Simultaneously, he and Rose caught him before he could fall. But Blake struggled even against them, fear and distrust coloring his eyes.

"Don't touch me!" he yelled, trying to pull away from them.

"He's bleeding so much!" Rose's eyes brimmed with tears.

Quinn slid his hand over Blake's, slowly prying it away from his neck. Rose was right; there was a lot of blood loss. It had to be stopped immediately.

"Don't be afraid, Blake, I'm not going to hurt you. I'll seal the wound."

Blake wildly shook his head, trying to get away from him. "No! Oh, God, no! Shit!"

"Hold his head still, Rose."

As Rose put her hands on Blake's head, his eyes shot to her. "You too? You're all like him aren't you?" he cried out in desperation.

Not losing any time, Quinn lowered his mouth to Blake's wound and let his tongue snake out. Quickly and efficiently he licked over the site. Twice, until he felt that the wound had closed due to the healing effects of his saliva. The bleeding stopped instantly.

Just as quickly, he pulled back from Blake, not wanting to cause him any more distress. He caught Rose's pleading look when he straightened.

"Wipe his memory," she urged.

A frightened widening of Blake's eyes together with a shocked gasp, made Quinn contemplate her request for longer than he should. Then he slowly shook his head.

"I think he has a right to know."

"No!" Rose's protest was instantaneous.

Reaching for her, Quinn sent a silent plea to her. "It's for his own safety. We can't keep on wiping his memory whenever he sees something he shouldn't. He needs to know what's going on."

When she squeezed his hand and gave a little nod, he knew she had finally seen reason.

"But I'll be the one telling him."

Then she turned to Blake again, whose entire face was a mask of worry and fear. As soon as she loosened her grip on him, he jerked back from her.

"Now, now, son," Quinn tried to calm him, still holding onto his upper arms. "Just stay calm. Nobody wants to hurt you. We're all here to protect you."

Blake's doubtful look darted past him. Quinn turned his head and saw that Cain and Amaury were talking soothingly to Oliver, who looked devastated. He caught Oliver's look.

"I'm so sorry, Quinn. I didn't mean to disappoint you. I couldn't help it. The temptation . . . " Oliver dropped his head and turned away.

"We'll talk about it later," he assured his protégé and turned back to Blake. "Why don't you sit down, Blake."

Wesley pulled a chair to assist.

Quinn shot him a quick look. "And weren't you supposed to keep an eye on him during the day?"

"If your grandson wouldn't be such an ass, it would be easier not to avoid his company," Wesley griped. "But if he keeps on pissing people off by invading their privacy—"

"That's enough," Quinn interrupted.

"Grandson?" Blake croaked. "What the fuck?"

Quinn looked at Rose who pulled another chair and slunk into it. Now eyelevel with Blake, she leaned closer. Instinctively, Blake shrunk farther back into his.

Blake watched them with suspicion. His hand went to his neck where Oliver had bitten him, yet the skin was now flawless as if it had never happened. It was freaky to say the least. But he knew what he'd seen: Oliver had fangs, and that made him a vampire.

And if he was one, then the others had to be vampires too. When Quinn and Rose had held him while Quinn had licked his wound to seal it, he'd felt the same kind of supernatural strength from them as Oliver had displayed.

Shit! How could vampires exist and how the fuck had he gotten mixed up with them?

"Blake, honey," Rose suddenly started. "There's something you need to know. We're vampires, but—"

"No shit!" he interrupted. He'd figured that out in the last thirty seconds himself. There couldn't possibly be anything new she could tell him now. "The cat's out of the bag."

And now that he knew their secret, what would they do with him? He cast an assessing look at the assembled crowd. Nobody was missing. Amaury and Cain were huddled with Oliver who had turned away so Blake couldn't see his face anymore. Zane stood at the door as if wanting to make sure nobody entered or left the kitchen. Thomas and Eddie were frowning. Nina looked concerned, while Wesley had a defiant look on his face.

Jerk! He was ready to bet his first paycheck that Wesley had purposefully not come running to his aid, because he was still pissed off about that stupid book. For good measure, Blake glared at him before looking back at Rose.

"Blake, please remain calm. I'm sorry you had to find out this way. I wish I could have spared you this, but—" Her gaze strayed to Quinn, who answered with an encouraging nod. "—you need to know who we are. Quinn and I, we're your great-great-great-great-grandparents. You're our flesh and blood, and we'd do anything to keep you safe."

As Blake pushed back in his chair, its legs scraped on the tile floor, making an eerie sound in the kitchen. Nobody was saying anything, as if they were all waiting for his reaction.

"Bullshit!" He reared up from his seat and instantly swayed, gripping the backrest for support. Clearly, the blood loss was still affecting him.

But his mind was sharper than ever. They were vampires, all right, but no way in hell was he related to any of them.

"I'm no bloodsucker!" he protested. "I'm not like you!"

"Of course not," Quinn interrupted calmly. "You're entirely human, because Rose's and my daughter was conceived and born when we were both still human, back in 1814. Rose and I became vampires after that."

Blake looked at him, allowing his eyes to inspect his face, then did the same with Rose. The two looked nothing like anybody in his family. And besides, they looked younger than he!

"You're barely 25!"

Unexpectedly, Rose smiled at him. "One of the advantages of being a vampire: you don't age." She exchanged a warm smile with Quinn. "We'll always look as young as the day we were turned."

"Well I knew that, of course! I watch movies. I'm not stupid," Blake quickly replied. "But that doesn't mean we're related. So spit it out, what do you want from me?" He glared at them, then motioned his head toward Oliver. "Cause I already know what *he* wanted. And he's not getting it. I'd rather slit my own throat!"

Because nobody could ever find out that he'd found Oliver's bite arousing as hell. That's why he'd fought him with all he had. Because, fuck, he was no homo! He loved women, one hundred percent, and no fucking bloodsucker would ever get another chance at making him doubt his sexuality. No fucking way!

For good measure, he glared at the other two gays in the room: Thomas and Eddie. No matter how masculine the two had looked when he'd met them the day before, all dressed in their biker gear, there was no doubt in Blake's mind that the two were queer.

When Rose suddenly stood up from her chair and took a step toward him, he shrank back, hitting the kitchen counter behind him. As much as he didn't want to display fear in front of these predators, he couldn't help himself. He was outnumbered, and that alone freaked him out.

"Men in Black, my ass," he murmured under his breath. "More like Dracula."

"It's the truth. Quinn and I are your ancestors. And you're here because somebody wants to take revenge on me by hurting you. That's why we had to come up with this ruse; so we could protect you twenty-four-seven."

He shook his head, because he didn't want to believe it. It changed nothing about the facts. They were what they were. And somehow he

had to get away from them. Outsmart them, since fighting them was not
an option. There were too many of them. And if they were all as strong
as Oliver, Quinn, and Rose, he had a snowball's chance in hell at
landing even a single punch.

Mixed emotions battled for supremacy inside him, stirring him up.
He'd never been so confused in his entire life. While fear for his
immediate future was still at the forefront of his thoughts, other
emotions invaded. Confusion and disbelief were paramount, but
annoyance crept in too. They'd tricked him into believing that he'd
landed a fabulous job, when they'd lied to him from the start.

He felt like an idiot that he hadn't spotted their deception any
earlier. Hell, they'd fed him all kinds of crap, and he'd eaten it up like it
was mother's milk!

"I'm not stupid, you know!" he ground out.

"Nobody says you are," Rose cooed, her soft tone only underscoring
that she thought him to be a dimwit.

When she reached for him, he recoiled from her touch. At any other
time, he would have welcomed her hand on his skin, but not now. And
hell, if she was really his great-great-whatever than the fact that he'd
thought her hot was just utterly gross and disgusting!

"Don't touch me!"

He tossed a warning look at the vampires that all stared at him like
he was food and they were starving. Instinctively, he pressed his hand to
the spot where Oliver had bitten him only minutes earlier. Shit, they
were all after his blood.

"Nobody will hurt you," Quinn assured him. "Oliver is young, he
hasn't learned yet how to control himself. It won't happen again, I
swear it."

"You're right about that!" Because he'd be out of here as soon as he
could find a way to escape. He had no intention of waiting around until
the next one of them got hungry and took a bite out of him. Not even if
that hottie Nina was the one to do it.

Blake thrust his chin up in a show of defiance, when inside him
everything was crumbling. He'd put all his hopes into this new
endeavor. When he'd moved to San Francisco, he'd hoped to finally
find something that interested him, a job he could dig into and make his
own. For a few short days he'd believed himself in luck. Scanguards

probably didn't even exist. It wouldn't surprise him if the whole thing was some front for a criminal operation. No wonder Quinn had made it sound so mysterious. And been so secretive.

"Are you feeling better?" Quinn suddenly asked.

Blake shrugged. "How do you want me to feel? You imprison me here under some pretense and then you let one of your guys attack me." He pointed at Oliver. "He would have drained me!"

Oliver whirled around to face him. "I said I'm sorry. I didn't mean to do it. I told you to run, I did . . . "

"Don't think I didn't try," he shot back.

Quinn shot a surprised look at Oliver. "You used mind control to paralyze him?"

Oliver shook his head. "I didn't. I don't even know how yet."

"I suppose your instincts kicked in." Then Quinn looked back at him. "As I said, I'll make sure Oliver behaves from now on. And from the rest of us, you have nothing to fear either. We don't attack humans."

He wanted to believe it, for his own sanity's sake, but when Blake looked at the other vampires, his gaze fell on Zane. There was something mean looking about him, and he knew that he never wanted to meet that guy in a dark alley. Something told him that he was dangerous. No, he wasn't safe here, even if Quinn and Rose tried to convince him of it. Even if they were his 4th great-grandparents.

"I don't feel so good right now," he pressed out.

"Of course, the blood loss," Rose agreed quickly. "Why don't you lie down in your room a little, and when you've rested, we'll talk more, okay?"

He nodded, then looked toward the kitchen door. Without saying anything, the others parted to make way for him. Zane even held the door open for him until he'd stepped through it.

Blake briefly eyed the front door at the end of the corridor, but remembering how quickly Oliver had moved when he'd attacked him, he knew that even a mad dash for it wouldn't succeed. He'd never reach it in time.

But he wouldn't give up.

Determined to find a way out, he walked upstairs, leaving the vampires and their quiet murmurs behind.

31

"Zane, Cain, Amaury, watch the doors," Quinn ordered as soon as Blake had walked upstairs. "Wesley, Nina, stand by. It's still daytime for a few hours. Thomas, Eddie, you might as well get some rest while you can so you can relieve the others in a few hours."

As his colleagues left the kitchen, Quinn was alone with Oliver and Rose.

"Quinn, I'm—"

He held up his hand to stop Oliver from saying anything else.

"Rose, can you give us a minute alone please?"

She nodded quickly and left the room. When the door fell shut behind her, he looked back at his protégé.

"I blame myself. I knew you were having trouble keeping the thirst under control. Hell, all of us struggled with it at the beginning. I should have been there when you needed me. Instead, I . . . " He glanced toward the door through which Rose had just left.

Oliver took a hesitant step toward him. "I understand. You have enough stuff going on right now. Rose . . . well, it's important that you and she work things out. She's worth it."

Quinn felt a smile tug at his lips. "She is. But it's no excuse for me to neglect my duties. I'm your sire, and you need to be able to rely on me to guide you through the worst. I haven't done that. Far from it. I've pulled you out of your familiar environment, made you move in here, and then practically abandoned you."

"I don't feel abandoned. All my friends are here. Cain's been helping me."

Quinn combed his fingers through his hair. "The point is he shouldn't have had to."

"Hey, man, don't take it so hard. I'm the first one you've turned, right? I suppose it's like being a new parent. They don't get everything right at first either."

Surprised at Oliver's no-nonsense answer, he stared at the kid. Was he really as grown up as he pretended? But even if he was reacting rationally to this situation, it didn't change anything. Quinn was still responsible for him.

"How are you feeling now? How is the thirst?"

Oliver's gaze shifted past him, suddenly uncomfortable. "It's ok. I can handle it."

Quinn put a hand on his shoulder and squeezed it. "It's fine if you want to lie to me, but don't lie to yourself."

Oliver sighed. "I didn't want to believe you when you told me it would be hard at first. You guys all make it look so easy. I've never seen any of you go off the rails like that and attack somebody for blood. I thought it would be the same for me. I never realized . . . " His voice died.

"That the thirst for blood would have you in its grip, control you, guide your every thought? That you could smell a human hundreds of yards away? That even now Blake's blood smells more delicious than any of the stuff that's sitting in the pantry?"

Oliver's eyes widened. "How do you know that? That's exactly how it feels."

Quinn smiled. "We all went through it. We had to learn to control ourselves, to bury that part of us so we could begin to function in human society. It's a choice we make. For some it's easier than for others."

"Zane never made that choice," Oliver added, a hopeful glint in his eyes.

"Don't go there, Oliver. Zane had his reasons. And he had himself under control even when he was feeding from humans. The point is not to never feed from humans again, but to make sure that if you ever do, you won't put their lives in danger—and you make sure they don't remember. Both things you're not capable of yet."

"So you mean later I can feed off humans again, when I have myself under control, I mean?"

There was an eagerness in Oliver's voice that Quinn couldn't dismiss. The kid wanted fresh human blood, not the bottled stuff. And who could blame him? Fresh blood still held the life force of a human and carried more strength and healing power.

"The idea is to get you used to bottled blood so that you won't resort to biting humans unless it's an emergency."

Oliver pushed his lips forward in a stubborn gesture. "But if I always drink bottled blood, how am I going to control myself when I do have to bite a human? I mean if I never really practice it on a live human, how would I know when to stop?"

Quinn shook his head. "They're not guinea pigs. We don't practice on them. And that's an order."

"But—"

Oliver's protest was interrupted by an angry shout coming from upstairs.

"Fuck!" Zane cursed. "Wesley! Nina! Blake's outside! Go get him!"

"Shit!" Quinn echoed and immediately ran into the hallway.

Wesley and Nina already came running from the living area.

"Back or front?" Nina asked.

"Back of the house!" Zane yelled as he shot down the stairs. "He's running toward the neighbor's fence."

***

Blake tossed his bag over the fence and followed.

Vampires! Fuck, he couldn't believe what he'd gotten into. At any other time he would have liked the idea of meeting a bunch of vampires, hanging out with them, finding out how they lived, what it was like to be immortal. All that shit. The idea was way cool. But to be bitten by one? That went too far for his liking! Maybe if one of the women had bitten him, he wouldn't have panicked like that, but to feel the fangs of a guy in his neck, that was just too creepy. He wasn't swinging that way.

Grabbing his bag, he ran through the garden, heading for the street, not caring that he was trampling through flowerbeds. He had to get out of here.

"Blake!"

Shock coursed through him when he heard Wesley's voice. Tossing a quick look over his shoulder without slowing his pace, he saw him vaulting over the fence.

What the fuck? Why wasn't he turning into dust under the rays of the sun? What kind of vampires were they? Could they go out in the sun after all? Shit, that meant they could hunt him down even during the day.

Next to Wesley, Nina appeared too, jumping over the fence just as gracefully. Knowing he had no time to lose, he ran faster.

"Wait, Blake!" Nina called out now. "You're safe with us! Come back!"

Her voice came closer, but he didn't dare waste any time looking over his shoulder again. He needed to put some distance between him and those vampires. The extra 20 pounds of his bag were slowing him down. No wonder they were gaining ground on him.

Shit! It was either getting caught by them or parting with the designer clothes that he'd packed. The decision was easy. He dropped his bag when he hit the street corner. Without the added weight, he instantly ran faster, crossing the street like a bullet.

Panting for air, he felt his lungs burn from the exertion, but he didn't stop. He had to try to lose his pursuers.

"Stop, Blake!" Wesley shouted after him, and Blake could hear that he too was exhausted from the chase.

Maybe vampires weren't that much stronger than humans after all. Maybe he had a chance. Blake chanced a look over his shoulder and saw that both Nina and Wesley were about a half a block behind him, not giving up.

Odd, he wondered as he crossed the next quiet street without checking for traffic, Oliver had moved so much faster when he'd stormed into the kitchen. His movements had been a blur, so fast, Blake had barely seen them. Why didn't Nina and Wesley employ that same speed? And why were they the only ones chasing him?

Could it be that Nina and Wesley weren't vampires after all? Was that why they were the ones running after him and not Quinn or Rose who'd claimed to be his third or fourth great-grandparents?

There was no time to wonder about this now and waste any energy on thinking about it. He could contemplate what all this meant later when he was safe. For an instant, he wondered where to run to. He couldn't go home; they knew where he lived. He would have to find another place to hide for now.

Blake was about to cross another intersection when a dark van cut him off, nearly knocking him over. Before he could even give the driver the finger, the door slid open and gloved hands grabbed him. He tried to fight his attacker, but the bastard was stronger and pulled him into the van.

"Nooooo!" Nina screamed from half a block away.

Her scream died as the door of the van slammed back shut, shrouding the inside in darkness.

"Let me go!" Blake yelled.

An evil chuckle was the answer.

Slowly his eyes adjusted to the dark, and he was able to make out three figures. Large men. They wore heavy clothing and gloves. Their faces were covered with large ski masks, the exposed skin around their eyes covered with zinc oxide. When they removed their masks, their faces reminded Blake of raccoons.

"Welcome, Blake," one of them said, his voice devoid of emotion. "I'm Keegan. And you've just become a bargaining chip."

When Keegan opened his mouth, Blake noticed the white of his teeth. He focused his vision.

"Oh, shit! More vampires."

"That's right. And we're not as tame as the ones you just ran away from."

All three men laughed, and the chilling sound ran down his spine.

He'd just jumped from the frying pan into the fire.

32

Rose stared out the window. The sun had just set, and she was beside herself with worry.

Quinn had done everything he could. During the day, human Scanguards personnel had roamed the city to find Keegan's hiding place, but they had come up empty-handed. Even though Nina and Wesley had witnessed Blake's abduction and taken note of the van's license plate, the information hadn't helped locate her grandson. The plates belonged to another vehicle and therefore wouldn't lead them to Keegan.

Thomas was busily looking at all available surveillance videos from businesses and schools in the neighborhood to see where the van had disappeared to, but so far nothing had shown up on any videos. As if they'd been swallowed up.

Nervously, Rose chewed on her fingernails. Quinn had urged her to rest a little, but instead of lying down, she paced in her room. She had to do something. Sitting around and waiting for Keegan to contact them was driving her nuts.

Determined to bring this charade to an end, she pulled out the cell phone from which she'd texted Keegan a day earlier. For many long seconds, she stared at it, composing a message in her mind, which would compel Keegan to act.

She still had what he wanted. Now it was time to use her bargaining chip.

If you touch him, I'll destroy it, she texted and hit *send.*

Her heart beat into her throat as she waited anxiously for a reply. Quinn had explained that despite the fact that the cell phone was untraceable, anybody whom she'd texted from it, could text back to this secret number.

From downstairs, sounds drifted to her. Everybody had a job to do, everybody but she. Quinn had tried to assure her that they were professionals and knew what they had to do. But even though she believed him, it made no difference. Blake was her flesh and blood, and she couldn't just sit idly by while he was suffering at Keegan's hands.

She wasn't a shy debutante in Regency London anymore; she was a woman of action.

A humming sound interrupted her thoughts. Her eyes shot to the phone in her hands and read the message that flashed on the display.

You destroy it, and I'll tell Quinn what you did to Wallace.

Panic made her heart stop. How did Keegan know? She'd never told anybody. Never confessed her crime to anyone.

Another hum announced a second message.

After I turn Blake.

Keegan had the upper hand, and he knew it. How long had he known about her secret? Had he been sitting on this piece of information for a long time, waiting for the right moment to use it against her? She assumed as much. It was exactly what Keegan did: blackmail people. And now he was blackmailing her.

Ready to talk? the next message came.

What do you want? she asked, even though she knew the answer already.

The data. Meet me at the top of the Lyon's steps in ten minutes. Alone. Be one second late, and Quinn finds out about Wallace.

She wasted twenty seconds on her smartphone trying to find where the Lyon's steps were located, then realized she would have to run full speed, once she'd snuck out of the house, if she wanted to make it in time. Keegan obviously knew that and wanted to make sure that she had no time to notify anybody or take any precautions for herself. Luckily he had no idea that her own cell phone contained several pre-programmed alert messages. She scrolled through them, selected the protocol labeled *Hostage Scenario,* took ten seconds to modify it with a couple of specifics and pressed the *send* button—now her hope was that the recipient would execute her orders swiftly enough. Then she tossed the phone into the closet.

Rose used the side door leading to the tradesmen entrance to sneak out of the house undetected. Not telling anybody about her exchange with Keegan was a risk, but knowing that her adversary wouldn't think twice about telling Quinn that she'd killed his maker, such disclosure was a deadly chance she couldn't take. Not only would she forfeit her own life, but Blake's too. Now her only hope was that the people who owed her loyalty would be able to help her.

As she sprinted through the night, her body cutting through the crisp air so fast any human observing her would merely see a blur, her mind frantically worked on a plan of how to defeat Keegan and snatch her grandson from his clutches.

Checking her watch in mid-run, she increased her speed, knowing that Keegan wouldn't hesitate to execute his threat should she arrive late. Looking ahead, she spotted a sign and the gate for the Presidio. To its right, the Lyon's steps descended into the Marina district. From their top, they afforded an unobstructed view over the Palace of Fine Arts below, and the Bay beyond.

Two dark vans were parked next to several sedans where the street ended and the Park began. Rose came to an abrupt halt.

"Always loved the way you could move," Keegan's icy voice came from the opposite street corner.

Her head whipped in his direction. He stood in the shadow of a hedge. Slowly, as if he had all the time in the world, he emerged and crossed the distance to her.

"Let's cut to the chase, Keegan," she said, her chest barely heaving from the run.

The moonlight cast a shadow on one side of Keegan's face, illuminating the other. There was something eerie about the sight. It only underscored the seriousness of her situation. If the hasty plan she had concocted in the short time she'd had didn't work, she would be out of luck.

"Where's Blake?"

"In good company."

"I doubt that."

Keegan chuckled, shaking his head at the same time. "And you think your company is more appropriate? After all you're a murderer too. Just like the rest of us. And to kill your own maker in cold blood . . . tsk . . . tsk. That's very bad of you. Very bad indeed."

At the recollection of that event, Rose suppressed the chill that traveled down her spine. "How did you find out?"

She'd been careful never to reveal anything about her past to him.

"It's funny what kind of information surfaces if you keep digging long enough. You remember Charles, the gentleman who witnessed your dirty deed?" He released a short laugh. "What am I saying? Of course you do. After all, you stayed with him for a few months, before you robbed him blind and disappeared. Hard to forget that, isn't it? A man like that is more than willing to share information with anybody who asks the right questions."

"He deserved it. He was using me." She'd believed him at first when he'd pretended to want to help her, but in the end, he had turned out to be just as selfish as everybody else. He'd used her to lure unsuspecting humans and vampires into his trap. She'd been his bait.

"How ungrateful of you. After all, he helped you survive. Had he not warned you that Quinn would avenge the death of his maker, you wouldn't even be here tonight."

Rose clamped her jaw together. "I don't need a history lesson."

She understood well enough what Wallace's murder meant. Charles, the vampire who had witnessed it, wasn't the only one who had explained it to her. Years later, when she'd been with a clan, she'd seen how such a revenge killing had taken place: A vampire had killed his long-time lover after finding out that she'd killed his maker, a female vampire, out of jealousy. She'd never witnessed such a brutal killing before.

"Well, then let's talk about the present. I want the data back. And I want it now."

Rose sucked in a quick breath. "First I need to know that Blake is still alive—and that he's still human."

"Very well."

Keegan pulled a small walkie-talkie from his pocket and pressed a button. "Open up."

When she heard a sound coming from one of the dark vans a moment later, her gaze shot to it.

The side door opened. Blake's head and upper torso were held by strong arms, shoving him just outside of the van, keeping the rest of him inside. He appeared uninjured, yet he looked fearful. At the same time, relief flooded her: His aura was still human.

"Rose?" he croaked.

"Blake. Just hold on! I'll get you out of this. You'll be safe soon."

Before he could reply to her, he was pulled back into the van, the door shutting behind him.

"I hope you have every intention of keeping your promise to him," Keegan said.

Rose turned back to face him. "As long as you keep yours. I want him freed, now."

He laughed out loud. "You're funny, Rose. You really are. First the data, then Blake. That's how it works. I'm sure you've seen enough movies and are familiar with how an exchange works?"

She narrowed her eyes.

"Of course you are. So I won't need to explain anything else, will I?"

She hated his condescending tone, and under any other circumstances, she would have robbed him of the ability to spout any more insults by driving her fist into his mouth, but at present, he held all the cards. She would have to wait her turn.

"So where is it?" he repeated.

"I hid it."

"Where?"

"In San Francisco."

"Good. We'll go together. Hope you won't mind, but considering that you shook me off last time, I'm sure you won't mind if I'll stick to you like glue on our second attempt, will you?"

He motioned to the second dark van. "Get in there."

"I want to ride with Blake," she insisted quickly.

"Not a chance. His van will follow us. If you lead us into a trap, my men have orders to hurt him."

Clearly, Keegan had learned from his mistakes. She hadn't expected anything else. Now she could only hope that leading him and his men to a place where she had allies would provide her with sufficient advantage to fight him off.

When she stepped into the van and felt the door close behind her, she closed her eyes and allowed her nerves to calm. She needed all her wits about her now, because one false move, and she and Blake would perish.

33

"She's gone," Thomas confirmed from the top of the stairs.

Panic flared up in Quinn as his suspicion was confirmed. Rose had left the house without telling anybody.

"Shit! What is she up to?" he wondered out loud.

"She's meeting Keegan," Thomas continued as he rushed down.

"What? Why the fuck didn't she tell me?" Quinn cursed, furious now. Rose had to understand that alone she was more vulnerable. Only if they stuck together as a cohesive unit, did they have a chance at defeating Keegan.

As Thomas reached him, he held his cell phone out to him. "I just got an alert that text messages were sent between the cell I fixed up for you and Keegan's number."

"How? I thought it was untraceable," Quinn said, confused.

"I mirrored the number on my phone so I would receive a duplicate whenever a message was sent or received. Just in case." He paused for a brief second. "Who's Wallace?"

Quinn nearly stumbled backwards at hearing the familiar name. "What does my sire have to do with Keegan?"

"It appears he has something to do with Rose." Thomas handed him the phone. "Read this."

Quinn's eyes darted over the text messages, reading them twice.

"Fuck!"

His mind worked overtime, trying to put all the pieces of the puzzle together. If Rose knew Wallace, it could only mean one thing. He didn't want to follow that thought to its conclusion, because if he did, it would only lead him to a place where guilt was waiting for him. Too well he remembered the night when he'd quarreled with Wallace. The night he'd left. He recalled the last words they had exchanged as if it were yesterday.

"You want to help me?" he had accused Wallace. *"Then help me! Help me make her love me again. Or get out of my sight!"*

"Very well," his maker had replied.

Quinn had seen it as an answer to his last words, to get out of his sight, when in fact Wallace had agreed to his earlier words: *Help me make her love me again.*

How wrong he had been. And how blind not to see what had been right in front of him for so long. Wallace had turned her so she would have no reason to reject him any longer. No wonder she had never come back to him, because he alone was responsible for Rose's turning. He had asked Wallace to help him. He had begged his sire. And his sire had listened.

Quinn didn't waste any more time guessing what had happened to Wallace in the end. In his heart he knew the answer already. It all made sense now. He understood what had happened and why. Now all that mattered was getting to Rose and closing this chapter of their lives. It was time to bury the past for good.

"Do you know where those Lyon's steps are?" Quinn asked Thomas, who instantly nodded.

"She'll be long gone. The message was sent over ten minutes ago."

"Can't you trace the phone we gave her?"

Thomas shook his head with a sad look. "You wanted an untraceable one. Sorry. No can do. Besides, Keegan has probably already gotten rid of it."

The thought of Rose in Keegan's hands made his blood boil. "She should have trusted me. She shouldn't have done this on her own."

Thomas pointed to the phone message. "Whatever it was that she didn't want you to know, Keegan is obviously using it against her."

"That's not important right now. We've gotta find her before it's too late." Quinn ran a shaky hand through his hair. "Send two people to the Lyon's steps to see if they can pick up her trail from there."

Thomas nodded. "Eddie," he called out, and his mentee appeared within seconds. "You and Cain, go to the Lyon's steps and search for any trace of Rose or Keegan. Report as soon as you're there."

"On my way!" Eddie replied and called out for Cain.

As the two left, Thomas turned back to Quinn. "And the rest of us?"

Quinn lifted his head and looked at his friend. "Keegan will force her to give him the data. She'll have to lead him to where she's hidden it. When you swept her room, you didn't find anything, did you?"

"Not a trace." Thomas cleared his throat. "Nothing in the rest of the house either."

Not at all surprised that Thomas had searched the entire house for it,

Quinn nodded. "Then she must have hidden it before she ever went to Gabriel to hire us."

"But where would she consider it safe enough to hide the flash drive? She doesn't have any friends here in San Francisco. She knows nobody here. Sure, we can search Blake's apartment, but I doubt it's there, and besides, Keegan has most likely already looked for it there," Thomas wondered.

"I agree that it's not in Blake's apartment. However, Rose does know somebody here besides us and Blake."

Thomas gave him a curious look. "Who?"

"She owns a brothel here."

"There are no brothels in San Francisco as far as I know," Thomas claimed.

"I suppose they're called *Massage Parlors* here. She mentioned a fancy place near the Ritz. It's the only place I can imagine her hiding the flash drive. She said the women are loyal to her."

Thomas nodded and started typing on his cell phone. "Let's see what comes up. It can't be that hard finding a massage parlor near the Ritz."

Bent over Thomas's phone Quinn waited for the search results to display, hoping that his hunch was correct.

34

Rose looked up and down the street as she stepped from the darkened van, Keegan on her heels. The driver remained inside as did the second vampire who had accompanied them. Her eyes darted to the second van that pulled up behind them.

"Let's go," Keegan ordered.

"Do you really think I'm an amateur?" She shook her head. "The minute I hand the flash drive over, you'll have one of your men turn him, just to spite me."

When she glared at him, he answered with a nonchalant smile. "So you did learn from the time we spent together? How sweet. And how utterly inconvenient."

Had he really thought she would trust him to keep his word? "I want Blake by my side when we do the exchange."

"Very well," Keegan conceded. "But don't think that'll change anything. One false move and I'll personally bring him to the brink of death and you'll be begging me to turn him. And then we'll see what I decide."

Keegan made a motion toward the van and a moment later, the door slid open. One of his thugs pushed Blake onto the pavement, making him stumble.

Instinctively, Rose rushed to him to prevent him from falling. But behind Blake, three of Keegan's minions had already stepped from the van and grabbed him.

"Are you all right? Did they hurt you?"

Rose ran her eyes over his body, but couldn't see any visible injuries.

Blake thrust up his chin, gave a quick shake of his head, then glared at her. "If you'd told me everything from the start, this wouldn't have happened. You thought I couldn't handle the fact that you and your friends are vampires? You didn't even give it a try. You thought I was weak."

"You didn't take it well when you found out."

"Well, how would you take it if you found out about vampires, because one of them was trying to suck you dry? You should have told me earlier! Fuck, I could've helped you defeat these guys."

Keegan chuckled behind her. "He doesn't lack confidence, your grandson. Or shall I call it arrogance?"

"I'll give you arrogance, you jerk!" Blake shot back, making an attempt at raising his fist, but the vampire behind him quickly restrained him.

"No respect, the young. Don't you agree, Rose?"

Rose didn't bother replying to Keegan's remark and searched Blake's eyes instead, trying to connect with him. "I'm sorry, Blake. But everything will be all right. I promise you. Just trust me."

At the same time she used mind control to send her thoughts to him.

Do what I'll tell you. If I say jump, you'll jump.

"Let's not waste any more time," Keegan ordered.

Rose turned toward the corner house. Only a brass sign next to the opulent entrance door gave away the fact that the residential property housed a business.

Executive Services, the sign said.

She'd always hated neon signs. Besides, her business didn't rely on foot traffic but on word of mouth. And the more exclusive each of her brothels appeared, the higher the fees she could charge.

The intercom crackled. "Yes," a female voice inquired.

"Rose Haverford."

Instantly a buzz sounded. Rose pressed against the door, opening it. Next to her, Keegan entered. She cast a quick glance over her shoulder, making sure Blake followed. At the same time, she counted: Keegan had brought six or seven thugs. Two stayed with the vans. One of them remained outside of the door as it snapped shut. The others followed her up the five steps into the large foyer.

The place had once been a hotel and had retained its Victorian charm. A crystal chandelier hung from the high ceiling, and beyond it a grand staircase led to the upper floors. To the right, a small bar and lounge invited patrons in for a drink. Several women and men sat on the comfortable sofas while soft music dripped from the speakers above. They only briefly glanced at the newcomers, then returned their attention to their companions.

To the left of the lobby, there were two doors, one marked *Private*, the other *Cloakroom*.

Rose raised her head as she perceived a movement from the stairs. A beautiful Asian woman swept down the stairs in an elegant business suit that accentuated her delicate features.

"You neglected to mention that there were vampires here. What are you trying to play at?" Keegan hissed under his breath, grabbing Rose's elbow at the same time and squeezing it painfully.

She narrowed her eyes when she looked at him. "You didn't think I would leave the protection of the flash drive to a human, did you?" She jerked her arm from his hold. "And don't get all bent out of shape, she's the only vampire on the premises."

"I'm Vera," the Asian beauty announced as she stopped in front of them. "I'm honored that you grace us with a visit, Miss Haverford."

Rose nodded. "I'm sorry I wasn't able to give you any notice. But circumstances—"

Keegan cut her off with an impatient hand movement. "No more pleasantries. Let's get to it."

Vera raised an eyebrow. "A very eager gentleman you brought us. Maybe I should bring down a selection of girls?"

Rose smiled inwardly. She'd met the manager of her San Francisco operation only a couple of times, but she'd always known she was smart. Despite the fact that she'd been alerted by Rose's text message, she didn't let on that she knew that this wasn't a friendly visit.

"I have girls to suit every taste: Asian, Caucasian, African American, blondes, redheads. You name it."

Rose sighed. "Alas, my . . . associates and I are not here for pleasure. If you would please lead us to the executive office so I may retrieve an item I deposited for safekeeping."

Vera's face instantly changed. "Oh, but of course. Follow me."

She turned and walked to the stairs.

As they followed in silence, Rose reacquainted herself with the layout of the place. The house had only three floors. One large suite on the top floor had been converted into the executive office, from which the manager of the establishment conducted business, and where she entertained private clients if she chose to do so.

The room Vera led them into was larger than Rose remembered. It easily would have fit a dining table for twenty. Instead, it was furnished with a large desk containing a single computer, a comfortable sitting area in front of a fireplace, and a four poster bed with gauzy fabric hanging from its wooden beams meant to hide whatever happened there from time to time.

The one thing Rose noticed immediately was that the room was stifling hot.

"Apologies about the heat in here," Vera said quickly. "I've already opened a window, but unfortunately we've had problems with the thermostat and haven't been able to fix it yet."

Rose noticed how one of Keegan's men tugged on his shirt collar, opening a button or two, clearly uncomfortable in the hot room.

"No worries," Rose replied and walked toward the desk.

Keegan clamped his hand over her forearm.

"I'm getting it already, no need to be so unpleasant," she hissed.

"We'll do it together, shall we?" Keegan's mistrust was clearly visible in his eyes.

"If you insist."

"Don't mind if I do."

With Keegan by her side, Rose rounded the desk and faced the wall. She tapped the painting that hung there, and it swung toward her, revealing the safe behind. Rose hesitated.

"Open it," he ordered.

"It's not in there."

Keegan bared his teeth in a flash of anger. "You fucking bitch!" He turned his head toward his associates, ready to spout another order.

"It's here," Rose said quickly, pointing to the back of the painting.

As Keegan turned back to her, she put her hand to one corner of the frame. The little wooden piece that held the corners in a 90 degree angle, created a little pocket between frame and canvas. She fished for the flash drive, pulling it out of its hiding place a moment later.

Keegan instantly snatched it from her fingers, inspecting it.

"Looks like it. But I'd like to make sure. You understand, don't you?"

Of course she did.

Slowly she turned to their host, connecting with her dark eyes. "Vera, you don't mind if we use your computer for a moment, do you?"

"Be my guest."

Rose nodded briefly then glanced at Blake, who was watching them intently. She also noticed how the three thugs weren't standing as close to him as before, the two heavier set ones now fanning themselves in obvious discomfort.

Get ready, she advised Blake using mind control. *You can trust Vera.*

She brought her attention back to Keegan as he inserted the flash drive into one of the USB ports on the computer. He drummed his fingers on the desk, impatiently waiting until the drive was recognized and the explorer opened.

When the window popped up and he clicked on the only folder that was on the drive, a curse was already forming on his lips.

"Bitch!" he screamed as he realized that the folder was empty.

Within a split-second he had her by the throat. But Rose didn't care. From the corner of her eye she saw how the thugs made a step forward, toward them, ready to help their boss if need be. For good measure she thrust her knee up, aiming for Keegan's jewels.

It did the trick, and one of the thugs rushed toward them, ready to help his employer.

It was all the distraction she needed.

"Now!" she screamed and saw the blur with which Vera charged toward Blake and grabbed him before the other two vampires could react. Without stopping, Vera flung Blake toward the open window.

Jump! Rose sent her order to him, employing mind control. Her grandson would have no choice but to obey. *Now!*

Vera used karate kicks to fend off the two thugs, preventing them from stopping Blake as he launched himself out of the window.

Relieved, Rose's heart finally started beating again, only to stutter to a halt when Keegan's hand squeezed her throat harder and his fangs approached her face, murder in his eyes.

Fuck! Now he was pissed.

"Reinforcements, now!" she heard one of the vampires order into his walkie-talkie.

"You tell me now where it is, or your friend is toast," Keegan threatened, motioning his head toward a spot behind her.

She twisted her head enough to see that Vera had been captured by two of the vampires. One pointed a stake to her heart.

I'm sorry, she mouthed.

"Don't be," Vera said, lifting her chin in defiance. "I've been spoiling for a good fight. It'll be fun bashing those guys' nuts in."

35

The two vans in front of the building were empty and unlocked. One of them still carried Rose's scent and in the other Quinn could still smell Blake.

"We're at the right place," he confirmed to his colleagues, then gave the address to Cain and Eddie who were on the other end of the phone, on their way back from the Lyon's steps. "Get here as fast as you can."

Then he quickly assessed the situation and motioned to his friends. "Zane, Oliver, you'll take the front door, then take the second floor. Wesley, Amaury, check if you can break a window on the other side and gain access that way. You'll secure the first floor. Thomas, you'll come with me. We'll take the fire escape to the top. Once your floors are secure, work your way up."

As everybody nodded and dispersed, Quinn rushed down the little alley next to the house. He'd seen the fire escape from the street. It wouldn't take much to get up there.

As they reached it, Thomas put his hands together providing a step. "I'll catapult you up."

Quinn put his foot into Thomas's palms and jumped, reaching his arms over his head. His fingers grabbed the fire escape, and he pulled it down, landing back on the ground.

"Let's go."

As fast as they could, they rushed upstairs, heading for the third floor. The window at the top provided no barrier. Quinn pushed it up and stepped through it, landing in a corridor. Behind him, Thomas squeezed through it and joined him.

Quinn's sensitive hearing picked up sounds from downstairs: music and people talking. Then he concentrated on the sounds on this floor, his ears perking up when he heard a loud thud.

"This way!" he ordered Thomas and ran along the corridor, past the many doors until he reached a double door.

He pressed his ear against it. Taking a deep breath, he recognized Rose's scent instantly.

"In there," he whispered, looking over his shoulder.

He watched as Thomas drew his gun and nodded. "Ready when you are."

Quinn pulled a stake from his pocket and held it tightly in his right palm.

On a nod, he turned the door knob and jerked the door open, bursting into the room. His eyes instantly took in the situation: two vampires were restraining Rose while two others were fighting against a struggling female—an Asian vampire. Quinn could only assume that she was a friend of Rose's.

Thomas fired his gun, felling one of the vampires fighting the Asian woman as Quinn rushed to help Rose. From the corner of his eye, he saw the bastard combust, then disintegrate into dust as a result of the silver bullet Thomas had planted in him.

At the sound of the gunshot, the heads of the other vampires snapped toward them. One of Rose's attackers released her and launched himself at Quinn, but he was prepared and struck him with a hard blow to his head, sending him reeling for a short moment before he caught himself.

As his opponent dealt an equally severe punch, Quinn shot back with an uppercut to his chin, then kicked his leg into the jerk's knees. He toppled over, but before Quinn could deliver the deathblow, he was alerted to activity behind him.

He whirled around quickly, and as it turned out, just in time: two hostile vampires crowded into the room. Behind them he heard footsteps on the stairs. He could only hope those were Scanguards' men.

As he attacked one of the vampires and Thomas lunged for the other, he saw two women reach the door. They were barefoot and dressed in skimpy outfits.

Their shocked screams added to the fighting noises and curses that now filled the room.

"No!!!!" Rose suddenly screamed.

Momentarily distracted, Quinn turned his head, just as more men stormed the room. He kicked his opponent to the ground and ran for Rose. Keegan—and he had to assume it was he from his determined look—had her in a chokehold and dragged her toward another door. As he pulled it open, Quinn reached him.

When Keegan saw him, he pulled a stake from his jacket and held it at Rose's chest.

"You come any closer and I'll kill her."

Quinn stopped in his tracks.

"Got you, bastard," he heard Amaury's voice from the door. Good, his friends were here. But it didn't solve his immediate problem.

The screams of the human women intensified, and from their direction, Quinn knew they'd entered the room and were now in the middle of the battle.

"Eat that!" came Zane's triumphant growl.

Rose's eyes stared at him, silently begging him to help her. But he knew that Keegan would be faster. There had to be another way to free her from his hold.

"Kasper!" Thomas's stunned voice suddenly drowned out everything else.

Keegan's head spun toward the sound, then his eyes widened in shock. "Thomas," he murmured as if he'd seen a ghost.

It was impossible. Thomas flung his opponent against the door with so much force that it left a large crack in the lath-n-plaster, and stared at Kasper. Thomas hadn't seen his sire in almost ten decades. But the vampire restraining Rose was clearly the man whose blood he carried in his veins. The vampire he'd divorced himself from, because he didn't want to be part of what he represented.

Thomas stalked closer.

"Let her go!" he commanded, knowing at the same time that Kasper, or Keegan as he called himself now, didn't believe in orders unless they came from him.

"You're once again fighting on the wrong side, Thomas."

His sire's eyes were mocking him, trying as so many times before to plant doubts in him. But Thomas had long ago stopped doubting his choices.

"You're wrong, as always. I've chosen the right side."

Keegan intensified the chokehold around Rose's neck, making her gasp. Instinctively, her hands came up, digging her claws into his skin, but Keegan didn't even flinch.

Quinn stood only a few feet from them, his face one of anguish, ready to attack despite the hopeless situation. He would never reach Rose in time to save her from Keegan's stake.

"What's it gonna be, Thomas? Are you joining me, or would you rather perish with your friends?"

"You leave me no choice." And he hated his sire for what he was about to do, because he'd sworn never to use his skill to kill.

When he locked eyes with Keegan, he realized that his maker understood what he meant to do. A flicker of apprehension crossed his face, and he heard his opponent's heartbeat spike for an instant before it returned to normal.

"Very well, son, so you think you're better than I?" He let out an evil laugh. "Maybe you would be if you hadn't left and abandoned the gift I've given you."

"Gift?" Thomas hissed. "It's no gift to carry evil in your blood."

Thomas allowed his mind to calm, preparing himself for the battle ahead of him, the outcome of which was by no means determined. Keegan was right: he hadn't honed his skill in all those years, and using it now was a risk.

Collecting all his energy, feeling the warmth as it settled in his center, Thomas focused on his enemy, then sent his first thought to him.

Drop the stake!

A faint trembling of Keegan's hand was the answer. Then his laughter.

"Is that all you've got? Haven't I taught you any better?"

Anger and hate surged, forming a ball in his stomach. With a shout he sent it toward Keegan, aiming at the hand that held the stake. The invisible burst hit Keegan.

"Now!" Thomas screamed at Quinn, hoping his friend would get the idea and act. Giving any more detailed instructions would destroy his concentration and make him lose the little control he'd just gained.

As he saw Quinn move toward Keegan, Thomas sent another blast of his mind's thoughts to him.

Release Rose. Drop the stake.

He noticed how Keegan's jaw clamped shut as he tried to fight the invasion.

Quinn's kicked his foot high, catapulting the stake from Keegan's hand in the next instant. Simultaneously Rose pushed her elbow into his ribs.

With a curse, Keegan kicked his knee into her back, pushing her to the ground. Then his eyes glared at Thomas. "Your mind or mine. Only one can survive."

Lifting his hands in a dramatic gesture, his body seemed to harden. His fangs elongated, his fingers turned into sharp claws, and his eyes glowed red.

The first invasion stabbed him like a silver knife, sending a burning sensation through his entire body. Thomas cried out in pain. Then Keegan's thoughts entered his mind, pushing through the protective walls around his brain, searching for weak spots to annihilate first.

Thomas pushed back, collecting his own energy to combat his sire. He concentrated on the hate and disgust he felt for his maker and hurled it toward him, using those emotions to enter Keegan's mind and create devastation there. Drawing on every ounce of energy his body possessed, he reached for his opponent's mind, trying to crush it like a mouse beneath an elephant's foot.

But Keegan was strong and his mind a minefield, a booby trapped maze. Whenever Thomas felt he was gaining ground, he was catapulted back, the shockwave blasting him back, robbing him of more energy by the second.

Thomas noticed Keegan draining of energy too. They were equally strong, and equally determined to see this to the end. Only one would emerge alive.

Quinn reached for Rose, helping her to her feet, pulling her away from Thomas and Keegan.

Locked in a deadly fight, there were few outward signs of it. The air in the room crackled. From time to time, tiny bolts of lightning traveled between the two, as if two electrically charged bodies fought against each other.

"Oh, God!" Rose said. "Keegan is using mind control on Thomas. We have to help him."

Quinn pulled his silver knife from its sheath. He might be a lousy shot, but his knife always found its target. It wouldn't kill Keegan instantly, but a well-placed knife wound would disable him sufficiently so he could finish him off with a stake. As he aimed at Keegan, he flicked his wrist, sending the deadly instrument toward him. But Keegan's head turned suddenly, and a blast of energy struck the knife, reversing its path. He'd never seen anything like it before.

"Shit!"

Quinn jumped, grabbed Rose and sent them both tumbling to the floor, covering her with his body.

Breathing hard, Rose stared at him, stunned. "How are we gonna help him now?"

Before he could answer, a scream coming from outside, made Quinn jerk up.

He exchanged a brief look with Rose.

"Blake!" they said in unison.

36

Blake had landed on a balcony on the second floor. Oddly enough, he hadn't fallen too hard—a mattress had cushioned his fall from the third floor. As if somebody had planned it that way. But he'd hit his head on the railing, and it had knocked him out briefly. Why he'd jumped in the first place, he had no idea. But the urge had suddenly overtaken him, and he hadn't been able to stop himself.

Not that it mattered right now: he wasn't any better off than in that room with Keegan and his vampire friends. Because one of those fucking vampires had just joined him on the balcony.

With extended fangs and claws instead of fingers, the menacing creature stalked toward him, his hulky body blocking the door to the room behind. Shrieks and screams from within the room accompanied his approach.

The vampire bared his fangs, pulling his mouth into an ugly grimace.

Fuck, he was so done with this crap!

"Fuck off!" he yelled.

The fear he'd previously felt when confronted with vampires, had made way for frustration. If only he were as strong and fast as them, he'd show those bloodsuckers where they could stick their fangs. He'd seen how fast they moved, and how strong they were, and hell, if he wasn't a tiny bit envious of those skills. Okay, he could admit it: a lot.

However, that wouldn't get him out of this situation right now.

Casting a quick glance down to the ground, he realized that jumping wouldn't be wise. Metal debris lay on the ground beneath, and if he jumped, he would most likely be impaled by one of the spiky metal rods that stuck out from the hovel of junk.

"Gotcha, boy," the vampire growled.

"Not yet," Blake retorted, gripped the railing behind him and hoisting himself up, kicking his legs into the aggressor's torso in the process.

The vampire tumbled back, but instantly caught himself, pushing away from the doorframe in the next instant. It appeared the attempt at tossing him on his ass had angered him, because his eyes now glared

red.

The thug pulled a knife and charged him.

"Shit!"

Lunging to the left, Blake barely escaped him, but was now wedged against the corner of the balcony with nowhere else to go.

An evil grin swept over his opponent's face as he took a step toward him. But he didn't get far.

From above, somebody jumped onto the balcony, landing in front of the vampire. As Blake's eyes adjusted, he recognized Rose. Her knee came up and kicked the bastard in the nuts before he could even react.

As Rose jumped to the side, avoiding the toppling vampire, Quinn landed right behind him. He too, had jumped from the third floor. A stake in his right hand, he lifted it and aimed, but the hostile vampire fell forward, his hand extended, still clutching the knife.

His eyes glared at Blake, who had nowhere else to go.

"Fuck you!" the vampire ground out.

In obvious agony, he drove his knife into Blake's side. The piercing pain was paralyzing, so much so that he barely noticed how his attacker disintegrated into dust as Quinn staked him from behind.

Dizziness overwhelmed him and he swayed. His hand went to the wound, his look following in the same direction, pain radiating through his body.

Shit, he was going to die!

"Oh, God, no!" he heard Rose scream and catch him as he fell.

Her arms around him felt comforting, and for the first time since finding out about vampires, Blake felt oddly safe.

"Quinn, do something, he's hurt!"

The panic in Rose's voice was undeniable, and despite the pain he was in, Blake tried to put a smile on his lips. "You really are my grandmother, aren't you?"

"Of course, I am."

Quinn crouched down next to her and examined the wound. When he pried Blake's hand from it, Blake let out a helpless cry.

"I'm sorry, son, but I need to see how deep it is."

His hands were gentler than he would have expected from a vampire, and Quinn made no attempt to drink the blood that was so freely oozing from the wound. Maybe not all vampires went crazy at the smell of human blood.

Rose stroked over his hair, diverting his attention from Quinn for a moment. When another bolt of pain wracked his body, he closed his eyes, trying to breathe through the pain, but it didn't go away.

"I'm dying, aren't I?"

He looked at Rose who cast a scared glance at Quinn.

"You'll have to turn me into a vampire too, so I won't die, won't you?" he asked. Well, if that was what needed to be done, he was ready for it. Rose and Quinn would take care of him. They were his family after all.

Quinn's chuckle came utterly unexpected. "Turn you? Not a chance, Blake."

Blake tried to sit up, but winced from the pain it caused him. "I'm dying. Forget what I said at the house. I was in shock from Oliver sucking on my neck. I'm better now. I know I can handle it."

Quinn shook his head and exchanged a smile with Rose. "Blake, it's a flesh wound. It'll heal in no time. There's no need to turn you."

"Are you sure?"

Rose interrupted. "He's sure. But," she hesitated, "maybe we should give him some blood to ease the pain and speed up the healing process?"

She looked at Quinn who slowly nodded. "Agreed. No need for him to suffer needlessly."

"What blood?" Blake asked. Were they going to give him a transfusion? Surely, the paramedics would take care of that.

Quinn brought his wrist to his mouth and elongated his fangs. Instantly Blake realized what he was about to do.

"Fuck no!" he shouted.

"It'll help you heal faster," Quinn claimed and lowered his mouth to his wrist, ready to bite into it.

"No!" Blake motioned his head toward Rose. "If I have to drink anybody's blood, I want Rose's."

"No way!" Quinn protested, his eyes suddenly glaring red.

Rose put her hand on his arm to calm him. "Maybe just this once. He *is* our grandson, and we got him into this."

A silent battle seemed to rage between the two as they stared at each other. Then finally, Quinn nodded and looked at him.

"This will be the first and last time you'll ever drink Rose's blood. And if I see you enjoying it, I'll bash your brains out later. Do you get that?"

Blake nodded hastily. Why would he enjoy it? Blood tasted gross!

He watched with fascination as Rose pierced her own wrist with her fangs then set the open wound to his lips. When the first drops of her blood reached his taste buds, Blake jolted in surprise.

Shit, it tasted good!

Now he also knew why Quinn was so mad at him: he was jealous that Blake got to drink Rose's blood.

37

As soon as Blake had stopped drinking from Rose and he had left them in the nearest room, Quinn rushed upstairs again, bumping into Eddie who came running up the stairs, followed by Cain.

"Did we miss the fight?" Eddie asked.

Quinn listened for any sounds from upstairs. It had gone quieter, but some fighting was still going on.

"Almost. Cain, stay with Rose and Blake." He motioned to the room he'd just left. "Eddie, come with me."

It was time to finish this. Quinn only hoped it wasn't too late for Thomas. He and Rose had left Thomas only three minutes earlier, but in a battle of mind control, three minutes could be an eternity.

He hoped the others had defeated their opponents and were somehow able to help Thomas. But deep down he knew that he hoped for the impossible. Nobody could interfere in a fight of mind control without risking his own sanity and life.

Quinn burst through the door into the room just as Zane dealt a deadly blow with his knife, severing the head of his opponent, covering himself in a cloud of dust as the vampire disintegrated.

"Oh God no!" Eddie cried out when he entered the room, his eyes instantly falling on Thomas and the battle he was still locked into.

He rushed toward him, but Quinn was faster and pulled him back.

"We have to help him!"

"You can't get between them. If you do, the energy that's traveling between them will incinerate your mind," Quinn warned.

"Then shoot the guy!" Eddie ordered, looking around the room for who had a gun.

Quinn looked at Thomas and Keegan, but they weren't stationary anymore. They moved back and forth at varying speeds, circling each other like prize fighters in a ring.

"And risk killing Thomas?" Quinn shook his head.

"Then what are we gonna do? Don't you see, he's in pain."

Eddie was right, Thomas's face was contorted in pain, yet his body still held up. But for how long?

"I've got it," Wesley's voice suddenly came from behind them.

Quinn turned to him, but before he could inquire what Wesley meant, he ran past them, lifting his arm, swinging it, then throwing something. A small item, a bottle or something, flew through the air, then landed on the floor between the two fighters, where it smashed into pieces.

Blue smoke rose from the spilled liquid, making the air sizzle as if acid were burning through metal. Thomas instantly tumbled back, freed from the invisible hold Keegan had had on him.

Keegan too stumbled, but seemed less affected. His eyes instantly roamed the room. Realizing that only one of his associates was still alive and would soon be dead, he jumped to the bed where one of the human women had taken refuge.

He grabbed her amidst her high-pitched shrieks, dragged her against his body like a shield and made for the secondary door that led out of the room.

"One move, and she dies!" Keegan warned.

Thomas, lying on the floor, unable to lift himself, issued his own warning. "Next time you die, Kasper."

"There will be no next time," Keegan predicted instead, shaking his head.

"You've got that right," Quinn murmured under his breath and pulled a knife from Eddie's belt, having lost his own earlier in the fight.

He flicked his wrist. The weapon lodged in Keegan's throat a split-second later. A surprised gurgle was Keegan's response before he lost his hold on the panicked human. As the woman scrambled from him, stumbling to the floor in the process, Quinn pulled his stake from his pocket and lunged for him.

A gunshot stopped him. For a split-second he was in shock, but then he saw Keegan as he combusted, then disintegrated into dust. Quinn whirled his head around, trying to locate the shooter, when he found Rose standing in the door, still holding the handgun that had fired the deadly shot.

She smiled. "You were right. Small caliber works best." She shrugged. "I borrowed it from Cain."

Quinn returned her smile then let his eyes sweep over the room, confirming that all enemies were dead. Eddie was kneeling next to Thomas on the floor, helping him to a sitting position. Quinn rushed to him, crouching down.

"Thank God you're all right."

Thomas gave a tired nod. "I almost had him. Just a little longer, and I would have had him." He dropped his head.

Quinn exchanged a silent look with Eddie, who shook his head, confirming that he too doubted Thomas's statement.

"I've never seen anything like it . . ." He knew what he wanted to ask, but the condition Thomas was in, Quinn wasn't sure he had the right to question him. It appeared he didn't have to.

"His real name was Kasper. He was my sire."

Shock spread on the faces of his colleagues as Thomas confirmed what Quinn had suspected from the heated exchange between the two, and the fact that Keegan had called him son.

"I'm sorry," Quinn murmured.

Thomas lifted his head, an effort which seemed to cost him all his strength. Quinn watched how Eddie supported the weight of his torso to keep him sitting upright, allowing him to lean against him.

"I left him decades ago. I wanted nothing to do with him. He was evil to the core. And his mind control abilities were unparalleled . . . I carry his blood."

Quinn guessed what Thomas was insinuating: he had inherited the same skill. And Quinn had seen it in action.

"He was your sire, yet you were prepared to kill him," Quinn said, then his gaze involuntarily drifted to Rose who stood watching them just as his friends and colleagues did.

"Because he threatened my family. You all, you're my family. He meant nothing to me." Pure hatred colored Thomas's voice. "And if I hadn't been stopped, I would have killed him myself. It was my duty, not yours."

As Thomas's gaze fell on Wesley, Quinn put a calming hand on Thomas's arm. "I'll have a serious word with Wes about that."

Thomas nodded.

Quinn rose. "We need to do damage control." He looked at his colleagues. "Guests and employees will have heard the fighting. Let's get to work."

Then he turned to Eddie. "I trust you'll get Thomas home?"

"Leave it to me."

"I'll take care of Vera," Rose interjected, looking at him.

Quinn walked to where Rose was helping Vera, assisting her to sit on the sofa. Her arm hung limply from her shoulder.

"I'm Quinn. Thank you for helping Rose," he offered.

She gave a quick smile then winced when she tried to lean back in the cushions. "We all owe her. When I got her message, I knew what I had to do."

Quinn felt a stab in his chest. She had trusted her friend, but she hadn't trusted him. Could he even blame her for it?

"You showed up just in time," Vera added. "Lucky coincidence?"

"Not exactly." He cast a glance at Rose. This wasn't the time to talk to her about Keegan's text message. He would have to wait for a private moment. "I'm assuming Keegan got mad when you didn't give him the flash drive."

"Oh, I gave him a flash drive, but an empty one." Rose motioned to Vera. "Vera was so kind as to make sure there was one that looked identical to the real one. While Keegan was checking it, we had just enough time to get Blake out of the room and—"

"But not enough time to save yourselves," Quinn interrupted.

"No." Rose hesitated. "How did you find me?"

"We'll talk about that later. First, I've got to take care of this mess here."

Quinn turned, then looked at Wesley who was standing near the door. "A word."

As soon as they reached the corridor, he turned to Wesley, who appeared apprehensive and immediately went on the defensive. "Hey, I only wanted to help."

"I wanted to thank you," Quinn interrupted.

Wesley looked at him, stunned.

"No matter what Thomas says, if you hadn't broken their concentration, Thomas would have died. You saved his life."

"I did?" He paused, then smiled. "I did."

Quinn gave him a friendly slap on the shoulder. "Now, what was that stuff?"

"Just something I've been working on. I found the recipe in Francine's books. It's supposed to paralyze a vampire." He grinned sheepishly. "Guess it didn't quite work that way, but hey, it worked out fine anyway, right?"

Quinn rolled his eyes. "No more using any untried potions, are we clear on that?"

A hopeful look spread over Wesley's face. "You mean I can try them out on you guys first?"

"I didn't say that! And no, you can't."

"Oh. But, if you want me to help you guys, you should support my research."

Quinn exhaled. "Research?"

"Yeah. I mean, next time we get attacked by evil vampires, we should be prepared."

"I think you should leave that up to us. And not a word of this to Thomas. He's going to be pissed at you for a while anyway. No need to stir more shit up by telling anybody that you're working on your witchcraft."

"Fine."

As he looked at Wesley, Quinn guessed that the last word had not yet been spoken on that subject.

38

By the time all human witnesses to the fight had had their memories wiped and the injured had been taken care of, it was almost daytime.

Blake's injury had healed quickly, and he seemed to suddenly be all excited about the fact that he was related to two vampires.

"So, tell me more. What was it like to see history happen?" Blake asked Rose, his eyes wide.

She smiled. "You don't think it's history when you're right in the middle of it. It becomes history later."

"There you are."

Rose turned to see Quinn enter the living room. Her heartbeat instantly spiked. They hadn't had a single minute alone since the fight, and she yearned to feel his arms around her. But she also knew that she owned him something—the truth.

"Can we talk?" she asked him. "In private."

"Of course." Quinn smiled at his grandson. "Excuse us, Blake."

As Quinn followed her out of the room and up the stairs, her body tensed. The moment they entered their bedroom, she turned to him.

"Now that Blake is safe, it's time for the truth."

His expression was serious when he nodded without saying anything.

"We have to talk about Wallace, your sire."

She avoided looking at him, tears threatening to overwhelm her. She forced them back. Once he knew the truth, her life would be over. But she was ready. Blake was safe, and Quinn would make sure it remained that way. She had fulfilled all promises she'd made to Charlotte.

"Wallace turned me against my will. He attacked me as I tried to flee London, murdered my coachman, and made me into this. Wallace is dead. I killed him the night I awoke as a vampire."

Lifting her chin, she looked at Quinn. Her revelation didn't seem to surprise him much.

He simply nodded. "I know."

Shock coursed through her veins. "You do? How?"

"I guessed it when I read Keegan's text messages. Thomas set it up so he got duplicates of everything that was sent. I put two and two together. I realized that the only reason why you couldn't tell me about your turning had to be because it would lead back to Wallace."

She swallowed hard, wondering why he had even bothered saving her, knowing what she'd done.

"Now that you know, do what you need to do. Kill me to avenge your sire's death."

She closed her eyes, waiting for the blow that would end her life.

Quinn stared at her. She had confirmed what he'd assumed ever since he'd read Keegan's message. And it made his heart bleed. Anger welled up, made his chest heavy with pain and guilt. How could his sire have betrayed him like this? How could he have let it happen?

"I would have killed him myself if I had known what he did to you!"

Rose's eyes shot open, her surprised gaze pinning him. "You would have . . . but . . ." Her voice faltered.

"Of course I would have. He hurt you! Wallace hurt you. And I promised to keep you safe. When I married you, I pledged my life to you. And I failed you." Because he now realized that it was all his fault. He had caused this.

"But I thought you would avenge your sire's death. It's an unwritten law. An urge . . ."

"Where do you get that notion from?"

"You mean it's not true? But I was told by multiple vampires. And I've seen it happen, I've seen a vampire kill his lover because she'd killed his sire. I've seen it," she insisted.

"It's a vampire law, all right. But I don't subscribe to it. I never did. It's savage. And it's certainly not an urge. It's an excuse vampires use as an outlet for their rage." He stretched his arm out to stroke her cheek. "I would have never hurt you."

"Oh God," she whispered, a tear running freely down her cheek. "I wasted all those years."

He pulled her into his embrace. "You hid from me because you thought I'd kill you. Oh, Rose, I wish you would have come to me, talked to me. We could have . . ."

He stopped himself, easing her away from him. She'd come clean; now it was for him to tell her the truth too. He had no right to hide his own guilt.

"It's all my fault, Rose. What Wallace did to you . . . it's because of me."

She stared at him, an expression of dread on her face. "What do you mean?"

Quinn ran a shaky hand through his hair and dropped his lids. "I told him that if he couldn't help me gain your love back, he might as well leave. He left. But I didn't know he would turn you. I didn't realize that's what he thought would bring your love back."

There was a long pause. He listened to Rose's breathing, to her steady heartbeat, but he didn't dare look into her eyes, didn't want to see the realization in them that he was the reason for what had happened to her. She'd hated this life for two centuries. Would she hate him for it, knowing he had caused all this?

"I never stopped loving you, not even when you came back a vampire. I was afraid for our daughter and for myself that night, but I still loved you."

He sensed her step closer. Her hand came up to cup his cheek. "You're not responsible for Wallace's actions. You didn't know what he intended. He told me that night that you didn't know. He was deranged, Quinn, misguided. He had no idea what love was. And that you can't force it. Just as you can't will it to stop."

He lifted his lids, looked at her. "Forgive me, Rose."

She shook her head. "There's nothing to forgive. You loved me all these years, you grieved for me, and I hid from you. I made you believe I was dead. I'm so sorry." Rose slanted her lips over his. "Make me forgot those years. Make me forget the pain. Show me how wonderful this life can be. Pretend the last two hundred years never happened."

Quinn snaked his arm around her waist, dragging her against his body. "In that case, my love, I owe you something. I believe you've never gotten to enjoy a honeymoon."

"A honeymoon?" she whispered against his lips, but he drowned out the sound by capturing her mouth with his.

Quinn felt her love radiate through him as her body molded to his and her lips yielded to his kiss. They had wasted two hundred years because Rose had not trusted him, because he hadn't been gentle enough when he'd come back as a vampire; because he'd scared her. He would never make the same mistake again. He would never give Rose another reason to be afraid of him and not trust him. From now on, there would be no secrets between them, only openness and trust.

And there was one way of assuring this.

Quinn released her lips and peeled from her embrace, taking her hand in his in the next instant. Her eyes widened in apprehension, then softened when he dropped to one knee.

When she smiled at him, he chuckled. "See, I remember how it's done. You taught me well."

"Are you intending to propose marriage to me, Quinn Ralston? If that is the case, I shall tell you that I'm already married, and I have no intention of getting a divorce."

Her playful tone trickled down his body like a sensual caress.

"Alas, I can't offer you marriage since, like you, I am already wed, so would you, my impetuous Rose, please give me a chance to speak?" He looked into the depths of her eyes, drinking in her beauty and grace.

"Why, Quinn Ralston," she began, sounding exactly as she'd sounded on their wedding night. "You are still a scoundrel, because if it isn't marriage you're after . . ." She suddenly stopped herself, then let out a soft "Oh" as she realized his true intention. Moisture suddenly rimmed her eyes.

He tried to do his scoundrel nature justice and let a wicked grin play around his lips.

"So, what's your answer then?"

"Quinn Ralston, you've still not learned how to propose!"

"Because you keep interrupting me!"

"Well, then do it and don't keep me on tenterhooks," she urged.

He cleared his throat, pressing his hand over his heart. "Will you, Rose Haverford, become my blood-bonded mate?"

A second later, he found himself lying with his back flat on the mattress, having been catapulted there by Rose who now straddled him.

"I'm assuming that's a yes?" He smirked and pulled her down to him.

"Before I can say yes, there's just one more thing you need to know. I hid the flash drive in—"

He pressed his finger to her lips, interrupting her. "I don't need to know."

"You do. There's no need to keep the flash drive anymore. I've decided to destroy it.”

“Are you sure?”

Rose nodded. “Keegan is dead, he can’t hurt us anymore.”

Then she lifted her left arm and allowed the fingers of her right arm to turn into claws.

“What are you doing?”

She made a three inch incision into her bicep before he could stop her, then dug into the open wound, pulling out a rectangular item covered in blood.

“The flash drive,” she whispered.

Surprise and relief collided in Quinn. “Oh my god, you kept it inside you all this time!”

“It was the safest place.”

She lifted her arm to her mouth to lick the wound so it would close, but this time he was faster and grabbed her arm.

“Allow me.”

His tongue licked over the incision, lapping up the blood that dripped from it. Within seconds, the wound closed, leaving only the delicious taste of Rose in his mouth.

Instantly, more blood pumped to his loins.

“And now?” he asked.

She balled her hand holding the flash drive to a fist, crushing the item. When she opened her palm, it had broken into a thousand tiny pieces. Leaning toward the nightstand, she let the debris fall onto it, then wiped her hand.

“It’s done.”

All obstacles between them were gone. They were free to love now. “Thank you.”

“Now there’s nothing between us anymore.”

He winked mischievously. “Only those clothes. And I believe you still owe me an answer.”

“Can’t you guess?”

“Rose, you still haven’t learned how to properly reply to a proposal.”

“Well, let me try again then.” She snatched his wrists and pressed him down into the mattress. “Yes! I’ll be your blood-bonded mate.”

As her mouth descended on his, he freed his hands and ripped her top in two, exposing her breasts. Capturing them, he allowed the flesh to mold to his palms and her warmth to seep into his body.

He finally had her back. Rose was in his arms, arms that would never let her go, arms that would always protect her. Quinn drank in her kiss, letting all tension drain from him. Every one of her moans acted as a stone thrown against the wall around his heart, tearing it down one by one. And every sigh that left her breathless body drove into his heart, lodging there for good.

As he frantically tore her clothes from her body, he lifted her off him and dropped her to his side, so he could pull her pants off her.

"Dresses were so much easier," he complained.

"For you maybe," she chuckled and helped him, then turned the tables on him and undressed him just as impatiently.

Wherever she touched him, his skin burned with desire. As soon as he was naked, he reached for her to bring her under him, but Rose had other ideas.

"Oh, no," she whispered seductively and let her eyes trail down to his groin. "First I get to do what I never had a chance to do on our wedding night."

When he followed her look to where his cock stood hard and heavy, he almost choked. Rose had never sucked him. She had been a virgin on their wedding night, and he hadn't suggested it then, but now . . .

Rose pressed him back into the mattress. "Don't move."

"I can't promise that," he answered.

"I might have to bite you if you do."

Her words coupled with the lusty gaze she ran over him, made his heart pound into his throat.

"You don't like biting," he reminded her, even though he knew that tonight she would bite him as part of their bonding ritual.

"We'll find out," she murmured and dropped between his spread legs, lowering her head to his erection.

As she gripped his eager shaft, his entire body jerked involuntarily.

"So impatient," she said and licked over the head of it.

Rose barely heard his words, his taste and smell drugging her. She knew instantly that she'd missed out on something by never having licked his gorgeous cock, and promised herself not to make the same mistake twice. Without letting him recover from the first lick, she wrapped her lips around the throbbing head and slid down on it, taking him into her mouth in one long and smooth glide.

With a harsh breath he let out a curse. "Fuck, Rose! You're killing me!"

She pulled back and blew air against his hard flesh. "Shhhh."

Then she descended again, sliding her tongue against the smooth underside of it to capture more of his taste.

Her hands released his thighs, which she'd gripped tightly, and now moved upwards, one cradling his balls. As she scraped her fingernails lightly against the soft sac, Quinn moaned and pumped his hips, demanding more.

Her other hand gripped the base of his shaft and together with her mouth, moved up and down on it.

"Oh God, Rose!"

Her own body throbbed in concert with Quinn's heartbeat. Tasting his arousal, allowing his scent to engulf her, to drown her, turned her own body into an inferno despite the fact that Quinn wasn't touching her. His hands were gripping the sheets, his sharp claws slicing them to pieces. The cords in his neck bulged from the obvious effort not to scream out as she unleashed more wicked caresses on him.

Still, she wanted more, couldn't get enough of him, of licking his aroused flesh, of giving him pleasure and igniting her own in its wake. How had she ever lived without this, without Quinn? It had only been half a life. But starting tonight, she would live to the fullest, the way it was meant to be. No more holding back, no more regrets.

As she sucked him harder into her mouth, she suddenly felt him pull away from her.

"Stop it, Rose!" he cried out and freed himself.

A split-second later, he catapulted off the bed, his eyes staring at her, full of untamed lust. It thrilled her to see him like that. She ran her eyes over his naked body, admiring his hard muscles, and particularly the one that now pointed straight at her.

"Am I not doing it right?" she asked coquettishly.

He growled in response and moved behind her, his hands gripping her thighs, spreading them. She fell forward, landing on all fours.

"You're doing it too well, but then, you already knew that, my wicked wife, didn't you?"

Her tongue came out to lick her lips. "You taste good."

"Just good?" he asked and moved between her legs, nudging his iron-hard cock against her core.

"Delicious actually, but then, you already knew that, my wicked husband, didn't you?"

On her last word, he drove into her with one perfect thrust. Had he not held her hips in a vice grip, she could have flown off the bed on the other side.

His cock, long and hard, reached all the way to her womb, his balls slapping against her flesh, the sound amplifying in her ears.

"You're mine, Rose!"

His words knocked at the door to her heart, which already stood wide open, asking him to enter.

"Always have been, always will be," Quinn added as he pulled from her sheath, only to plunge back in with more force.

Her sex clenched at each thrust and each withdrawal, and her clit throbbed in the same rhythm as her heartbeat.

"I'm yours," she murmured between pants.

And he was hers. She felt it with every fiber of her body. Her heart filled to the brim with love, with trust, and with the knowledge that they had a future together.

"I want your blood," she confessed. "I want it now."

He pulled from her sheath only long enough to turn her onto her back, then settled between her legs again. As he looked down at her, she noticed his fangs elongate. Excitement filled her as she sensed her own fangs descend, longing for a bite.

This would be different from all other bites. She knew it even before he drove back into her and lowered his neck to her lips.

"Take me," he demanded.

The vein in his neck pulsed invitingly, the blood beneath his skin rushing through it, whispering encouragements to her. *Take me, take me*, it repeated over and over again.

When she scraped her fangs against his neck, she felt him shudder. It sent a bolt of electricity into her sex. Then her sharp teeth pierced his skin and the scent of blood intensified. The moment the first drop of it reached her tongue, tremors shook her entire body. Her clit was on fire, and her sex clenched. Then it hit her: like a massive ocean wave she was swept up and crested, pleasure flooding her body without end.

His blood tasted like heaven on earth.

Quinn drove his fangs into Rose's shoulder, pulling on her vein. She was trembling, her tight channel convulsing around his cock so violently that he couldn't hold onto his control. Without a thought, he let go and gave himself over to the sensations that rolled over his body.

His orgasm took him and whipped him like a flag in a gale. He didn't fight it, instead he let himself fall, knowing Rose was there to catch him just as he would catch her. A sense of weightlessness befell him, of floating on a cloud. It was better than on his wedding night. This time he wouldn't have to leave the next day; this time no uncertain future was waiting. This time he would not leave her behind. If they fought any more battles, they would fight them together.

But most of all, they would lead a life of love together, just like they had promised each other that night in London.

When Rose's spasms stilled and his own subsided, he withdrew his fangs and felt her retract hers. Then he rolled to the side, cradling her in his arms, planting soft kisses on her eyes and cheeks.

When a sob unexpectedly tore from her chest, panic struck him.

"Did I hurt you? Did you not like my blood?"

If she didn't, he would be devastated.

Rose shook her head, fighting tears. "No. I did. I loved your blood. I want more of it."

His heart rejoiced at the same time as his mind continued to wonder why she appeared sad. "Then what is it, my love?"

She looked at him. "I wasted so much time. I deprived us of this for two hundred years."

"Shh, my love." He wiped a tear away with his thumb. "Don't think of it anymore. Think only of the future. Our future. We have eternity now."

He kissed her tenderly and she responded by pressing him closer. When she severed the kiss, a smile sat on her lips. She opened her mind to him, and for the first time he could hear her thoughts.

Eternity. Just you and me—

A knock sounded at the door. "Uh, Quinn, Rose?"

". . . and apparently Blake," Quinn added dryly before raising his voice to respond. "Not now, Blake."

"It's just," Blake continued, "there's something . . ."

Quinn rolled his eyes and caught Rose's suppressed grin. "Your grandson has bad timing," he whispered to her.

"He's yours too."

He stole a quick kiss, then turned his head toward the door again. "Why don't you hang out with Oliver?"

"Like I wanna get bitten again! And besides, that's what I wanted to tell you: he isn't here. I think he's still at the brothel."

"Oh crap!" Quinn exclaimed and reared up.

Rose pulled him back down to her.

"Blake," she called out. "Don't worry about it, Vera will make sure he doesn't cause any trouble. Why don't you go and help Wesley pack?"

A grumble came from outside the door, then the sound of footsteps.

"Did you just use mind control on him?"

She shrugged. "Is that a problem?"

He grinned and shook his head. "No problem at all. Saves me from doing it. But Oliver? Are you sure Vera will take care of him for the day? There are an awful lot of humans in that house."

"Trust me on that."

"I do." Quinn sighed contentedly. "So now that you have me all to yourself, what are your wicked plans?"

She winked at him. "Now *that* would be telling. I'd rather show you."

~ ~ ~

ABOUT THE AUTHOR

Tina Folsom was born in Germany and has been living in English speaking countries for over 25 years, the last 14 of them in San Francisco, where she's married to an American.

Tina has always been a bit of a globe trotter: after living in Lausanne, Switzerland, she briefly worked on a cruise ship in the Mediterranean, then lived a year in Munich, before moving to London. There, she became an accountant. But after 8 years she decided to move overseas.

In New York she studied drama at the American Academy of Dramatic Arts, then moved to Los Angeles a year later to pursue studies in screenwriting. This is also where she met her husband, who she followed to San Francisco three months after first meeting him.

In San Francisco, Tina worked as a tax accountant and even opened her own firm, then went into real estate, however, she missed writing. In 2008 she wrote her first romance and never looked back.

She's always loved vampires and decided that vampire and paranormal romance was her calling. She now has 32 novels in English and several dozens in other languages (Spanish, German, and French) and continues to write, as well as have her existing novels translated.

For more about Tina Folsom:
http://www.tinawritesromance.com
http://www.facebook.com/TinaFolsomFans
http://www.twitter.com/Tina_Folsom
You can also email her at tina@tinawritesromance.com

Made in the USA
Middletown, DE
26 April 2022

64793325R00154